PRAISE FOR RUSS

## GOOD NEIGHBORS

"Connor's ability to richly develop each character and plot thread is fascinating even when the horror is reserved... the constricting pressure as the dread piles on makes this book hard to put down and even harder to go to sleep after reading. This is a great novel..."
  -David J. Sharp, *Horror Underground*

## SECOND UNIT

"Intricately plotted and vividly layered with suspense, emotional intensity and strategic violence."
  -Michael Price, *Fort Worth Business Press*

"Drips with eeriness...an enjoyable book by a promising author."
  -Kyle White, *The Harrow Fantasy and Horror Journal*

## FINDING MISERY

"Major-league action, car chases, subterfuge, plot twists, with a smear of rough sex on top. Sublime."
  -Arianne "Tex" Thompson, author of *Medicine for the Dead* and *One Night in Sixes*

## THE JACKAL MAN

"Connor delivers a brisk, action-packed tale that explores the dark forests of the human--and inhuman--heart. Sure to thrill creature fans everywhere."
  -Scott Nicholson, author of *They Hunger* and *The Red Church*

Also by Russell C. Connor

*Indicates Dark Filament Ephemeris supplementary connection

# The Halls of Moambati

## THE DARK FILAMENT
## EPHEMERIS
### VOLUME IV

## RUSSELL C. CONNOR

DARK FILAMENT
BOOKS

DARKFILAMENT.COM

Contact the author at
facebook.com/russellcconnor
Or follow on Twitter @russellcconnor

Cover Art by SaberCore23 Artwork Studio
For commissions, visit sabercore23art.com

ISBN:
978-1-952968-40-2

First Edition: 2021

This one is for a lot of people who have shown
overwhelming support for my writing,
and probably long overdue.

For Dean Toland, founder and moderator of the
Book Lovers Club discussion group on Discord,
for always remembering to post about my books
even when I don't. Check out the group if you're
looking for some great literary discussion.

For JB Sanders, a fantastic writer, and someone
who encouraged me to start on these books when
the universe was contained in just one short story.

For Tom Bont, my bookselling partner in crime,
and a man who can bring traffic to
a booth like nobody else.

For the DFW Writers Workshop, Simone Alli
Ruggeri, Brandy Herr, Steve Ogden,
David Dugas, Jr., and many more I'm probably
forgetting.

Also, for everyone who has discovered, read, and,
most importantly, reviewed the books
on Amazon, you have my thanks.

# TABLE OF CONTENTS

The golden grasses of the *pasto* rippled in the breeze, as though a giant, invisible hand brushed back and forth across their tops. Onjel sat on the pebble-strewn banks of the river with his back to the water so he could watch the hypnotic motion of the blades swinging in perfect harmony, shifting through a range of flaxen shades as the sunlight hit them from different angles. His father had told him the wind was one of the ways *el Padre de Cielo* made His presence known to the earth. Onjel wasn't sure if he believed in the god his people worshipped in *Casa Sur*—what the white people in Wilton called 'the Mex'—but it was certainly a beautiful sight to behold.

He'd became so engrossed in the spectacle of nature that he didn't hear the familiar creak of a wooden wheel approaching from downstream. Gaulbriel Hernandez sat on the coach seat of their rickety wagon, behind a pair of elderly mules named El Cid and Zorro. The man drove the beasts carefully along the dry edge of the bank toward his son, but when he saw where the boy's attention lay, he jumped to his feet and shouted in their language, "*Onjel! The traps!*"

Snapped from his reverie, Onjel scrambled on all fours to face the river. The fish traps had overturned in the sluggish current while his attention was on the meadow, releasing the catches within. Onjel seized the ropes tethering them to the shore and worked to haul them in as Gaulbriel leapt from the wagon to help.

They dragged the traps onto the beach to find the bait gone, the interiors empty save for one scrawny, thrashing trout. Onjel hung his head in shame, but Gaulbriel placed a hand on the nine-year-old's thin shoulder and gave it a reassuring squeeze. "It is fine, *mijo*. Mine all came back full. We have a haul large enough to feed the entire village. But you must learn to be more watchful. Someday you will do this on your own."

"I know," the boy agreed, then added with a plaintive moan, "But it is just so *boring*."

Gaulbriel smiled as he wound the rope around his arm. "You are lucky to be bored. Boredom is a luxury that few children get to experience."

"It does not feel lucky," Onjel argued. But he knew what his father meant: the endless stories about red-eyed *demonios* that hunted down children in the lands that lay beyond this river. Onjel's mother had died in childbirth, and his father traveled far to seek sanctuary here, in the shadow of the great mountains the people of Wilton called 'the Skyreach,' where the *Encarnarios* feared to tread.

"We cannot always see the blessings that *el Padre de Cielo* bestows upon us, but that does not mean they are not there," Gaulbriel said.

Onjel looked up at his father. "Papa, the other children in Wilton...they say *el Padre* is not real."

"Then it is good that His existence is not dependent on their belief."

The boy nodded but said nothing. However, something on his face must've given his thoughts away, because Gaulbriel deduced, "You have stopped believing in Him as well."

"I'm…not sure," Onjel admitted.

"That is all right." The words came easily from his father's mouth, but Onjel could see that he was hurt all the same. "That is a luxury you have as well. In the lands beyond, most people would force you to worship the Aged Lord. And they would consider your very existence to be a slight against him. But belief cannot be forced; it must be voluntary, for it to mean anything. Someday, perhaps, you will see evidence of the love *el Padre* has for us."

On the heels of this statement, a deep boom like thunder sounded over their heads. Both looked up into the clear blue sky in alarm. A soft, reverberating hum filled the air, growing slowly louder. At first, Onjel saw nothing, then a tiny speck of motion in the endless azure swathe caught his eye. In moments, it resolved into a shiny, white, oval-shaped projectile that streaked down toward the field on the far side of the river with incredible speed. He cringed, anticipating a monumental impact that would shatter the earth, but, at the last second, the pod pulled upward and shot over their heads, so close that Onjel could feel the heat and wind of its passage. He caught sight of a pulsing white light on its tail as it flew across the golden grasses he'd just been admiring.

"Come!" Gaulbriel shouted excitedly. He ran toward the wagon, waving his son to follow. As they climbed onto the bench, he grabbed the reins and declared, "Let us see what *el Padre* has sent us!"

# The Sisters

# 74 Seconds

## 1

The display screens at the front of the stratoliner lit up with the bold message, **IMPACT DETECTED IN 74 SECONDS. A.I.N. NAVIGATION IS UNAVAILABLE AT THIS TIME. REDUCE SPEED AND CORRECT ANGLE OF APPROACH.** The timer began counting down as the heavy belts across Korden's shoulders and lap jerked even tighter, locking him in place against the thickly padded seat. Behind him, Zeega squealed in pain; he could only imagine what the sudden compression of the retraints had done to the riftling's squishy, malleable body.

"*What's happening?*" Rand demanded over the deafening wail of the ship's emergency klaxon.

"*I don't know!*" Korden answered. "*Stone's not answering!*" The telepathic computer's last communication had been full of buzzing distortion and urgent warning before he went silent.

"*Hellsuva time for our pilot to check out!*" Doaks strained against the belts and craned his neck to look out the side of the ship's wraparound windshield, where the ground rushed upward to meet them. "*We hit head-on at this speed, there ain't gonna be enougha us left to fill a tea kettle!*"

Korden thought briefly of the downed stratoliner he'd found in the mountains so many weeks ago. That craft had been much larger than this one, and, though badly damaged by the impact, no one had died in the wreck. The circumstances of that crash, however, were very different from this situation.

For starters, the engines were still on, pushing the ship downward at incredible speed. The velocity pressure was even more severe than when they'd taken off, preventing Korden's lungs from fully inflating and making the skin feel taut on his frame, as though his cheekbones sought to tear through the flesh. Outside, their view of the ground slowly rotated as the capsule corkscrewed without a pilot to steer it. He could see the banks of a languid river snaking across the yellow plains below—the scene somehow familiar for reasons he couldn't discern—and even a wooden cart parked on the shore. As he took in the mesmerizing sight of the earth growing larger, another tremor rocked the ship, so violent it made his back ache.

"*Do something!*" Lillam pleaded. The timer now gave them 52 seconds until collision.

"*Like what?*" Doaks asked. He tugged at the control sticks jutting from the panel in front of them. "*Nuthin's respondin! If yah got some better ideas, I'll gladly switch places!*"

"*What about this?*" From between Korden and Doaks, Meech strained forward to slap a red button overhead labelled **EMERGENCY ENGINE CUTOFF**, but the thrum of the ion engine didn't change tempo.

"*See? It's like this thing is TRYIN ta kill us!*" Doaks looked past Meech at Korden. "*Boy, if yah got another magic trick up yah sleeve, best play it now!*"

**IMPACT DETECTED IN 39 SECONDS.**

Korden reached out with his mind, focused past the shaking and blaring alarm and his own dragging breath. Through the conduit's eye, he could grasp the ship as surely as if his hands were on it, the sleek shape and smooth texture of it. With the reality of the craft fixed firmly in his head, he imagined the stratoliner reorienting, envisioned the nose nudging up and away from the ground.

The sheer mass and speed of the craft ripped through his efforts like an arrow through a single sheet of paper. Psychic feedback sent a sharp spike into the center of his brain. Korden cried out and clutched his forehead.

**26 SECONDS.**

"*It's too much, we're going too fast for me to do anything!*" Korden gasped, as-mah scratching at his constricted lungs. He'd told Rand that trying to lift the wagon across the crevies in the Valley of Bones would be too taxing, and this was worse by magnitudes.

"*Don't worry, we're gonna be on the ground soon!*" Doaks yelled. "*One way or another!*"

From the back row, Lillam uttered a terrified cry.

*You wanted a way to get rid of all that extra artcraft the Moambatis pumped into you.* The stern voice in Korden's thoughts sounded like Redfen. *Might as well use it all up now.*

He sent the fingers of his mind out again, gritting his teeth in determination as they seized hold of the ship once more.

Then he tore away the mental dam he'd built to keep that excess magic at bay, and let the conduit stretch open wider than ever before.

**13 SECONDS.**

The overflowing fount of artcraft exploded out of him. Raw power set his body aflame. Dear sweet Upper, there was *so much of it*, more than he could ever hope to rein back in on his own; last time he'd unleashed a mere fraction of this, and only Zeega's call could halt the flow.

But Korden had no desire to stop it now.

Instead, he let it run free, trusted his subconscious to sculpt it into a tool devoted solely to taming this juggernaut. His focus sharpened until the world seemed to be not just around him, but *inside* him. And when the pain tore open his head this time, he didn't let up, not even when something wet trickled from his nose and ears, he just concentrated harder, and set his will to realigning reality…

Cupit by agonizing cupit, their course shifted. The stratoliner broke out of its corkscrew as the nose pulled up. On the monitors, the impact timer stuttered up and down between numbers, attempting to recalculate…but the ground was still coming at them fast.

"*Don't stop, boy! Get us level!*"

Korden gave one last massive heave.

The ship performed a sweeping curve that left his stomach behind. Someone in the back row noisily vomited. The earth shifted, swinging beneath them, and then the stratoliner was skimming above the prairie floor. They were so low now, the golden grasses whipping by on either side looked close enough to reach out and touch.

The impact timer disappeared. A new message advised them to **REDUCE SPEED BEFORE LANDING.**

Korden barely saw it. The artcraft continued flowing, filling the world with blazing color, making him feel alive in ways he'd never known possible. This was a sensation he could get lost in; his thoughts, his consciousness, his entire *being* reduced to a stick bobbing along in a swift current, his problems and fears dwarfed by a power that would never let him fall. But it wouldn't last forever; already he could sense the tide ebbing. Before the wellspring could run dry, he cast his mind into the bowels of the stratoliner. Unlike the exterior, he didn't know what it looked like in there, not really, but he created a picture in his head of the various wires and circuits and computer chips that made up this amazing vehicle, his own interpretation of the mechanical innards. Then he imagined them being destroyed, parts crushed and wires shredded. His mental image must've been close to true, because the roar of the engine fizzled out.

Their speed reduced drastically. The pressure stealing Korden's breath disappeared. Their height lessened until the underside of the ship scraped the ground.

The glancing contact tossed them back up. Something in the stratoliner's structure gave a tortured groan. A web of cracks raced across the windshield, obscuring their view.

Then they came down again and again and again, skipping across the land like a flat stone hurled across a pond, and Korden directed the last of his will and dwindling artcraft into cushioning their impacts amid the screams and pounding cacophony of collisions and the sense of being pulled in every direction at once.

When the disorientation cleared, he found himself upside down, arms dangling over his head, blood dribbling into his eyes, held in his seat only by the restraints. Acrid smoke filled his nostrils, drifting from the demolished control board in front of him. The interior of the craft was in shambles, cracks in the walls as wide as his wrist allowing sunlight to stream inside. Every cupit of his body was somehow in pain at the same time, his mind as wrung out as a crushed grape, and from all around the cabin came groans and moans and coughs.

But all of that was forgotten when the face of a young boy pressed against the other side of the shattered windshield to peer in at him.

# WHOLENESS

## 1

WE'RE SORRY, THIS UNIT IS EXPERIENCING TECHNICAL DIFFICULTIES! The voice was female, and so cheerful you could hear the smile in her words. PLEASE DROP BY ANY NAMENCO OUTLET OR AN AUTHORIZED REPAIR LOCATION FOR SERVICE ON YOUR S.T.O.N.E.

Always the same message, no matter how many times Korden squeezed the computer's casing to wake it up. Stone's presence—his most constant companion since fleeing his home almost a full season ago—had vanished from his mind, leaving a yawning void in its place. This was far more frustrating than when Zeega blocked him from interacting with the computer, because this time he had no idea how to solve the problem, or even if there was any way he *could* solve it. Despair would surely come later, but right now Korden was too mentally debilitated to comprehend the loss. All he could do is lean back against the side of the wooden cart he'd seen from the sky as it bumped along through the prairie.

In front of him, the boy turned to grin and wave from the

driver's seat behind the two mules. His name was Onjel, and, from what they'd gleaned, he was only nine years old. Both he and his father—a lean, dark-eyed man named Gaulbriel—had the same deep tan skin color as Santo, and spoke a rapid, tongue-twisting language that Doaks identified as Mex. They'd been fishing in the river when the stratoliner streaked across the sky like a giant, gleaming bird and crashed down less than a span away from them. Gaulbriel had helped cut them free from their restraints, got them out of the smoking wreckage and, after asking a hundred enthusiastic questions that they couldn't interpret, urged them to climb onto the rickety cart he used to haul his spoils. None of them had been in any shape to reject the offer.

Korden gave Onjel a warm smile and returned the wave.

"This is so strange," Rand said from his right.

The others were also stretched out amid the fresh-caught fish in miserable heaps, along with all the personal belongings they could salvage from the debris. They'd been severely banged and shaken in the accident—Doaks had twisted one leg at the knee, Meech received what might be a broken arm, Lillam's jaw slammed shut on the meat of her tongue, Zeega lost a few more tentacles, and all of them sported bruises in the shape of the restraints across their torsos—but considering the state of the stratoliner, Korden found these injuries very fortunate. According to Onjel's pantomimed recreation, the aircraft bounced along for a thousand pargs, leaving gouged trenches in the earth like fresh scars, before going into a wild tumble and coming to rest on the savannah that cradled the river. The glossy white outer hull had been torn away, the tubular body crushed, and wreckage scattered across the prairie in a fan.

It was the second vehicle accident they'd survived in a week—the first being Gwenita's spill during the maelstrom in the desert—and, as Rand muttered when they crawled from the remains, the experience was getting a little old.

"What's so strange?" Korden asked blearily. His thoughts were mushy after the massive amounts of artcraft he'd expended to land the stratoliner; he had little enough magic left to peer into the emotional spectrum. And, while that emptiness was scary, it was also wonderful in its own way, like the pressure released from lancing a boil. Now that he'd drained the wellspring of its excess, he felt more like himself than he had in a long time.

Rand nodded at Onjel. "I haven't seen a human being that young since Meech was his age."

Korden shared his awe. He'd never met anyone younger than himself. Even now, seeing the boy was like catching a glimpse of a fairy or leprechaun or some other fantasy creature from the books he used to read. Despite that he'd known, logically, there must be other children somewhere in the world, some part of him had believed he was the last one.

When the shock of the crash wore off, they'd all expressed similar reactions to the child, staring and fawning over him. Onjel accepted their attention with jubilant delight, jabbering away in his strange tongue. He'd been particularly amused by Zeega, trying to pet her head and feed her bits of raw fish. The riftling accepted these grudgingly but refrained from speaking, either reading Korden's thoughts or coming to her own realization that matters would only be complicated if these strangers knew she could talk.

"Look at them." Lillam sat propped on Rand, gazing at the father and son duo. "They don't even seem worried. They're not on the run, they were just...catching fish, without a care in the world."

"We have to make them understand about the Incarnates," Korden said. "That army won't give up. *Heater* won't give up. They're probably heading this way even now."

"We will," Rand assured him, wrapping his arms around Lillam. "But for now, can't we take five minutes to enjoy the fact that we're not on the ragged edge of death for the first time in weeks?"

Korden decided to take that advice. Their survival was nothing short of miraculous. Two hours ago, they'd been in the middle of the Valley, dying of thirst and surrounded by hundreds of the Filament's demonic footsoldiers, with Heater Kay at the forefront. Korden had been preparing for death, truly coming to accept that it would happen, and the situation had changed so rapidly that relief hadn't fully sunk in yet.

*Just further proof that the Upper provides.*

Across from him, Meech shifted, moaning as he jostled his broken arm. "Wish we knew where these two were takin us."

"Why?" Rand asked harshly. "Afraid you won't be able to get your next spin?"

Meech flushed with embarrassment and dropped his gaze. The man had spoken little since abandoning them in the desert to find more of his drug, and with good reason; they all still harbored resentment, but none more than his brother.

Korden was intensely curious about their destination also, mainly because he'd grasped why this open prairie looked so familiar to him: it was the same meadow from his dream, where he'd held hands with Denise and Charlotta Moambati while they urged him to come to them. He didn't know if their arrival here, at this exact spot, was coincidental, orchestrated, or preordained by the Upper Himself, but it made him uneasy.

Gaulbriel drove the mules away from the river, cutting across the prairie due east, toward a series of hills populated by healthy pine and spruce. Beyond them, no more than a few day's walk away, was another sight that gave Korden an acute case of what the Olders called 'déjà vu': the spine of a formidable mountain ridge lay across the sprawl of the horizon, like a lower mandible full of purple teeth biting into the sky just beneath the dark well of the Shroud.

"Is that the Skyreach?" he asked, already knowing the answer.

"Ayuh, that's it, all right." Doaks grumbled. He lay with his injured leg propped on the cart's sideboard and stared into the distance. "Part of it, anyway. Damn thing stretches for spans upon spans. Hadn't seen it in years, but yah don't forget a sight like that."

"Is it hard to cross?"

"Harder than that ring of peaks 'round Tay-ho, that's for sure. Hafta know where yah goin, and make sure not to get caught in the snow."

A pang went through Korden when he remembered the similar advice Stone had given him. "What's it like? On the other side, I mean."

Doaks raised a shoulder. "Bigger city wastes. More Incarnates. Some angry little men playin at kings and knights. Wouldn't recommend goin there if yah didn't have to, rubo. I crossed the Skyreach thirty years ago and never felt the urge to go back."

## 2

Rand nodded off at some point while pillowed on Lillam's breast, waking to discover the sun low on the flat land behind them. Gaulbriel was steering the mules down into a ravine that carved through the foothills of the Skyreach. His son slumped against him, also asleep. Every time he looked at the boy, Rand experienced a brief shock, as though his brain simply couldn't reconcile seeing someone so young in such a casual setting. As he watched, the father leaned over to plant a kiss on top of Onjel's dark hair. The gesture made Rand think of that tiny, golden flame he'd seen inside Lillam's stomach when Korden opened their minds, and the rush of emotions it inspired in him. Before that moment, he remained unsure if he'd chosen the right course for his life, had agonized constantly over the rash decision to leave Ida.

But afterward...he knew there was no place he would rather be, no matter what the future held.

He was about to try communicating with their benefactor to ask how much farther to their destination, when Lillam lifted her head and whispered, "Do you hear that?"

Rand sat up. Voices echoed through the canyon ahead, along with shouts, laughter, and the ring of metal on metal. His nose caught a faint whiff of woodsmoke and cooking meat that made his stomach growl. He recognized the intricate mixture of sensations immediately.

A town.

They were nearing some manner of civilization.

He peered ahead until he spotted the end of the gorge. Nestled amid the gentle hills was a wide plain with a stream running along the northern edge, the perfect location for a settlement.

Wood and mud mortar buildings filled the expanse, solidly built two- and three-stories high, clustered around dirt roads. Most looked to be dwellings, but some on the main avenue were obviously tradesmen facilities; he spotted what must be a tavern, a baker, a farrier, and a blacksmith, with a fire stoked and ready. Smoke leaked from chimneys and a watermill straddled the stream behind the tavern, rotating steadily in the current. There were people out and about as well, their clothes simple and homespun without any real fashion to speak of: knee-length denim dungarees and rough-weave tunics.

All in all, it was a flea speck village, nowhere near the refinement and luxury of Ida, with its power and cobblestone streets.

Yet Rand sprang to his feet on the fish cart and stared in astonishment as they drew closer. At the same time, he heard Lillam let out a small murmur of surprise behind him as her hand latched on to his ankle.

Because there were children here. Children *everywhere*. In fact, most of the townsfolk currently outside were below the age of twelve, and the majority quite a bit younger. Both boys and girls, in a variety of colors and sizes. The largest group kicked a deerskin ball around in the middle of the trampled dirt trail that led into town, but when they saw the cart approaching, they broke the game to begin shouting and waving. Their cries brought more curious onlookers from the surrounding buildings, and soon a crowd of more than fifty men, women, and children waited to greet them, without any sort of division between genders.

Rand felt his jaw hanging open but couldn't remember how to close it.

Yes, he'd listened to Mikolt's rumors. Yes, he'd convinced Lillam to trust in the security they promised. And yes, he'd chased those stories all the way across the Valley of Bones.

But only now did he grasp that he'd never actually *believed* they could be true.

Even seeing the evidence with his own eyes, the more rational parts of his mind screamed that it must be a trick, a mirage, a hallucination.

While he marveled, a muscular, late-forties man with muttonchop sideburns and a stiff-brimmed straw hat stepped forward from the crowd. He flashed a broad grin and raised both arms, the left of which, Rand noticed, ended at the wrist where a leather cradle capped the appendage. "Looks like you came back with more'n just a loada fish, Gaulbriel," he said, his timbre deep but tone friendly. His accent was reminiscent of Dabber Knox, the stranded caravan boss they'd encountered in the desert. "'Less you're pullin whole families outta the river now!"

Both Gaulbriel and Onjel spoke rapidly in Mex while they switched between pointing at their passengers and jabbing fingers into the air. A few in the crowd must've understood their words, because they turned and whispered to those around them until an excited murmur had built throughout the townsfolk.

The man with the muttonchops hiked a skeptical eyebrow at Rand beneath the brim of his hat. "If I ain't losin somethin in translation, ol' Gaulbriel here says you folks fell outta the sky in some kinda 'magic pod.' He thinks his god sent you. Don't suppose you'd care to explain what that's all about?"

"It's…a long story," Rand said distractedly, unable to tear his eyes away from the young faces peering at him from the crowd. The story of the stratoliner might hold these people in thrall, but it wouldn't be anything compared to what their town's mere existence was doing to him. From the way that Lillam dug her fingers into his calf, he knew that she must be in just as much shock. "What…" He swallowed and tried again. "What is this place?"

"Oh! Sorry 'bout that, I forgot my spiel! Ahem…welcome to Wilton!" the one-handed man proclaimed. "Been here two years and three seasons, population 259 and growin! My name's Baryus Mellory, and it's a pleasure to meet ya all!"

"Rand. Rand Holcomb. Are you…the mayor?"

Mellory barked laughter. "Oh hells, no! We don't have anything that formal here, Mr. Holcomb! Not yet, anyway. But I s'pose I'm the next best thing: a tavernmaster!" He winked, but when no one reacted, his smile faltered into a look of concern. Mellory removed his straw hat and held it reverently to his chest with his lone hand, revealing a thatch of wispy blond hair. "From the looksa you all, you've gone through a lot. Why dontcha come in and—"

"We can't!" Korden shouted suddenly. The boy leapt up to stand beside Rand in the cart. "There's an army of Incarnates heading this way! We left them far behind in the Valley of Bones, but they could be here in days! You all have to leave immediately!"

Rand didn't know what sort of response he expected to this declaration, but it wasn't the one they received. Hearty laughter boomed from the assembled crowd. Even the children covered their mouths and snickered as they looked at one another. Mellory waited for it to die down, then favored Korden with a sympathetic smile. "You prob'ly run from those devils your whole life, son, but I promise you... those days are over. You're safe here. You're *all* safe here."

Behind Rand, Lillam burst into tears. He bent and helped her to her feet in the cart, then slid an arm around her waist and let her bury her sobs in his shoulder. "I'm sorry," he told Mellory as his own eyes moistened. "Like you said, we've... well, we've been through a lot."

The other man nodded. He replaced his hat on his head and snapped his fingers at people in the crowd. "Let's find these folks some place to wash up, and some clothes, too. Jansa, go get Doc Timpett and tell 'im we got injuries. And somebody throw together a meal."

"We don't have anything to trade for all that," Rand cautioned.

Mellory waved the sentiment away. "This is hospitality, not business. We can figger all the rest out once ya settle in. If you *want* to settle in, that is."

He'd hardly finished speaking before Doaks heaved himself up, slid off the end of the cart and hobbled past

Mellory, favoring his hurt knee.

"Where're you going?" Korden called after him.

Doaks spun, fire in his eyes. "Yah wanted me to get yah to the Skyreach, here yah go. 'Cept yah don't have any way to hold up yah end of the bargain, now do yah? So if I never see any of yah dumbskulls again, it'll be too frammin soon." He raised both arms straight and rigid in front of him, extended the ring-laden small fingers of both hands in a vulgar display, then stalked away, disappearing into the crowd.

"Pleasant fellow," Mellory remarked.

Rand climbed down from the cart as well and helped Lillam do the same. Korden and Zeega had been surrounded by the town's children, who were all trying to touch the latter while babbling questions at the former. The riftling looked uncomfortable-bordering-on-murderous, but a huge grin uncurled on Korden's face as he told his peers about his 'pet'. Rand couldn't imagine what the boy's isolation from other kids must've been like; even on their own travels after their abandonment, Rand and Meech always had each other.

"How is this possible?" he asked Mellory. He wanted to believe this man, he really did, but it was all too good to be true.

Mellory grinned and laid the stump of his wrist on Rand's shoulder. "You folks get fed and rested, then come to the tavern and we'll have a good, long chat."

## 3

"Would you stop staring and lie down?" Rand urged. "You heard what that doctor told you."

Lillam turned from the window she'd been standing at for the past ten minutes, through which they had a sweeping view of one of Wilton's southernmost thoroughfares and the people of all ages and sexes who traveled it. Joy made her face glow as she moved toward him. "I'm sorry, I just can't believe this is happening! I keep thinking if I look away for too long, they'll all be gone!"

They were given a spare room on the second floor of a quaint home owned by a couple a few years older than Rand and Lillam, who built the dwelling with the intention of filling it up with children. The space was smaller than their dormitories back in Ida and outfitted with only a feather mattress, a chair, and a homemade chest of drawers, but after the confines of the wagon and the ravages of the desert, it was profound luxury. Hot water was boiled for a bath, which they took together in the large metal tub down the hall. Scrubbing away weeks of sweat and sand felt wonderful, but the freedom of being able to do it at the same time—without worrying that someone would break down the door to exile them for fraternization—made them both giddy with relief.

It was also the first time Rand had seen her completely bare since the day before they'd left on this journey, and he'd been startled when she showed him the small but noticeable rise to her stomach which his baggy clothes had previously hidden.

That was his offspring, growing inside her. A child that would one day be no different than the ones outside. He thought again of that golden fire and realized he badly wanted to meet the being who generated it.

By the time they finished bathing, the town had donated enough clothing to give them both a whole new (if somewhat dour) wardrobe, a charity Lillam needed far more than he. Then, after a hot meal of fresh river pike and carden beans, a hunchbacked little bodla named Timpett arrived to give them an inspection and patch up their various scratches and wounds. He was most concerned with Lillam's stubbornly festering shoulder wound, which he treated with an herbal paste and bade her to rest before going to the room next door to examine Meech's arm.

Rand was thrilled to see her smiling as she flew from the window into his arms. He pulled her close and kissed her deeply, drinking in the clean smell of her. All the enmity and sore feelings from their last fight in the desert was forgotten amid the jubilance of their escape and arrival in this miraculous place. "I know," he said, when they parted, "but they won't disappear, I promise. Right now, I want you in that bed."

She smirked wickedly as she caressed between his legs. "You read my mind."

He sighed with pleasure but gently removed her hand before he became too stiff for his new pants to contain. "When I get back from talking to Mellory, you can have your way with me."

Lillam scowled and flopped backward across the mattress in a huff. "I don't see what's to talk about," she pouted. "This town is perfect in every way. I want to have our baby here."

"And that's one of the things I'll speak to him about. But I don't want you to get your hopes up about staying yet."

"Get my—? Aged Lord, Rand! Isn't that the reason we came all this way? To get our hopes up?"

"I just want all the facts before we make any rash decisions. We need to understand how this is possible before we let our guard down."

"I don't care how it's possible." Lillam sounded resolute as she stared longingly at the window. "This place... something is different here. Don't you feel it?"

He did. Oh Lord, he did. Even aside from the shock of the children, there was an energy in the air, an intangible spark that he'd never experienced in Ida or anywhere else. It was evident in the way people moved, in the easy lilt of their conversation and laughter, and Rand thought he knew what it was.

Everyone he'd ever met was ruled by an undercurrent of fear. Fear of procreating, fear of someone else doing so, fear of encountering a child or having an Incarnate think they did. It drove every decision in their lives, from where to live to who to love to how far that love could go. Hells, Ida had been ready to tear itself apart over one pre-ager in their midst.

But here, within the boundaries of this magical town, that ubiquitous, subconscious fear just didn't exist. As Lillam pointed out when they first met Gaulbriel and Onjel, the citizens of Wilton didn't have a care in the world.

The result was a heady, intoxicating sense of...of *wholeness*, as if a missing piece of one's soul had been fitted back into place.

"Is this what it was like?" she asked softly. "Before the Purges? Before the Filament? When parents didn't have to go on a Rearing to give their children a future?"

"Maybe," he conceded. He lowered himself to the mattress and stretched out beside her. "But what if Korden was right? You saw how many Incarnates chased us through the Valley. Enough to roll over this town without even breaking stride. They could be rolling toward us even as we speak."

"These people didn't seem to care."

"And I, for one, would like to know what gives them so much confidence."

Lillam squeezed her eyes shut. "You told me we'd be safe if we made it to the Skyreach."

Rand leaned over her and put a hand on that firm bump in the middle of her stomach. "And I want to make sure we will be."

"So it's definitely 'we' then? You're not planning to steal away and abandon the girl who 'duped' you?"

"As long as she promises never to get 'banged up' by anybody else."

"I wouldn't count on that. You're certainly not the highest man in town anymore."

He laughed and kissed her forehead. "Let me see what I can find out from Mellory, and we'll go from there."

She nodded grudgingly and curled up in bed. He tucked her beneath the blankets before slipping out.

## 4

As twilight descended, oil lamps on poles were lit along the wide dirt avenue running through the center of Wilton. People gathered beneath them, talking, singing, and eating in the cheerful glow. The custom was charming, but it was their *mohols* that were truly fascinating; the auras were in harmony with one another, emotions flowing easily from one person to the next in an unending ribbon of peaceful, content color that reminded Korden of the sandman's method of communication. He goggled at the spectacle even as an eleven-year-old boy named Arrin explained the rules of the game to him for a second time.

"So then, if you get tagged on the way to base, you gotta count next time." Arrin squinted at him. "You really never played Hidey Sneak before?"

"No," Korden answered. "I...well, I never had anyone to play with at all, until now."

The children digested this information with reverent nods, as they did everything that came out of his mouth. Of the fifty-eight pre-agers Korden had been told resided in Wilton, there were twenty-four gathered around him. The rest were all infants, a massive crop of births that occurred within the last year. Korden was older than anyone in his new entourage, the closest being a fourteen-year-old girl named Debress with brown curls and warm blue eyes whose gaze stayed fixed on him as the children showed him around the town. They asked him a thousand endless questions—about his parents, his shoes, his companions, where he'd travelled, what his favorite food was, on and on and on—and he answered them as honestly as possible without revealing too much about his past. Zeega had taken refuge in the eaves of a nearby dwelling, out of reach of the small hands who wanted to touch and poke at her squishy form.

"Did you weawwy see Incawnates?" one of the younger boys inquired, his eyes wide. He was so tiny, Korden could've stowed him in his carry pouch. It was mind-boggling that a being so small could grow into a full-sized adult.

"I did," he confirmed.

"What did they wook wike?"

"Like anyone else, I suppose. Except with red eyes." Korden frowned. Talking with children was so different than with adults. They knew so much but understood so little. "None of you have ever seen one?"

"*I* have," Arrin proclaimed, puffing out his chest. "Me and my dad killed one before we came here. Ran it through with a spear. I saw its soul come out and everything!" The bland reaction from the other children told Korden they'd heard this story before.

Debress toyed with the end of her hair as she asked, "So an actual *army* of them was hunting you? How come?"

"That's...um...well, I guess the easiest way to put it is that their leader doesn't like me."

"And you think they'll come here?"

Korden shrugged, caught between not wanting to cause panic in these innocent children and a need to be honest about the danger they faced. "I hope not. That's why I shouldn't stay too long, so hopefully they'll follow me and leave your town alone."

"No, don't go!" Debress blurted. Her aura ripened with a vivid, rosy color very similar to the one that surrounded Lillam whenever she looked at Rand. The younger girl composed herself quickly before adding, "I mean, you can if you want, but it'd be kye if you stayed..."

"Oooo, Debwess has a boyfwiend!" the younger boy sang, bringing laughter from the group. Debress's cheeks reddened as she swatted at him, her *mohol* darkening a few shades into embarrassment. Korden tried not to let his bafflement at the teasing show.

"Yeah, don't leave!" Arrin agreed. "I ain't scared of any Incarnates!"

"And why is that?" Korden asked, unable to keep from grinning at the bravado.

"Cause the Sisters'll take care of 'em!"

The proclamation stiffened the hair on Korden's neck. He grabbed the boy's shoulders and bent until their eyes were level. "What do you mean? Who are 'the Sisters'?"

Arrin opened his mouth, but his eyes flicked over Korden's shoulder. He let go of the boy to follow his gaze. Rand was coming up the street in a new—if somewhat ill-fitting—set of clothes.

"Sorry to interrupt," he said, "but I'm going to talk to Mellory. I figured you'd want to come."

"Yes, just a second." Korden turned back to Arrin, but the children were already running up the street, whooping and laughing. Debress went with them, but she flashed a shy smile at him over her shoulder that made his heart flutter.

"I see you made a new friend," Rand said, biting his cheek to suppress a grin.

"Yeah, they're nice."

"I'm sure *they* are, but I meant *her*."

"Oh." Korden squirmed and found a rock on the ground to nudge with his foot. "I've never talked to a girl before. It's strange."

"Believe on, it won't get any easier."

After checking to make sure Zeega would be all right on the rooftops, they walked up the road toward the warm lamplight and raucous noise drifting out of the tavern.

# RELIGIONS OF NECESSITY

## 1

Baryus Mellory's establishment was a single room about half the size of any of the taverns back in Ida, but otherwise it looked the same: long wooden tables where men—and even a few women—gathered to drink and sport. Gaulbriel was among them, sitting on a bench at the rear of the room playing the narrow corner in a game of Burdens. The tart smell of fruit mead and fried fish was overpowering. A serving bar took up the right wall, behind which Mellory and a second, younger man pulled drinks from tapped barrels. When Rand entered with Korden in tow, the patrons all looked up and cheered, whistling and raising their mugs in salute, a few moving their flattened hands through the air as if in imitation of a soaring bird. Rand and Korden gave awkward waves and headed for the bar while the rest of the room returned to their business.

"My new friends from the sky!" Mellory greeted as they took up empty stools. His hat was gone, hair combed, and he wore a vest that might've been made from beaver pelt, the nicest article of clothing Rand had seen in Wilton thus far.

"Are people ever going to stop talking about that?"

"Not 'til you set the record straight, I reckon. Gaulbriel's painted quite the pitcher. I admit, I've got a bad case of o' curious myself." The tavernmaster retrieved copper mugs from a drying rack on the bar. "How's 'bout a drink for you and your son. He looks old enough for a little imbib'fication."

"He's not my son," Rand corrected. "We...met on the way here."

"Wow. Just guardin him then?" Mellory gave an admiring nod. "Takin responsibility for a pre-ager that ain't your own blood is an admirable thing. Not too many would dare. I hope you 'preciate all the things this gentleman did for you, young man."

Struggling to contain laughter, Korden said, "Oh, sure! I never would've made it this far without him!" Beneath the bar, Rand launched a swift kick into his leg.

Mellory gave the boy a suspiciously amused frown, then turned away to fill the mugs beneath a keg spigot, a daunting task for a one-handed man. "But the bun in the miss'um's oven; that one's yours, correct? Doc Timpett says she's a good ten or twelve weeks along."

"Yes. It's mine," Rand confirmed. The admission caused a spur of guilt even though there seemed to be little cause for it here. In Ida, he'd've been marched to the stocks and shamed for a week. He imagined it would be a long time before such cultural standards faded from his mind, if they ever did.

"Then you came to the right place. We got plenty o' folk here that un'erstand the birthin process, if you wanna know what to 'spect." Mellory set the dark brown drinks on the scarred bartop in front of them. "My own recipe, brewed right here. On the house, a-course, 'til we can figure out a work detail for ya to ply against."

Rand lifted the mug to his lips and tasted the liquid within. It was a heady, thick brew, flavored with lemon. "'Work detail?' Is that a nice way of saying we're to be indentured?" Beside him, he sensed Korden tense. The boy had strong but understandable issues with forced servitude.

Mellory laughed. "No whips here, my friend. But, as you've prob'ly seen, we're too small and off-the-beaten-track to have muchuva barter 'conomy. At the present, we survive on commune princ'ples. All of us workin together for the betterment of Wilton." Despite the twangy accent it was delivered in, the explanation caused Rand to reevaluate Mellory. He'd assumed the man was another bumpkin, but perhaps there was more to him than met the eye. "If ya don't take to our ways though, there're other Filament-free cities strung all along the Skyreach that'd take ya in. No hard feelins, I'd be happy to point the way."

"You mean there are *more* places like this?" Korden blurted through a mouthful of mead.

The tavernmaster winked at him before addressing Rand. "You got any skills that might be o' use?"

"I can read and write. And…well, I used to be the personal assistant to a mayor, helping run an entire city."

Mellory's face brightened as he hooked his thumb into a buttonhole on his vest. "Now, that's interestin! This place is desperately in need o' leadership. Which city was this, if you don't mind me askin?"

"Ida."

"Oh, *that* place." The other man blew a dismissive

raspberry. "Separatin the guys and gals. Humans weren't meant to live that way. No offense to you or your work."

"None taken. That system was in place long before I came there." Rand could feel heat in his cheeks as he added, "Obviously, I didn't follow the rules."

"No, I s'ppose not." Mellory shook his head. "Y'know, between settlements like Ida and all this 'Aged Lord' nonsense, we're just helpin the Filament along."

Rand chuckled.

"What's funny?"

"If you don't worship the Aged Lord here, Lillam's not going to be as thrilled about this place as she thinks."

"She's free to pray however she likes. But that religion... it's one o' *necessity*. I can guarantee you, after a season or two here, she'll wanna wash the taste o' that name right outta her mouth. I sure did."

"Why is that? Because people aren't scared of the Filament here?"

He hoped the question would prompt Mellory for the information he'd come for, but instead, the man walked down the bar to the other tender. "I'd like you both to meet my son, Harek." The younger man—a rugged guy with greasy black hair and a scraggle of goatee encircling his mouth—nodded in their direction after being tapped on the shoulder by his father.

"Harek turned nineteen last season," Mellory continued with a wistful grin. "Didn't think he'd ever see it, even after we ended up here. When he hit free age last year, I threw 'im the biggest party you could imagine. Kept halfa Wilton soused for three days." His face darkened. "Before that…we were on the Rear for years. Got cornered in a siege down south with some other families. I lost my hand fightin those bastards off. Harek and I escaped. No one else did. Includin his mother."

"I'm sorry for your loss."

Mellory nodded at the condolence. "These days, most o' us know what runnin's like. I'm sure you did it when you were a pre-ager. Exhaustion settles into your bones, becomes a way o' life. Steals a peace o' mind you can never get back. But now…you have a chance to give your child somethin *better*. Don't pass it up."

Rand moved his drink aside and leaned over the bar, eager to steer the conversation where he needed it to go. "Look, I admit, your setup here…it's very impressive. I can't speak for Korden or my brother, but Lillam and I would very much like to live here. She's…she's so tired, just like you say, and she wants to believe all of this is real. Which is why I have to be the one keeping my eyes wide open."

"Meanin?"

"Meaning that before I gulp down a fairy tale, I need to understand what makes this place so special. Why doesn't the Filament come here?"

All expression fell off Mellory's face. He regarded Rand with hooded eyes and said in a flat tone, "Don't play coy with me, Mr. Holcomb. You wouldn'ta gone east, come all the way across that burnin valley, if you didn't hear the rumors. So why don't you go ahead and say it?"

Rand hesitated, taken aback by his sudden change of demeanor, so the answer came from the boy beside him.

"Moambati," Korden said.

## 2

Since coming to this town, Mellory—and most of the other adults—had more or less overlooked Korden, directing their conversation and inquiries at Rand or Lillam or even Meech. He was confused until he observed the other kids being treated the same way, and then the answer came to him in a flash: here, being a pre-ager didn't make him an oddity. He'd been the sole focus of attention his entire life, from Redfen's overprotection to the Olders' teachings, and in every settlement he'd set foot in since leaving the village. Being able to slip into anonymity for a change proved enormously relieving.

But now he needed Mellory to hear him, to take him seriously as more than just another child. "What do you know?" he asked urgently. "Please, tell us."

"Prob'ly not much more'n what you've heard," Mellory said evasively, while he busied himself wiping down the bar.

Korden thought about Arrin's last, cryptic declaration. "I doubt that very much."

"Start by telling us how Wilton and all these other towns came to be," Rand encouraged.

Mellory stopped cleaning and cocked a bushy eyebrow at him. "Ask yourself this, friend: does that *really* matter?"

"If I'm ever going to feel comfortable here, then yes, it does."

Mellory sighed and dropped the rag. Conversation around the room fell quiet. Korden glanced back to see all eyes on the tavernmaster. "Four or five years ago, the settlements around here weren't much diff'rent than anywhere else. Wide places in the road, mostly bodlas and crones. Way stations for trade caravans headin to the eastern kingdoms or folk fleein west to put some distance between them and the Shroud. Then, alluva sudden, people started noticed somethin peculiar."

"What was it?" Korden urged impatiently, denying the urge to shake the answer out of the man.

Mellory walked his fingers across the bar top. "Those on the run from Incarnates saw that if they could make it up into the peaks of the Skyreach, those Incarnates met with… an unpleasant end."

"How? What killed them?" Rand asked.

"These people didn't know. Never saw. Just heard the shouts and the sounds o' battle, and then the Incarnates— those that even got found—were torn to pieces. Pretty soon, the Filament wouldn't even pursue folk up there anymore. When a person got their child as far as these foothills, the Incarnates turned tail and retreated. And boy, what a sight *that* musta been." Several bar patrons cheered this sentiment before Mellory continued. "So they started puttin down roots. Buildin stable lives and homes for their offspring in a way no one has in hundreds of years. But all the time stayin wary, in case the phenom'non or miracle or whatever it was ended. Then…the dreams came."

Korden froze. His head was buzzing a bit from the mead, but he didn't believe this was the reason his body seemed to belong to someone else as he whispered, "Dreams?"

Mellory nodded. "A vision shared by all who take up residence in the shadow o' the Skyreach. Dreams o' two identical blackenfolk women. Dark and strangely-accented and so gorgeous most men wake up with a puddle in their pants." He grunted. "Ladies too, for that matter."

"What happens in them?"

"Always the same. They speak in rhymes, and tell us the Filament can't touch us so long's we're under the protection of Moambati. They say not to worry, to just stay where we are and enjoy life." He closed his eyes as if conjuring the image of these midnight reveries. "Makes you feel like someone snuggled you up in a big ol' blanket of happiness."

"Wait on," Rand interrupted. "You're telling us you've experienced these dreams *yourself*?"

Mellory looked past them at the rest of the tavern. "Raise your hands if you had a meetin with the Moambatis this past week!"

A majority of the hands in the room went up. Someone near the back called out, "Wish they'd meet with my cock!" to boisterous laughter.

The tavernmaster raised an eyebrow at Rand. "We all have 'em at diff'rent times, completely random. You stay here long enough, you will too."

Korden frowned. "A boy here in town...he said something about 'the Sisters.'"

"That's what most've taken to callin 'em." Here Mellory hesitated again. "A lot o' folk're comin around to the way of thinkin that they're...some kinda gods."

"But that can't be right!" Korden argued. After they'd controlled him, threatened him, and tried to use him to dismember one of his friends, the idea of someone revering Denise and Charlotta Moambati—or whatever masqueraded as them—made him sick. He thought about his last conversation with Winstid and his deputies as he exclaimed, "Everyone beyond the Valley of Bones is terrified of them! When I first heard the rumors, I was told no one could cross to the other side of the mountains anymore, and that entire towns had disappeared!"

Mellory's expression remained placid, but his *mohol* revealed an emotion akin to horror growing in him. He leaned over to whisper something to his son, then gestured for Rand and Korden to follow him around the end of the bar and through a door that took them out to a narrow alcove behind the tavern, where the water wheel spun around and around in the stream. The man sat down on a stump of rock beside the creek and regarded them like someone working a difficult puzzle.

"From what I un'erstand, there was a lotta that sorta talk near the beginnin." Mellory loosened the leather cap at the end of his arm and slipped it off, then rubbed at the knob of gnarled flesh beneath. "Back then, folk didn't know what to think, so they got every bit as scared o' the Moambatis as the Incarnates. And, fact is, those early stories are prob'ly the reason we weren't overrun with refugees." He swallowed and shook his head. "But no one takes too kindly to the Sisters bein badmouthed anymore."

"Is any of it true though?" Korden pressed.

The tavernmaster shrugged. "After awhile, it wasn't just Incarnates that vanished in the Skyreach," he admitted. "There's been no word from the eastern side in years. And those who try to cross never return. For all we know, there are settlements like Wilton croppin up over there."

"And what about these missing towns?" Rand asked.

"There was only one that I know of. Place called Farrowbend. A day's ride northeast o' here, up by Red Creek. And before you get too worked up, nobody knows for sure what happened there." Mellory shifted on the rock. The conversation seemed to've taken a toll on the usually cheerful man. For a time, the only sound was the babble of the stream and the incessant creak of the water wheel. "Farrowbend was a town long before the Incarnates stopped comin around, so they were in a better position to take people in. Their pop'lation exploded from a hundred people to close to five in two years. Magnificent place, closest I've ever seen to an old-world city. If things'd kept goin, we'd prob'ly've been absorbed into their community by now. Then, last year, the whole town—from the smallest babe to the oldest crone—up and vanished. Overnight. Not a one o' 'em seen since. Farrowbend is still sittin there, just as they left it. But nobody'll go near it, not even looters."

Korden suddenly recalled what the Prophet said before they'd launched the stratoliner, about a city close to their destination being abandoned. If there had been more time, he might've connected this to the rumors Winstid first told him about.

Rand was gaping at Mellory. "And people think Moambati did this?"

"For a time. Now, like I said...no one speaks ill o' the ones protectin us. They think those two women hung the moon and lit the stars. That's why when you all showed up, babblin 'bout Incarnate armies headin this way, they laughed it off. None of 'em wants to believe things could go back to the way they used ta be."

"Talk about a religion of necessity," Rand muttered. He sounded somehow offended.

"But it doesn't make sense." Stone's absence hit Korden all over again; the computer's counsel always gave him much-needed insight to human behavior. "Why would they all stay here and worship these Sisters if there's a chance they could disappear too?"

Mellory studied him with a mixture of pity and disdain, the way one looks at a horse that needs to be put down for its own good. "Because folk will accept a lotta curse just to feel safe."

# BLINDERS

## 1

Korden awoke sore and bruised in the hayloft where he was given quarter, after a tortured night of tossing and turning. It hadn't been easy falling asleep without the security of Stone's watchdog mode, especially in light of their alarming conversation with Baryus Mellory.

Even before his eyes opened, his stomach was in knots. He'd come to a decision about his next step after leaving the tavern, and he didn't like it any better this morning than he had in the dark.

He sat up and looked around the small, triangular loft. Zeega roosted in the rafters to his left, where she could emit her call to keep his slumber free of intrusive dreams. Her five yellow eyes were already open and fixed upon him as she silenced the buzzing mental drone with the power to choke off his flow of artcraft.

"Zeega, I—"

"You are going to travel to the abandoned town you were told of last night," she surmised, reading his thoughts, "in order to seek answers about Moambati."

"Yes." It was a slim hope, but it might keep him from blundering into the mountains of the Skyreach completely blind about what waited for him.

The riftling bobbed her small head forward in curt acknowledgment. "Zeega will accompany you."

"Are you sure? You're free now. You could go wherever you want."

She considered this, but only briefly. "Zeega wants to continue your practice of 'asking questions.' She would like to learn more. To seek the truth, so she is never lied to again."

"Yes, that's important," he agreed. "But you don't have to be with me to ask questions."

"Then who will hear them?" She jumped down from the rafter, landing nimbly beside him in a flurry of purple tentacles. "Zeega wishes to follow Korden, wherever you go."

He smiled, unable to hide his relief. "All right. Let's go tell the others."

2

They found Rand and Lillam sitting on a grassy knoll outside the home where the couple had spent the night, watching several of the town's children as they attempted to get a diamond-shaped swatch of fabric mounted on wooden sticks to ride the wind currents. Lillam laughed and cheered them on with Rand's arm resting comfortably around her shoulders. Their *mohols* were more relaxed and at ease than Korden had ever seen them, in sync with each other and even the scampering children. Korden was relieved that Debress and Arrin weren't among the other pre-agers; he didn't want to answer their endless questions about his departure.

Rand noticed Korden approaching and took his measure. "You look determined."

"I am." He told them his intentions. "I'm leaving this morning, as soon as I can. And even though we don't have Gwenita anymore, you're welcome to keep traveling with me."

The couple exchanged a glance filled with as much subtle communication as any aura. Then Rand shook his head. "Thanks for the offer, Korden. But we'll have to decline."

"I understand." The disappointment was bitter, but not unexpected. The arrangement had been for him to get them across the Valley of Bones; why would they want to endanger themselves any further by staying in his presence before their own child was even born? "Where will you go then?"

"Go?" Rand spread his arms. "We're staying right here."

This answer, however, jolted Korden. Getting distance from him was one thing, but remaining in the haunted shadow of the Skyreach? He looked to Lillam. "Didn't he tell you what Mellory said?"

"He told me everything," she assured him. "It doesn't matter. I want to live here. I want to be like these people, and have my daughter be as free as *them*." She nodded at the group of children, who laughed gleefully as they fell on top of one another in the dirt.

"But Moambati—!"

Rand cut him off. "We're not jumping into this willy-nilly, Korden. All right? We talked about it. Stayed up most of the night talking about it, actually." He used two fingers to rub his eyes as if to illustrate this claim. "It's creepy, sure. Neither of us is excited about having the weird dreams. And we have no intention of worshipping these 'Sisters.' But, even more than that…we don't want to run for the next eighteen years. If there's a chance we won't have to, we intend to take it. Besides, these people aren't worried about Moambati; maybe it's vain of us to show up here for a day and think we know better."

This reasoning was just more evidence of the theory Mellory put forth: that people would accept a lot of curse to feel safe. Something about this place dropped blinders across a person's vision, and Korden wondered if the residents of the other 'Filament-free' cities were of the same mind. "Then what about the Incarnates?" he asked. "What if they're coming here?"

"And what if the sky falls?" Rand countered. "What if a herd of wild ramlars tramples us all to death? There'll always be what-ifs. We'll have to deal with them as they happen. That's what we decided to do: take it one *if* at a time."

The sentiment reminded Korden so much of Fortholm's life philosophies (and a parable he loved to tell about chipmunks) that his heart ached for home. Still, he might have argued on if Lillam hadn't struggled to her feet with a little help from Rand and moved toward him. He cringed, thinking she might mean to slap him, but she took his hand and placed it gently on her stomach. Korden could feel a tiny lump beneath the fabric, in the same place where that golden aura had blazed.

"Thank you," she told him softly. "For everything you did for us. For *her*. We never would've made it here if not for you. I...I was wrong to treat you so poorly. I'll remember that the next time I meet a Crafter."

Korden threw his arms around her. She hugged him back, bent to kiss the top of his head. It was then that he understood how much he'd become used to having these people in his life, and how much he would miss them.

From behind her, Rand said, "Excuse us for a minute, sweetlove. I'd like to have a minute alone with Korden."

Lillam knelt to say goodbye to Zeega while Rand led Korden to the opposite side of the house. The position was far out of earshot, but that didn't keep Rand from glancing nervously back at his lady when Korden said, "You can still practice your artcraft. Just keep doing the exercises I showed you. As soon as you can open your conduit, the rest should come quickly."

"Well...I'm hoping now that we're here, I won't ever need it."

"You should at least try. You were given the gift for a reason. The Upper wants you to use it."

"Then the Upper should make it easier to do so."

Korden nodded sadly. The man's prejudice and fear of his own artcraft ran deep. Korden suspected they might be part of Rand's inability to use his magic reliably, but he couldn't help feeling as thought the failure were his own. He'd taken the man as his *den-ret*, yet taught him nothing. All their sessions in the desert seemed so pointless now.

A scowl on Rand's face indicated they'd come to the reason for the secretive conversation. "Are you planning to take Meech with you?"

"I guess I'll offer…"

"Don't. As much as I want him gone from my life, he would only be a liability to you. And that's the last thing you need."

It was no more than what lurked in the back of Korden's mind when Meech first made his proposal back in Ida. Still, it saddened him to hear his friend and 'bodyguard' spoken of so harshly. "Will you ever forgive him?"

"I don't even want to waste the time it would take answering that question on my worthless excuse of a brother. He is a degenerate with no redeeming value. A squandering of the life our parents bestowed upon him."

Korden stared at his sneakers, unsure what else to say.

"You know, you don't have to go either." Rand said this as if stating the obvious to a very dense individual…but Korden saw hope threading through his *mohol* and was touched by it. "Wherever you're going, whatever you plan to do…forget about it. In two years, when you hit free age, you can leave then. Or not. I'm sure that girl Debress could give you plenty of reasons to stay."

"I can't," Korden told him, wanting nothing more.

"Then I guess this is goodbye." Rand stuck out his hand. As Korden shook it, he added, "I'm sorry for what I said. About you…taking the moral high ground, or whatever foolishness I spouted back before we left Ida. You always see the best in everyone, find the positive in any situation. I don't understand how you do it, but I think you made even me a better person. And whatever you're seeking, I hope you find it."

Korden wiped at his moist eyes. "May all your choices be true."

"Right back at you." He glanced down at Zeega as the riftling joined them. "Take care of him, all right?"

"Zeega will endeavor to do so."

Rand walked away, and Korden went inside the house to say goodbye to Meech.

3

No one answered when he knocked at the bedroom door. Korden opened it to reveal a room steeped in darkness, the window covered by a blanket. Meech lay on the mattress with his splinted arm across his chest. He appeared to be sleeping, but, as Korden approached, he saw the man's eyes were open and staring at the ceiling. Sweat beaded on his forehead like dark jewels.

"I'm leaving," Korden said. "I wanted to…well, to say goodbye."

"Goodbye," was all the man returned, without taking his eyes from the ceiling.

"Meech…are you all right? Is it the gimmies?"

"Yes. But that certainly isn't all it is." He rolled on his side to face Korden, favoring his left arm. His aura was a mess once more, and responded little when Korden tried to soothe it. "I don't blame you for goin on without me. Rand is right; I'd just hold you back."

Korden glanced at the covered window, which was

positioned above where he and Rand had been talking. "You heard that?"

Meech sighed weakly. "Doesn't matter. Like I said, he's right. I'm not fit for human company. Might as well tie me up and leave me for the wolves."

"Don't say that…"

"*Look* at me. Look at what I've become. I'm a wretch with only one thought in my head. I mean, I'm talkin to you now, drude, and if someone told me all I'd have to do to get another spin is kill you…I'd have my hands around your throat faster than you could say 'jinkoid.'"

"You would never do that!"

Meech gave a thin, brittle laugh. "I *have* done that. I left you out in that desert without a second thought, remember? I can't be trusted. Not even by myself."

"It's not too late," Korden said. "You said you wanted to be free of it. So keep trying."

"I'm tired of trying." He lay back to stare at the ceiling. "I'm tired of everything. I'm going to wait here until it's all over."

Korden had no idea what he meant by 'all over,' but the phrase terrified him. He stood in the middle of the room, desperate for a way to fix this. The man on the bed was so unlike the cheerful, carefree man he'd met on a Tay-ho peak all those weeks ago. "Meech, if you would—"

"Just go. I don't have anything else to say."

Korden trudged into the hall. "You should talk to your brother," he said, before pulling the door closed.

## 4

Korden found Mellory and his son working outside their establishment and asked for directions to the town of Farrowbend. The tavernmaster gave him a quizzical look.

"Why would you wanna go pokin 'round there?" he asked.

"Because I intend to go east, across the Skyreach. Anything I can find out about the Moambatis might help."

"All right. I ain't your pappy. If you *do* make it through the mountains though, we'd appreciate you doin whatever you can to send word back about the situation there."

"I promise," Korden agreed. "And one more thing. Does the name 'Crested Butte' mean anything to you?"

Mellory's face scrunched in thought, but his perplexed aura was all the answer Korden needed. "Don't believe so. What is that, a nethers disease?"

"Not exactly." Korden could find the name of the town which the Moambatis had told him to go to on his map, but, without Stone, he had no way of gauging exactly where *he* was. For all he knew, he might be blundering right into the Sisters' hands.

The tavernmaster lifted a shoulder. "Then let's scrounge around for some vittles to send you on your way."

Ten minutes later, he and Zeega walked through Wilton one last time, intending to leave through the hills to the north. The town was coming alive for the day, people emerging to go about their business, and, as they turned a corner onto one of the dirt roads that crossed the main avenue, a familiar voice reached them.

"What about *you*, sah? Yah look like yah could use a little more spring in yah step! And miss'um, is takin care of all those kiddos gettin yah down? Try some of Doc Apocalypse's Miracle Cure to keep yah on yah toes! I'll trade fer whatever yah can spare!"

Doaks stood in the mouth of a narrow alley between two homes, wearing one of his fancy costumes—the only one he'd salvaged from the stratoliner wreckage—but the fabric was torn and soiled, and the gaudy rings were all gone from his thick fingers. A rickety table stood beside him on which were stacked various glass jars of some cloudy liquid. He hawked one of these to everyone who passed, but scowled when he caught sight of Korden and Zeega.

"Fantastic! Let me guess, yah just stopped by to drive off my customers? Shatter my goods? Maybe yank my knickers up over the backa my head fer good measure?"

"If Korden commands it, it will be done," Zeega growled.

"Yah know squiddy, for someone who does an awful lotta whining about her masters, yah sure have taken a new one pretty damn fast."

Korden stepped between them before the fight could worsen. "What are you doing, Doaks?"

"What does it look like I'm doin? I'm tryin to bring a little relief to these peoples' lives! But the framheads won't even talk to me!"

"That's because they don't need relief. They're happy here. Your slick tongue won't work on them."

Doaks's neck and cheeks burned so red, the color was visible even through his beard. "Well, what else am I supposed to do, eh? I gotta get supplies together to mount an expedition back out to the Valley to rescue Gwenita, since someone abandoned 'er out there! But I can't dance no more thanks to my new bum knee, and this crooked sausage in the middle of my face ain't doin me no favors, either!" He kicked the leg of the table beside him in frustration, causing the glassware to rattle and him to clutch at his injured leg.

Trying not to laugh, Korden picked up one of the frothy jars. "What is this stuff?"

Doaks hesitated, then waved a dismissive hand. "Mostly muddy stream water. A little flacker root mixed in to give it a kick. Oh, don't look at me like that, I built that concoction into an empire once, I'll do it again. Had to trade my rings to get the jars, but it'll all be worth it." He eyed Korden and noticed the carry pouch slung over his shoulder. "Where yah off to?"

"Farrowbend first. Then east."

"Right. Gotta continue the biiiiig quest. Those other rubos goin with yah?"

"No. They're staying here."

"I don't know if that's a sign of sense or lack thereof." His tone softened almost imperceptibly as he asked, "What about yah little computer friend? He get better?"

The question surprised him; Doaks was the first person who'd asked. "No. I still can't get anything out of him."

"That's too bad. That thing was one valuable piece of tech."

Korden hefted the jar, sloshing the liquid inside. "Have you considered giving this up? Making an honest life for yourself here? Everyone else thinks this place is paradise."

"No sah, I can't put down roots. My heart needs to roam. Soon as I get the capital, I'm outta here."

"If they don't throw you out beforehand."

"Wouldn't be the first time." Doaks watched as Korden put the jar back down, then reached out and grabbed his shoulders so fast that Zeega gave a warning growl. "Listen boy, I-I-I admit I did yah wrong, and I'm sorry fer that!" His eyes were wild as he pleaded, "But yah and me, we can make a lotta scratch together! With yah magic, surely we could find a way to do some good for people! *Real* good, not this snake oil hype! Yah be the talent, and I'll take care of the business side! Let's just...*let's stick together!*"

The desperation in his words would've aroused pity... but Korden could see the bright silver in his *mohol*, glinting like a knife. "I used to hate you, Doaks," he said, shaking free of the man's grip. "I don't anymore, but I could never forget what you did to me. To us. I can, however, wish you good luck, and part with no ill will."

It took Doaks a good ten seconds to compose himself. His face buttoned up as he smoothed down the front of his colorful vest. "Yah as well, rubo. Yah as well."

With Zeega at his heel, Korden walked past Tarmon Doaks and left the town of Wilton behind for good.

# FARROWBEND

## 1

The terrain roughened throughout the day as Korden traveled, spiking into steep ridgebacks that he was forced to either claw his way up or avoid by traversing winding ravines that often took him the wrong direction. A dense forest of slim-trunked aspens, alders, and willows made either choice unappealing.

But, worst of all, the directions Mellory had given proved to be disastrously vague. They could find none of the landmarks he'd listed, and soon gave up in favor of trying to keep to a northeastern direction. Zeega scouted ahead wherever possible, climbing the tallest trees to get the lay of the land, while Korden used the time to scribble lines of poetry and work on writing a new story. The creativity refilled his depleted artcraft coffers much faster than it used to, but the supply was far more natural than the borrowed power that had been pumped into him through the dreams.

After hitting their third impassable route and being forced to backtrack yet again, Korden declared in frustration that it was time to make camp for the night.

While Zeega gathered firewood, Korden huddled on his bedroll and held Stone's casing in his hands. Today was another bitter reminder of how much he needed the computer. He couldn't travel even a few hours through these foothills without becoming lost over and over; what chance did he have to find his way across the towering summits of the Skyreach and the uncharted country beyond? The endless spans ahead suddenly felt all the more treacherous to Korden.

But, aside from that...he missed his friend.

*I'm sorry*, he thought, as the tears he'd been holding back scalded his eyes. *It's my fault. I shouldn't have asked you to fly the stratoliner. I'll find some way to fix you. I* promise.

*Listen to yeh, ghammer.* The disgust in Tash's words was entirely authentic, modeled from years of hearing him sound that way in real life. *Mournin a 'lectronic gizmo?*

*He was more than that*, Korden told the imagined representation of his mentor. Without Stone filling the quiet places of his mind, he wondered if more voices from the past would speak up to break the silence. *He cared about me, worried when I got sick or upset...*

*Because he was* programmed *ta do so. Didn't he tell yeh as much himself?*

*Well...yes. But even if he was, that doesn't make my affection for him any less genuine.*

*He was naught but circuits and wire, ghammer. A digital ghost in yehr head. Yeh became too dependent on him. Put too much faith in technology. Jes' like the people o' the old world.*

"Who speaks to you this way?"

Korden jumped as Zeega interrupted his internal argument. The riftling scuttled out of the woods and dropped a claw-load of kindling on the ground in front of him.

"My old teacher," he said, wiping at his moist eyes.

"One of the male humans that reared you?"

Korden fastened the leather strap back around his neck and scooted forward to arrange the sticks for a fire. "Yes. The Olders. That's what I called them, anyway. They were Crafters who'd been alive for…a very long time."

She settled down on a pile of dead leaves and watched him with three of her eyes while the other two roamed. "These 'Olders.' They did not like technology? Like the *Exatraedes*?"

"No, they were *nothing* like the Incarnates," he answered, a bit too harshly. Korden softened his tone and continued. "It wasn't that they didn't like technology. They just believed in balance. And self-reliance. They didn't think you should use machines for any task you could do yourself. The same goes for artcraft, too."

Zeega considered this. "But there was much the disembodied one could do by his very nature that you would never be able to. Though Zeega was often rude to him, she would much rather have him present than absent. He was a useful ally."

Korden lit the fire in a burst of artcraft, then smiled at her over the crackling blue flames. "So are you."

She greeted this compliment with her usual stoicism, but her claws gave a few soft clacks in what he took to be contentment. Korden busied himself preparing some of the food Mellory sent with him, bread and cheese and fish fillets. He spitted one of the latter to lay across the flames, then threw a second to Zeega raw. She inhaled the meat with her disproportionately large mouth, sharp teeth a blur as she masticated, and gulped it down in one swallow before inquiring, "Your false broodsire was also one of these Olders?"

"My false brood...? Oh, you mean Redfen!" Korden chuckled. He wondered how the man he called father would've felt about this creature. "No, he wasn't an Older. He didn't even like artcraft. Wouldn't let me learn for a long time. But I wore him down."

"Zeega is confused. Why did this human have power over you if he was not your true broodsire?"

"Because, ever since I was baby, I thought he was."

Judging from the way her eyes blinked out of rhythm, he guessed this didn't clear up her confusion. "Who were your lifegivers?"

Korden flipped the fish over the fire as the flesh darkened. "That's a good question."

"Then honor it by answering."

"You're really taking this asking-mission seriously, aren't you?"

"If questions are the only true path to knowledge, then Zeega will pose them."

He sighed, seeing it was pointless to argue. But the last thing he wanted was another reaction like Rand's. "My mother was a Crafter. She told Redfen—my false broodsire—that I had no true father. But she was scared and weak and the Incarnates were closing in, so maybe it's not true.

In any case, I never met my parents, and I probably never will."

The jiggly flesh around the riftling's mouth tightened as she grimaced. "Zeega sympathizes. In the breeding farms, *hoshnitaths* are taken from the broodlayers at the larval stage. Zeega has never met her lifegivers either. The separation can stunt some *hoshnitaths*. Cause them to go feral."

This story reminded Korden of something that had been mulling in the back of his mind since their conversation with the sandman beneath the desert floor. He pulled the cooked fillet off the fire and took a steaming bite while he considered how best to broach the subject. "Zeega, this homeland of yours. Do you think it could be…on a different world than this one?"

"World?"

"Or maybe plane? Of the allverse?"

"Perhaps," she said slowly. "How do you know of the allverse?"

"I was told about it by two beings that came from these other planes. Do you know what it is? The allverse?"

Her multi-faceted gaze moved away. "These are things we should not speak of."

He laid the rest of the fish on his bedroll and moved around the fire to sit closer to her. "You're free now. You can speak of whatever you want. The Incarnates can't hurt you."

"What you ask concerns far more than the *Exatraedes*." Her tentacles twitched like a nest of rattlesnakes as she pronounced the word. "There are darker forces at work, masters that even *they* must answer to. Vast machinations neither Zeega nor Korden could ever comprehend. And if you think the Incarnates are the worst of what they have at their disposal, you are mistaken."

*Them and theirs*, he thought, recalling her words from before, during their mutual captivity with Doaks. The warning was chilling, but Korden didn't let it deter him. "Please," he persisted. "Anything you can tell me might help defeat them. It might even help free your people some day."

The riftling looked up sharply. "You believe...we can be free?"

"Of course! Your people have as much reason to be rid of them as we do. But we must work together. And you have information about the Filament that few others would."

She shivered, the motion like water ripples across her spongy body, but still did not speak. He started to press her again when she finally said, "The allverse is that which the Dark Filament wishes to spread the long, sweet silence to. The *Exatraedes* speak of it often. As Zeega understands, the planes are many; all the same, but different."

Korden frowned at the nonsensical answer. "How do they travel between them?"

"Zeega does not know."

"But don't your people travel with them? How did you get here from these breeding farms?"

"When transport is required, we are carried in sealed containers. The broods under Regent Torgas's command were brought here, to this hunting ground, many years ago, and kept in work camps until needed. However..." She paused to snap her claws and then lowered her gurgly voice. "There is a story that one *hoshnitath* saw out through a loose seam during transit. It spoke of endless corridors… huge, rusted machines…and powerful magics flowing through them like blood…"

Korden considered the description, then gazed up through the tree canopy, where the sky had darkened enough to show the first pinpoints of light. "When the Incarnates invaded my world—my plane—the people said something happened to the stars. Because of that, they called the story of everything that's happened since then 'the Dark Filament Ephemeris.' Do you know anything about that?"

"Zeega does not." The admission seemed to pain her. "But she can tell you this: your teachers were right to seek balance. Equilibrium and parity are the foundation upon which the allverse is built. The Filament detests such stability. They will accept nothing less than absolute annihilation of every plane."

A sudden flush of anger made Korden's hands tremble. "But if they want us dead so much, why don't they kill everyone and get it over with? There are so few of us left, they could do it in a season! So why do they only hunt the children?"

"Death is but the simplest form of destruction." All five of her unique pupils focused on him. "What they eradicate is not life, but *hope*. It is the one thing they fear, the single emotion that holds the Shroud at bay in every land they march upon. Hope means something different on each plane, but for most mortal species, you are united in the concept of a future beyond your own lifespan, and there is no greater symbol of this than the young. Children are pure. Unpolluted. Their slaughter is an atrocity that demoralizes all who are touched by it."

"That's horrible." A thought occurred to Korden, one that he tried to immediately hide away before it could be read, but he could tell from the way she stiffened that it was too late.

She closed her eyes one at a time until her face became nothing but a sheet of darkness. "Zeega did many things for the masters that she is not proud of."

He decided then and there that he didn't want to know about her past. It was no longer who she was. But there was one more thing she'd said that grabbed his attention.

"If hope is what keeps the Shroud at bay, then that means beyond it...all hope is gone?"

Zeega nodded with her eyes squeezed shut, a single dip of her small head. "Zeega has never been there, but the *Exatraedes* call that which exists beneath the Shroud...the Black Lands."

2

The following day dawned hot and bright; it was past the midpoint of Burning Season now, and Korden was thankful they'd gotten out of the Valley of Bones before the sluggish, miserable days leading up to the Harvest cooldown. After taking some time to faith and write, they set out. By late morning, he'd worked up a drenching sweat when he came to a wide, fast-moving waterway flowing down through the foothills in the opposite direction. He assumed this was Red Creek, though it looked more like a river and there was nothing red about it. They followed this stream toward the rising sun until an incline on the southern bank brought them above the forest canopy, and they got a first glimpse of their destination, a mere two spans away.

Or rather, the yellow cloud smothering it.

"That's a fear pathome," Korden said, thinking of the various fogs of leftover emotion he'd encountered. "Isn't it?"

"Yes," Zeega confirmed. "Many humans experienced the worst terror of their lives together in that place."

A cold breath of dread made every hair on Korden's body stand up. The jaundiced smog bank was smaller than the desperation *mohol* that had hung over Tay-ho, but much denser than the one inside the stratoliner, so thick that only a few of the closest rooftops were visible in its murky depths, like chunks of meat in a stewpot. He wondered if the reason for this might be because it was newer; a mere year old, rather than hundreds. And he realized he could see it even without the overabundance of artcraft, meaning that whatever the Moambati sisters had done to him, it must've altered his perception permanently.

"Can you block it out for me, like you did the one in the power center?"

"It will require extreme concentration. Zeega may be unable to avoid affecting your craft this time."

"That's all right. I'm still recovering from the stratoliner anyway."

"Very well." The riftling emitted her buzzing call. The pitch changed several times in Korden's head, growing more intrusive and shrill until the bones of his skull grinded against one another. He closed his eyes, and, when he opened them, the pathome in the distance was gone, revealing Farrowbend in all its glory.

The settlement was indeed much larger and grander than Wilton, full of stone and wood buildings of ornate design. Even from this distance, Korden could see painted shutters covering windows, beautiful ironwork decorating exteriors, and ivy-covered trellises—now overgrown—arching over the walkways between them. A low stone wall encircled the town, adequate to provide meager defense against ill-equipped marauders, but it was nothing compared to the battlements and heavy iron gates of Ida.

Zeega's cry grated on his nerves, but he thought he would be able to stand it long enough to take a quick peek around. "Let's get down there."

## 3

Fifteen minutes later, they crossed a sturdy horse bridge spanning Red Creek and pushed through a swinging iron gate into the settlement, following a rutted dirt road thatched with fresh grass from disuse. Narrow dwellings crowded the thoroughfare, quaint cottages with clay tile roofs and tiny rock chimneys jutting up from the rear. Many of their doors hung open, as if the occupants left in too much of a hurry to bother closing them. A few, however, were broken in, the wooden barriers reduced to splinters. With his artcraft regenerating, Korden was hesitant to open the conduit's eye to scan the area for *mohols*, but Zeega reported that she could sense nothing, save for the wildlife that had moved into the village in the absence of humans. Nevertheless, they peered through several windows and doors at random, studying the empty, dust-covered interiors before venturing deeper into Farrowbend.

From what he could tell, the town was situated circularly, with streets laid out like spokes on a wheel. As this avenue ran on, the construction became older stone structures that housed shops. Korden spotted signs for a tailor, a chemist, and a fletcher. He saw what Mellory meant now, about this place being close to an old-world city.

An outdoor marketplace much like the one at Ida soon took over. Vendor stalls were stationed along the building facades, leading to a central pavilion at the very heart of the settlement. They made their way to the middle and turned in slow circles, taking in the scene.

Korden had passed through many empty towns since beginning this journey, but they were mostly ruins, little more than rotted-out husks. That wasn't the case in Farrowbend. Everything looked so fresh and new, he kept expecting the residents to jump out at any moment, like the 'surprise parties' Eddas once told him about.

Aside from several overturned tables, vendor kiosks were stocked with wares, exactly as their owners left them. One stall held baskets of oranges, garrens, and bananas, the fruit long-since dried and shriveled. Horseshoes sat ready for fitting, slighty rusted after a few seasons exposed to the weather. Another counter was covered with small wooden horses carved from logs and strange burlap figures the size of his hand that were stuffed with straw and woven with yarn about the head for hair; it took Korden several seconds to comprehend that they were children's toys.

The emptiness—the glaring vacancy—gnawed at his nerves.

"They just…disappeared," Korden murmured, picking

up one of the dolls to study its tinted glass eyes.

"Zeega does not think it was that simple. There are signs of a struggle, though not many."

Korden turned from the table, clutching the burlap doll, and tried to figure out what to do next. He could spend time searching every building in this deserted town for clues, but it would likely yield the same results. Besides, it wasn't the aftermath he needed to see, but whatever had befallen this town and its people a year ago.

Unfortunately, he knew of but one way to do that.

He made his way back to Zeega, dropping the doll into his carry pouch. "You have to stop your call. I need to see the pathome."

The riftling's eyes widened in alarm. "Once they sense your awareness, the echoes within such a powerful emotional stain can be dangerous. Your mind could fracture if they infect you."

"I'm aware. But it's the only way we might be able to find out what happened to them."

"Then let Zeega open her awareness and experience it in your place."

Korden shook his head. "No. I need to see this for myself. If I get into trouble, you can block them out for me again, right?"

She hesitated. "The echo is so deep that a correct frequency is not easy to achieve. But yes, Zeega will try."

The buzz inside his head faded.

And Korden found himself thrust inside an ochre haze.

He gasped. There was no transition, just a sudden and total envelopment, as when the pathome on the lake descended upon him. A dirty yellow blur pressed in around him, unbroken and uniform in all directions. The fog grew so dense, he couldn't even see his own body below the knees. As with his past encounters, the emotional cloud gave off no taste or smell to hinder breathing, but he began to choke anyway as panic seized his weak lungs.

"Zeega is here." Her voice warbled even more than usual in the haze, but it gave sufficient reassurance to get his anxiety under control. "Give the pathome a chance to condense."

Korden waited, resisting the urge to close his eyes. His vision was indeed returning. Gradually, bit by bit, the surrounding buildings emerged as the mists thinned and withdrew. As inside the downed stratoliner and the casino, the pathome was solidifying, concentrating its mass into ethereal figures all around him. In less than a minute, the marketplace thrived with people made of yellow smoke. They went about their business in eerie silence: merchants hawking their goods as families strolled happily among them.

"Relay to Zeega what you see," the riftling urged, climbing up on top of a nearby vendor awning.

"They're just walking around like normal. I think it's called 'shopping,'" he whispered. "But I don't see any—Wait on. Something's happening."

The quaint atmosphere changed so slowly, it took seconds to catch his attention. Some of the yellow figures twisted their heads curiously to the east, as if drawn by a sound. Several ventured hesitantly in that direction. But they were soon forced to move out of the way as a mob of more smoke people stormed into the marketplace. These newcomers looked scared, and their fear spread quickly through the rest of the assembly. Within seconds, Korden stood in the midst of silent chaos as the emotional echoes of Farrowbend's townspeople stampeded like frightened sheep. They ran in all directions, crazed with fear, men holding their wives' hands, mothers carrying their children. Some of them headed for the other roads leading out of the marketplace, only to spin around and dive right back into the madness. Then Korden saw several of the ghostly forms jerking and spasming before they collapsed, and he understood.

*There was something among them in the marketplace.* A presence not represented in the pathome's reenactment, but one here during the event itself, terrorizing the townsfolk. And whoever—*what*ever—these unseen intruders were, they'd surrounded the remaining Farrowbenders. Their fright reduced those left standing to a pitiful huddle on the pavilion with Korden at the center. The unknown attackers moved in on them swiftly from all sides and, one by one, they fell limp to the ground, bodies writhing, mouths twisting in agony, until a pile of yellow bodies lay at Korden's feet.

4

He realized he'd been holding his breath and let out a ragged sigh.

In response, every incorporeal head in the marketplace lifted from the ground and focused on him.

Their play was over, and the actors wanted to greet their audience.

"They see me," he said. "Start your call."

The riftling's cry sounded in his brain, but nothing happened. The yellow bodies on the ground rose in unison, their rudimentary faces gaping as they faced him. They shuffled toward him on legs made of fog.

"Block them out!" Korden commanded.

"Zeega is trying to find the frequency," she muttered. The hum modulated rapidly, shifting through pitches.

Then it was drowned out as the emotional echoes let loose a collective scream.

Korden slapped hands over his ears, but it made little difference. Their terrified banshee wails clawed at his eardrums. He backed away from the mass in front of him, but there was little place to go in the crowded market. All around him, the yellow figures closed in, arms reaching for him.

His mind went back to his struggle beneath the freezing waters of Tay-ho. Positivity had countered the despair then.

And what was the opposite of fear but bravery?

He let his chest swell, banished all dread from his aura. The first of the ghosts—a woman with long hair—touched him. Frigid terror pierced him to the bone, but he fought against it, pushing out with the artcraft he'd managed to recharge, seeking to subvert her *mohol* the same way he'd soothed Meech's.

The echo disintegrated with a final, relieved moan, fading into yellow wisps.

More closed in around him. He was surrounded. Rather than wait for them to reach him, he pushed again, sending artcraft out as pure courage. The sapphire bursts of emotion shredded the echoes in reams, entire ranks blown to ragged smoke with each pulse. Their collective wail faded as their numbers dropped.

Korden didn't stop until they were all gone, until his brain felt like jelly and the marketplace and its surrounding streets stood empty.

"You exorcised the full pathome," Zeega said softly. "You are a powerful *craeftus* indeed."

## 5

"Something killed them," Korden insisted, but even as he said the words, he was thinking of the way the ghosts twitched as they acted out the attack. There had been something familiar about the spastic motions. "Something came from the east, swept through the town, herded them toward the center as they tried to run, and finished off the last of them there."

"*Exatraedes*," Zeega suggested. "Visiting revenge upon them for breeding."

Korden recalled his conversation with Winstid about the missing town. "I don't think so. If Incarnates did this, why remove all the bodies? Wouldn't they *want* people to know, as a lesson? To take away hope?"

She considered, then gave a curt nod. "Zeega agrees this is likely. Not only that, but upon discovering such punishment was possible, they would've done the same to Wilton and the other settlements taking in children."

"Exactly!" Korden whapped one fist into his opposite palm. "Whatever happened here...it had something to do with these Moambatis. I *know* it."

Upon leaving the marketplace, they'd headed east in Farrowbend, finding a house on the outskirts to stay the night in. Korden was leery of the idea at first, but Zeega assured him the pathome was cleansed, a danger no longer. The home they picked had faded red shutters and a door to match. Inside, they found an overturned dining table with an entire meal spilled on the floor that had decomposed to a gray smear. Korden checked each of the upstairs bedrooms, taking a few articles of clothing that would fit him, then settled on a chamber that had access to the chimney, so they could keep a fire. The room's sole window overlooked the eaves of the porch roof, and the street along the front of the house.

The riftling tossed more wood into the flames with her foreclaws. "What, then, would you like to do next? Continue east into the Skyreach?"

"If there's no other way." He took the last bite of his supper as he considered the question. "But first...I want to talk to them again. The Sisters."

"Through your dreams?"

"Yes." The last thing he wanted was to be pumped full of their artcraft, like a glutton unable to stop eating, but it would be worth it for one last chance at getting answers. Stone had given him so much information about these supposedly brilliant women from history, their resolute-but-murderous mother, and the technology company they all built, but it offered little explanation as to how the two of them were *here and now*, nearly three hundred years later, and what they wanted with him. "Let me sleep naturally tonight. But keep an eye on me. If I make any move to harm you, close my conduit like you did before."

She slithered up the dusty dresser, pulled open one of the drawers, and roosted atop the clothes inside, where she could watch him. "Zeega will do as you ask."

The moon had barely risen above the rooftops of Farrowbend, but Korden felt like he could sleep for a season. He settled into the strange bed and tried not to think about the previous occupants as he drifted into slumber.

6

When his consciousness returned, he found himself closer to those endless mountains now, standing before a gradual slope that wound upward for spans upon spans before disappearing amid the summits. The sun was bright, but a cool breeze blew down off the towering range, chilling his skin. That prominent, slanted peak rose above the others directly in front of him. A deep, natural cleft split its summit in two; amid that shadowy crevice, a vast structure glittered.

But his attention was quickly pulled away by the women standing on either side of him, who grasped his arms and pressed their dark, warm bodies against his, sandwiching him between them.

"Korden, we were so worried! We couldn't find you!" Denise's coiled braids brushed his cheek as she rested her head on his shoulder.

"Your mind was hidden from us; what did you do?" Charlotta's strangely-accented voice held the slightest hint of accusation.

They were as beautiful as he remembered, bodies works

of art on display in the sheer gowns they wore. He struggled against the sense of calm—and something far baser and more primal—that bled into his veins at their touch, fighting free of them. They reached for him as he stepped away, Denise grimacing as though in anguish at the rejection, Charlotta appearing to sulk. His rational mind knew their affections had to be an act, a way to enthrall him, and it was *very* effective. But no matter how much his body yearned to be close to these women, he couldn't let them bewitch him.

"What did you do to the people in Farrowbend?" he demanded without preamble.

He waited for them to deny involvement, but Charlotta shrugged nonchalantly as she ran a hand down her slender neck to the full breasts pressing against her thin, white smock. "What was necessary. Their service was called for."

Denise nodded. "Such a sacrifice was the only way." Her perfect mouth quivered as she finished the couplet. "And soon there will be more."

Korden's blood ran cold. "What do you mean? What sacrifice?"

"There is no time for this, darling. The cost of your distractions must be paid."

"We warned you there would be consequences, if from the path to us you strayed."

"Upper damn it, *what are you talking about?*" he roared.

The two identical women regarded him. Even now, in the midst of his fury, he recognized their exotic beauty, resisted the hunger they awoke in him.

Charlotta cocked one rounded hip. "You have brought an Incarnate legion marching toward our walls."

"So, now that you're alone, we need you secure within our halls." Denise clasped her hands in front of her bosom, pleading.

Korden crossed his arms. Shook his head. "I won't come to you. Not until I understand what you're doing and why you want me. I'll...I'll hide my mind from you again. Slip right through the Skyreach and go on my way."

Denise bowed her head. "Yes, dearest Korden, we believe you certainly would."

Charlotta glowered as she completed her sister's thought. "So remember, what happens next is for your own good."

## 7

He was shaken out of the dream, had a moment to take in the dark room around him before he registered Zeega sitting on his chest with one spongy tentacle pressed to his mouth.

"Someone is here," she hissed.

Downstairs, the door of their shelter crashed open.

# HUMAN CHATTEL

1

Rand spent his second day in Wilton meeting with Mellory and some of the other prominent merchants and tradesmen of the town, all the residents who held any sort of influence. He told them of his experiences in governing, pointed out what aspects of the settlement he recommended for improvement, and laid out a vision for its future largely improvised on the spur of the moment. When he finished his talk, not only were they ready to trot him out at the next town hall as a candidate for Wilton's first mayor, but that spot in the center of his forehead—he suspected it was what Korden called 'the conduit'—buzzed pleasantly, like a long-dormant muscle being stretched.

He returned to Lillam, whose infection continued to clear up at an astonishing rate, and told her the good news.

"Looks like I'll be the highest man in town after all."

"Then maybe we should take some time before your schedule gets too busy and decide on a name for the person growing inside me."

"I think that can be arranged."

That night, they sat down to a celebratory dinner with Grayhm and Nancer, the couple who had taken them in.

"Mellory thinks we'll be able to round a crew up next week to build a house," Rand told them, as Nancer put down a platter of roasted hen and malmo stalks. "I fear we've likely overstayed our welcome here by now."

"Nonsense!" Grayhm boomed. He had brown hair with a generous smattering of gray, thick sideburns to match, and was always in a jovial mood. "It's a delight having you! And we're sure not using those empty rooms for anything else at the present!"

His petite wife winced. The couple's plans for filling their large home with a family had met with complications. Nancer had yet to conceive, despite ongoing attempts since coming to Wilton two years before. Grayhm called it the ultimate irony: they'd spent their marriage terrified of accidentally creating a child, when it was probably never an issue to begin with.

Lillam noticed Nancer's discomfort also. "It'll happen," she assured the other woman. "My mother used to say the Aged Lord makes those wait who are foolish enough to try." Her face went white as soon as the phrase was out. "Oh, I'm so sorry, I didn't mean that you—!"

Nancer laughed and waved the apology away as she sat down. "Quite all right, dear. We're just thankful to have a place in the world where we can indulge such foolishness."

"Us too." Lillam reached out and took the other woman's hand. "You're welcome to play with our little one as much as you want."

"We would love that! Wouldn't we, Grayhm?"

"Of course!" He guffawed boisterously and slapped Rand across the shoulder. "And maybe her husband will give me some pointers on how to get my salmon swimming upstream!"

Nancer made an exaggerated sound of disgust, which just made Grayhm laugh harder.

The conversation was interrupted by slow steps on the stairs behind Rand. Meech slunk into the room and stood blinking wearily at the four of them gathered around the table.

Rand hadn't seen his brother since their arrival in Wilton. He'd stayed in his room, not touching the food Nancer left outside the door, not even emerging to use the outhouse. Rand heard him vomiting a couple of times through the thin walls as he suffered through another round of jinko withdrawals and, once, what sounded like sobbing. Meech appeared pale and listless now, so thin a stiff breeze could pick him up. His broken arm was held at a stiff angle by the splint and sling around his neck.

"Evening, stranger," Grayhm greeted. "Beginning to think you'd died in there. Come join us."

"We have plenty of food," Nancer added.

"No, thank you," Meech mumbled. "I just needed some air. I'll be…I'll be leavin in the mornin."

He wobbled past them, through the door of the house and onto the road, where peals of childish laughter could be heard.

Rand settled in his seat, preparing to tuck into supper, but Lillam caught his eye.

"Go talk to him before he does something stupid," she said.

"But stupid is the only thing he's good at," he told her.

"We owe him. We never would've made it here without him."

"The hells we wouldn't! Korden got us here!"

"And Meech got us to Korden."

"I don't care."

"Talk to him," she repeated sternly. "You'll regret it if you don't."

He sighed, nodded, and excused himself from the table.


# 2

Meech stood under one of the street lanterns with a wistful smile on his face, watching Onjel and several other children play leap rope in the deepening twilight. He jerked guiltily when Rand came up beside him.

"That sight never stops feeling odd." Rand gestured at the pre-agers as they cavorted. More Wiltonites huddled around the other lanterns up and down this small section of road, as they undoubtedly were throughout the rest of the town; youth-watching was a popular pastime in Wilton.

"You ever wonder what it would've been like?" Meech asked softly. His breathing sounded as wheezy as Korden's when the kid's lungs seized. "If we'd grown up with other kids around? Not havin to sleep in a different place every night? If...if Mom and Dad never left?"

"I used to. But wondering doesn't do much good. The past is the past, the present is the present, and the one thing we can change is where we're going." Rand looked at his brother. The warm radiance from the lantern above turned all the lines in his gaunt face into yawning chasms, aging him by decades. "So, the question is…where will *you* go?"

"I don't know. Away from here."

"You should stay until you have a plan. Or at least until your arm heals."

Meech's free hand stole up to his face and touched the place where Rand slugged him, now a fading bruise. "I'm just tryin to get away from you. Like you wanted."

Rand took a heavy breath. "I was angry, all right? Did I not have a claim to be? For Aged Lord's sake, you left us in the desert to die."

"I was gonna come back and get you!"

"But you didn't!"

"*Well…I'm sorry!*" Meech cried out, his voice rising into high-pitched tatters that drew stares from the people around them. "It was the spin, man! The need was eatin me up!"

"Then stop using it!"

"I'm *tryin!* You don't know what it's like!"

"That's right, I don't. Because I wasn't stupid enough to start." He shook his head in disgust. "Why do you have to be such a fram-up, Meech?"

His brother's face scrunched into a tight, wrinkled circle as frustration overtook him. "Because watchin life bestow blessing after blessing on you makes me feel like curse, all right?"

"What are you saying?" Rand demanded furiously. "What 'blessings' did I 'get'? Being abandoned by my parents? Having to care for an ungrateful brother?"

"See, that's just the thing, you only ever see the rotten side of the apple!" Meech rounded on him, counting each statement on the fingers of his splinted hand as he shouted them. "You were the oldest, the one in charge all the years we were running! As soon as we made it to Ida, you got a big, important job and everyone's respect! You have a woman and a child and a place to raise it! And fram drude, if all that wasn't enough, now you get to be a *Crafter*, too?"

Rand jumped at him, slapping a hand over his mouth as he glanced around to make sure no one could've heard. "Would you keep your voice down?"

His brother shoved the hand away. "Oh, sorry, wouldn't want anyone to look at you the way they always look at me."

Rand waited for his heart to calm before asking, "How'd you even know about that?"

"Like it was hard to figure out. You and Korden sneakin off into the desert every night. All the weird stuff happenin around you the last few weeks." He raised his shoulder inside the sling and let it drop. "Plus, Doaks kinda mentioned somethin to me."

"That conniving snake!"

Meech snorted. "So can you fling boulders and shoot fire from your fingers, or what?"

Rand rolled his eyes. "I can't even light a candle. Korden thought me a Crafter, but I could never get any of his tricks to work. Either I never mustered enough faith or found the right motivation or something of that ilk. I didn't understand half the piffle he spewed."

Again, the center of Rand's mind tingled, as when he'd fought the scorpigator and stopped the projectile. Something had definitely changed today as he spoke to Wilton's commerce leaders. If running a city was his personal form of creativity, then he had…what? Charged himself up today, like the batteries Korden brought back for the hovering wagon? That meant the artcraft he'd generated sat inside him this very moment, waiting to be used.

So how was he supposed to open the conduit to let it out, since he couldn't work up any faith in the Upper?

What was the trigger which fired that cocked crossbow inside him?

In front of him, Meech hung his head. "It's all just handed to you. Everything you could ever want. And I'm left to wallow in the gutter."

"Stop feeling so damned sorry for yourself." Rand put an arm around his neck and pulled the other man to him. Meech rested his forehead on Rand's chest. "You're my brother, and I'll always love you no matter how big an idiot you are. Now would you come inside and eat already?"

Meech nodded, the tension between them dissipating as easily as when they were children. Another sign of the magic of this place; it was impossible to let concern overtake you here. They started back toward the house.

But stopped when a scream pierced the night.

3

Grayhm and Nancer's house stood in the southeastern corner of Wilton, on a short avenue crammed tight with other homes. A few more such roads ran east, all the way to where the first rough slopes of the Skyreach took over the land, but the lantern poles hadn't been built out that way yet, and the farthest rim of town lay swamped in darkness after nightfall.

Both Rand and Meech stopped in their tracks and looked toward this murk, where the scream came from, as did everyone else standing outside. The cry had been too high-pitched to tell gender or age. As they squinted into the dimness, another shout came, this one angry, quickly followed by several more, and the sound of breaking glass.

"Drude...what is that?" Meech murmured.

"A fight," Rand answered. "Some sort of brawl, perhaps."

But the disturbance was still building; a constant litany of screams rolled up the dark road toward them, along with several pain-filled shrieks. The children playing in the road scattered like startled birds, running to hide behind their parents. Gaulbriel lifted his son off the ground and slung the boy onto his back as he stared into the darkness. Many of the people loitering beneath the lanterns backed away from the commotion uncertainly.

Rand's stomach twisted. Korden was right; the Incarnate army had come for them.

*If it's the Incarnates from the desert, then why are the screams coming from the* east?

All around them, other Wiltonites emerged curiously from their homes. Grayhm hurried outside with his cloth napkin tucked into his collar, Nancer and Lillam in tow. They, too, peered eastward, where people were now running out of the gloom, first one or two, then a crowd that filled the road. Many of them wore terror on their faces, glancing over their shoulders as they fled.

Rand jumped out the way before the throng reached him,

pulling Meech aside. The townsfolk hurtled by without stopping, but several encouraged the spectators to run also as they sprinted past. Gaulbriel and a few of the other people from the surrounding houses obeyed, dragging their children along, adding to the chaos. Grayhm marched past Rand, plucked a thin man out of the stampede by the arm, and spun him around.

"*Joshiah!*" he said sharply. "What is it, what's happening?"

"I-I don't kn-know!" the man stammered. "They c-came outta nowhere…busted into homes…started p-pullin people out into the street…touchin 'em with w-white fire!"

"*Who* did? Incarnates?"

Joshiah shook his head. "T-they're…dead," he whispered. "Dead people that m-move."

A sizzling squeal issued from one of the other roads to the south, accompanied by a white light that flickered briefly above the rooftops. Joshiah squirmed out of Grayhm's grip and resumed his flight as the rest of them turned toward the sound.

"Grayhm, what did he mean?" Nancer asked, having to yell to be heard over the panicked mob careening past them.

"He was rambling. Completely addled." Grayhm jumped as another burst of that strobing illumination washed over them, this time from the northeast. "But perhaps we'd better move away from whatever this is with everyone else, just in case."

The couple ran. Rand took Lillam's hand and entered the fray behind them, with Meech trying to keep up. More people came out of their homes, drawn by the uproar. A few retreated back inside, but most heeded the call to join the ever-increasing exodus. These folks had no idea what they were fleeing, but those sizzling pops came faster now, both at their back and on the parallel roads to either side. Strobing white lights tossed their shadows out long then reeled them back in. This town may not have held any fear before, but now it overflowed with a panic thick enough to taste, and Rand's heart squeezed into a painfully tight ball in the center of his chest as they were swept along. Within seconds, their mob joined another one on the main road, heading toward the bigger buildings on the west end. All of Wilton seemed to be in motion, one gigantic rush of frenzied bodies with no destination in mind, no thought except escape from whatever was sweeping through the settlement. Rand kept close to Lillam to make sure the crowd didn't knock her over, but Grayhm and Nancer were soon lost in the mayhem.

"*Hurry up!*" he called over his shoulder to Meech.

As he swiveled his head forward again, Rand caught movement on the rooftops to his left. A dozen shadowy forms leapt from house to house with uncanny agility, working their way ahead of the fleeing crowd. As he watched, one of them dove from the second-floor ledge and smashed headlong into the mob, sending seven or eight people to the ground in a tangle. That screeching buzz and flashing light started up, eliciting a chorus of wails, but Rand couldn't see through the crowd to tell what it was doing to those who'd fallen.

The stampede surged away from the altercation. Lillam's hand pulled out of Rand's grip. He saw her get thrown against the wooden front of a leatherworker's shop on the opposite side of the road. She cried out as the crush of bodies trapped her. Rand struggled to get through, but Meech got there ahead of him, using his splinted arm to shove people aside, making room for her protruding stomach and its precious cargo.

When Rand finally reached them, his brother shouted, "*What do we do?*"

He opened his mouth to tell them to keep running, but a hand snaked out of the narrow alleyway between the leatherworker and the shop next door, seizing Rand's bicep and pulling him into the dark crevice.

A familiar face swam out of the murk.

"This way," Tarmon Doaks hissed, beckoning him into the alley.

"But everyone else is—"

"If there's one thing I've learned, it's that yah never run the way the other sheep are runnin. Now c'mon or don't."

Rand followed the squat man deeper into the gap between buildings, signaling Lillam and Meech to come along. The sounds of the stampede faded as it moved west, but they could hear the screams. When they reached the back of the shops, where another alley crossed this one, a series of quick, furtive noises came from overhead. Rand looked up to see a flood of the same shadows springing across the rooftops directly above them.

Doaks froze and pressed himself flat to the wall beneath the eaves. "They're gettin ahead of the crowd, tryin to herd 'em all together," he whispered.

"Did you see what they are?" Rand asked.

Doaks shook his head. "All I know is, these things're damn fast and there's a lot of 'em. They came from the east, and I think they went house to house as quiet as possible 'til the jig was up."

"They're killing everyone!" Lillam gasped.

"No. I don't think so. That sound yah keep hearin? That's 'lectricity. Like my shock stick, only stronger." He swallowed. "They're *stunnin* these people, not killin 'em."

Rand recalled the sensation of being on the receiving end of these jolts, how his whole body went momentarily slack afterward. "What should we do?"

"There's a stable just a few roads over. If we grab some horses, maybe we can get outta town to the south before they finish moppin up the rest."

As much as Rand hated the idea of leaving Grayhm and Nancer and the rest of Wilton to fend for themselves, he could think of no way to help. He nodded. "All right, take us there."

They hurried through the dark back channels of Wilton, following Doaks as he limped through turn after turn. The man had learned his way around town a lot quicker than Rand. He'd led them into a wider alley where they could walk two abreast when the squat little shyster came to another abrupt standstill.

Ahead, where the alley let out onto the street, a body lay in the dirt on its stomach in a shaft of lantern light, a pre-ager girl with curly brown hair that Rand thought might be Korden's admirer. Only her upper torso was visible and, even from here, he could see that her back rose and fell as she breathed. He crept forward, meaning to wake her, but, when he was three steps away, the girl was yanked around the corner and out of sight. He bit down on a startled yelp before it could escape.

Doaks waved him back frantically and reversed their course, seeking a different path.

An unknowable amount of time later, they arrived at the mouth of an alley letting out on a section of the main road. Above the rooftops on the far side, the hills south of town loomed; they were almost free.

Doaks pointed at the wooden building directly across the road, from which frightened whinnying could be heard. "I'll go see if I can find any that're saddled up," he said in Rand's ear.

"Why don't we make a run for the hills?"

"Because I can't." He gestured at his injured knee. "And neither can yah brother, I'd wager. Besides, if those things catch wind of us or track us somehow, I'd like to have a way of outrunnin 'em, wouldn't yah? Just stay here and keep quiet."

With a quick peek up and down the road, Doaks limped across the dirt and slipped through the tall door of the stable.

4

"Drude, I don't understand what the fram is happenin." Meech paced back and forth in the alley next to a side door for one of the shops, scratching furiously at the jinko sores beneath his splint. Sweat drenched his tunic, but the perspiration was unlikely to have come from their flight, given the agonizingly slow pace Doaks set.

"I don't either," Rand told him. "But I should've listened to Korden. We should've gone with him."

Lillam buried her face in her palms and wept silently. Rand hated doing this to her, giving her this hope for a normal life and then snatching it away. He recalled something his father told him so long ago, before leaving him and Meech by the side of the road: never make promises that you have no control over.

There was no haven in this world. No paradise. No shortcuts. Whatever they wanted in life, they would have to fight for. He understood that clearly now.

Too bad the revelation came so late.

Beyond the alley, the night had grown unnervingly quiet. Rand wondered if anyone had managed to escape. Surely these things couldn't incapacitate the entire town.

*Why not? They did it in Farrowbend, didn't they?*

He thought of Mellory's story, about the residents of that settlement disappearing overnight, leaving behind an empty shell, and felt certain the same thing was happening here. How long would it take for someone to discover the residents of Wilton had vanished as well?

Meech abruptly stomped past him to the mouth of the alley and squinted across at the stable. He jittered with nervous energy. "C'mon, c'mon! What's takin him so frammin long?"

"Chill on and give him time."

Lillam dropped her hands to look at Rand, but her eyes slid past his shoulder. He saw the fear come into her face and spun around.

A silhouette stood framed in the far end of the alley. It

was human-shaped but wreathed in too many shadows to discern any detail. The figure stood frozen for a half-second, its stillness unnatural, then broke forward and bolted down the passage at them, moving with such incredible speed and unnerving silence it might as well be flying. Rand had time to shove Lillam aside before the shape lowered a shoulder and plowed into his midsection hard enough to knock him halfway out of the alley.

He landed on his back in the dirt with the thing on top of him, his brain rattled inside his skull and the breath knocked from his lungs. Now, in the glow of lantern light, he could see his adversary clearly, and Joshiah's words were clarified.

It had once been a young man not much older than him, but now it was something unmistakably dead. The flesh on its face was pale and waxy, shrunken to the bone as tight as drum skin, and the long hair sprouting from its skull lay so filthy and matted that the color was impossible to determine. Tiny spots of decay covered its cheeks and chin; its nose had begun to disintegrate, leaving a ragged, flattened beak. Any of this could've also described an Incarnate in a long-worn body, except the eyes peering into his were not glaring red but dull white, covered by a crystalline sheen that muted the irises.

Rand's breath hitched as it restarted. Rot filled his nostrils. The creature held him down with immense strength. It didn't snarl or grimace or even change expressions, just gazed at him with bland indifference while he struggled to push it away. Then it reared back, raising one bony hand that sparked with hot, white arcs of electricity, and, as the lamplight hit it more directly, Rand caught a brief glimpse of something glinting beneath the mop of crusty hair on its brow...

Meech barreled into the thing before it could touch Rand with its flickering appendage. He and the dead man rolled away across the dirt, giving Rand time to recover. His brother struggled with the creature, but, with his broken arm, he had little chance of defending himself. That buzzing squeal sounded, white light lit up the road, and Meech shrieked as Rand clambered up.

Close by, the dead man sprang to his feet as well, but Meech remained unmoving on the ground. Rand could see its clothing now: a strange, black, one-piece garment that fit to its skin as snuggly as a tailored calfskin glove. Some sort of insignia flashed on the right breast, too small for Rand to make out in the dim light. Instead of turning back to him, the creature's white eyes landed on Lillam, cowering in the shadows. It lunged at her.

"*NO!*" Rand roared. Something inside him cracked in two. In his head, he experienced a...a sort of *draining*, a great release of pressure so sharp and sweet that his eyes rolled back briefly in ecstasy. A gossamer green shimmer flowed off his skin and pulsed outward through the air, as when he'd fended off the scorpigator. It struck the dead man and sent him spinning down the alley like a leaf in a gust of strong wind. The creature struck a wall and fell to the ground in a heap.

Lillam stared at him, her jaw hanging. "R-Rand?"

There was no time to explain. Twenty pargs down the passage, the dead man attempted to stand up, but one of its legs appeared to be broken. Even so, Rand could see more flickering lights approaching beyond it.

"Get inside!" he ordered. As Lillam went to the side door of the shop, Rand ran to his brother. Meech's breathing came shallow, and his sunken eyes remained closed even after having his cheeks slapped. Rand hoisted the limp form over his shoulder and hurried after Lillam. The man's wasted body weighed next to nothing, so the chore wasn't taxing.

The door from the alley opened onto a descending staircase. They hurried down, went through another door, and into a basement workshop for the establishment above, illuminated by the moonlight coming through small, paneless windows high up near the ceiling that looked out on the street. There was no other exit, so Rand laid Meech aside, closed the door into the room, and began shoving whatever he could lay hands on in front of the entrance, tables and chairs and shelves. He was still building this barricade when heavy fists pounded on the other side.

Lillam squealed in terror and held her belly protectively. "What do we do?" she sobbed.

Through the windows, Rand heard the soft patter of hoofbeats. He rushed to an opening and stood on his toes to see outside. Doaks emerged cautiously from the stable across the road on the back of a small Quarter horse, leading two others by the reins.

"Doaks!" he whispered, waving through the narrow opening to get the man's attention. "Help us, those things have us trapped in here!"

The man held up his hands in a clueless shrug. "What the hells am I supposed to do about it?"

"Draw them away or something so we can get out!"

Tarmon Doaks frowned, took a slow breath, and shook his head. "Sorry, rubo. Looks like this is where our paths separate. Good luck to yah."

He wheeled his horse around and urged it to gallop, riding away between the buildings with the other two animals leashed at his side.

"*You bastard!*" Rand bellowed at his back. Had he honestly expected anything more from the man? He raced back to the door, which was already cracking down the middle on the other side of the barricade.

*Please work, please work*, he chanted, holding his hands out in front of him as he concentrated. He wanted to burn the things outside alive, but he would settle for tossing them all away.

Nothing happened.

He continued trying to use his artcraft until a pale hand shot through a hole in the door, grabbed his wrist, and filled his head with white fire.

5

Korden sprang off the bed, dislodging Zeega in a flurry of tentacles. Quick footsteps moved through the lower floor of the house, heading for the stairs without hesitation. Whatever was coming, it exuded no aura that he could discern. There was no time to prepare, no time to plan; all he could do is back into the center of the room and wait in the guttering light from the fireplace. Zeega scuttled up onto the dresser in the corner, positioning herself behind the bedroom door when it crashed open a second later.

Three figures entered the room, two men and a woman, bringing the overwhelming stench of decay with them. Though their dress was impeccable—matching, black, one-piece outfits that reminded him of the uniforms worn by the Trikers, except, these were made of some material that clung to their bodies much tighter than leather—all three were…well, 'walking corpses' was the only description that came to Korden's mind. Hair falling out, skin so pale it practically glowed, spots of greenish mold nibbling at their extremities. Beyond that, two of them had suffered horrendous injuries that they didn't even seem aware of: the woman's teeth were visible through a tear in her jaw, and an eyeball dangled from the socket of one of the men.

But, as much as their appearance surprised and repulsed him, his gaze was instantly drawn to their foreheads, where he stared in dumbfounded shock at what rested there.

All three of these unnatural creatures were adorned with a thin, metallic crown.

Exactly like the one Doaks used to take control of Korden's body.

"Wh-who are you?" he stammered. They stood in a line, still as statues, staring at him blankly, the pupils of their eyes crusted over with a white film. "What do you want?"

The woman opened her ripped mouth and said, in a monotone but otherwise pleasant voice, "Charlotta and Denise request an audience; no more, no less. Come with us Korden, and you will not be harmed."

He looked at those silvery bands running around their heads—bands which surely contained chips and circuits inside emblazoned with the words, MOAMBATI INDUSTRIES, INC., bands which seemed to be *imbedded in their flesh* rather than merely strapped in place—and his blood ran cold. "No, I *won't*. Go away, and tell the Moambatis to leave me alone."

He thought there would be further persuasion, but, upon his answer, the trio immediately moved toward him, spreading out across the room, their postures set for battle. Korden continued backing away, but there wasn't much space for retreating in here.

The man with the dangling eyeball lunged first, the movement startlingly fast. He raised a hand on which the flesh was worn away at the fingertips to reveal bone. Something buzzed inside his palm as lightning quick bursts of energy engulfed his hand.

Korden opened the conduit, tried to channel a blast of artcraft to repel him, but could find nothing there, not the slightest shred of magic. At first, he thought the effort of exorcising the pathome over Farrowbend had drained his reserves once again, but then he saw the truth.

He'd let the Moambatis back into his dreams, and this time they'd *taken*, rather than giving.

His moment of hesitation might've been his undoing if Zeega hadn't launched herself across the room, landing on the man's shoulder. She wrapped his head in tentacles, then snared his wrist in a few more and yanked the sparking appendage away from Korden. The man wobbled blindly away as he struggled with the riftling.

The woman and the second man—who was much heftier than either of his companions—closed in. Korden pulled the knife from his belt and rushed to meet the woman, taking the offensive toward the weaker individual as Eddas had always taught him in their hand-to-hand combat lessons. The dead woman grabbed for him, both hands crackling, but he ducked at the last second and pitched himself into her legs, bowling her over. He twisted around before she could get up, driving the knife hard through the back of her ankle and deep into the wooden floor below, pinning her.

Which just left the second man, with his broad chest and sloping gut beneath his stretchy garment, as an active aggressor. Korden regained his feet and dodged away as this one came at him, faster than his size would hint, a placid expression on his pale lips.

The fire-tending instruments stood in a rack beside the hearth. Korden grabbed the heavy metal poker and swung it without even aiming.

A high-pitched *clang!* reverberated all the way up his arms. The end of the poker had struck the metal band around the hefty man's head right at the temple, denting it in. He spun around in a stiff circle, smashed into the wall, and sank into the floor with his limbs thrashing.

Across the room, Zeega used her pincers to slash at the first man's throat while keeping his arms immobile, carving out huge chunks of black, fetid flesh. The injury didn't faze the dead man in the least. Muscles strained as he brought his hands together to lay palms on the riftling. Ripples of white electricity arced around Zeega's body; she shrieked before falling to the floor in a pile of limp tentacles.

The man faced Korden. His head wobbled on his shoulders now with so much flesh stripped away. His spine showed in the ruins of his neck, but no blood leaked from the injury. He came at Korden, who brought the poker whistling around again.

His aim was lower this time. The metal bar hit the man across the cheek and tore his head completely free from his ravaged neck. His body collapsed, the white fire in his hands sputtering out, but the head sailed through the air, bounced once on the floor, and rolled into the fireplace. Its white eyes continued to follow Korden as the flames consumed it, releasing a rancid odor.

By this point, the woman had freed herself, ripping her leg away from the knife rather than pulling it out, inflicting far more damage in the process. These things were quick and determined, but they weren't much for improvisation or forethought. She tried to attack, but her foot flopped uselessly, spilling her back to the floor. She finally settled for crawling toward him, holding out one sparking hand.

Korden went to his carry pouch in the corner, reached inside, and withdrew Redfen's shooter, still loaded with the two bullets he'd won in Carson City. He aimed it at the woman, trying to force his hand not to jitter, and commanded, "Stay back!"

"There is no time for this," she said in the same uninflected drone. She continued closing the gap between them, ignoring the weapon. But then, why should she fear the projectiler? No physical injury slowed these creatures much, besides damage to the crowns. "The Incarnates approach. Together, we can defeat them and save the world from the Filament. You only have to trust us."

"You've given me no reason to!"

Behind her, Zeega sprang up and scuttled toward the dead woman. Korden shouted, "*The band! Go for the band on her head!*"

The rifling ran up the woman's back as she crawled toward Korden, dug her pincers into the flesh beneath the band, and tore it away, taking half the woman's scalp with it. She fell over, truly dead at last.

Korden took a ragged breath of relief, glad that he didn't have to use the shooter. Two of the creatures were destroyed. The third had managed to sit up against the wall. His convulsions had slowed to twitching shudders, but he made no effort to stand or even look up. The dent in his metal crown made his head appear lopsided. He actually looked a little pathetic, like one of Bibb's mechanical toys slowly winding down.

Zeega moved toward him, snarling deep in her throat.

"Don't," Korden told her. "I've got an idea."

6

Korden squatted in front of the dead man with a lantern, remaining alert for movement. His limbs fluttered every few seconds, but the damage to the band had stolen whatever passed for his consciousness.

He was about Rand's age, perhaps a few years older, with a rounded head, bulbous nose, dark beard scruff, and lank black hair that hung to his fleshly jawline where it hadn't fallen out of his scalp, leaving thin patches. Veins were visible beneath his pale skin like dark, squiggly worms, reminiscent of Lillam's infection. Black mold grew out of both ears in a sludgy tumble, and a colony of rot had taken hold at the left corner of his mouth, but otherwise he had less physical damage than his companions, whose mutilated bodies were now stowed in one of the house's other bedrooms.

Korden studied the black bodysuit also. The material was unlike anything he'd ever seen, slick to the touch, but so stretchy that it snapped back into place when he pulled at it. Even so, the man's pudgy, overweight frame made the fabric bulge in odd places. His blubbery stomach, in particular, seemed to test the garment's limits.

A silvery symbol was embossed on the right breast, a shape that Korden recognized from his studies with Feegran.

The wrinkly outline of a human brain.

"Their physical *yans* were extinguished, yet they continued to move," Zeega observed from her position on the windowsill, where she could watch the street for more of the creatures. Although she wouldn't admit it, the riftling was weakened after the shock she'd received, her tentacles flopped haphazardly around her. "Not even the *Exatraedes* are capable of such a feat. Their bodies decompose when exposed to the sun, but they must continue to function to sustain their *animogas*."

Korden nodded in agreement. Steeling himself for the pungent scent of decay, he tried to find a pulse on the man's neck and chest, to make sure they weren't mistaken, but his heart no longer beat. His lungs didn't inflate. And he exhibited no mohol whatsoever, not even the black sludge that surrounded the Incarnates.

"This is magic beyond Zeega's comprehension."

"I'm not so sure it's magic at all." Korden pointed at the dead man's forehead. "You recognize this, don't you?"

Zeega's head swiveled, three of her yellow eyes studying their captive. "The same device the human Doaks used to enslave you."

"That's right. I suspect this was accomplished by means of technology, not magic." He bent closer to the dead man's face to inspect that thin, metallic band, ignoring the rotten stench that wafted from him. As he noticed before, the crown cut deep into the flesh, sealing it to his skull. And that wasn't the only modification made to his body. Black nodules protruded from the skin of both his palms, the source of the electrical jolts. Korden thought of the *mohol* ghosts of Farrowbend, the way they'd twitched and jerked during the reenactment, the same way he had when Doaks administered such shocks. "This was a person once. The Moambatis put this on him, and now they're using his body to do their bidding. These horrible devices must keep working even if the person wearing them dies." The implication simultaneously sickened and chilled him.

"Perhaps they placed it on *after* his death, in order to utilize the corpse," Zeega suggested.

"Does that make it any less of a desecration?" Korden demanded. Anger thudded at his temples as he recalled his last conversation with the dark-skinned women. He gestured at the other corpses. "This is what attacked the people of Farrowbend. But I think it's also *why* they were attacked. They were taken and...and converted into more of these monstrosities. In my dream, the sisters claimed it a necessary sacrifice. 'Their service was called for;' that's what they said." Korden blanched as a new thought occurred to him. "For Upper's sake, the Moambatis are only protecting the people in these towns so they have a ready supply of human chattel."

"Korden and Zeega must leave," she urged. "They could send more to claim you."

"Not yet," Korden set the lantern on the floor. "Even though this man is dead, maybe I can reach into whatever parts of his mind the band reanimated. See if I can discover anything about these women, or whatever they are."

"Zeega sensed nothing from any of these creatures, not even when the female spoke. Not a single thought ran through their heads."

"But you can only read the surface. I can go deeper, into the core of his emotional being. I have to try, anyway. If nothing else...maybe I can lay this poor man to rest with a little more dignity than the other two."

Zeega scurried from the windowsill to stand beside him, moving—Korden noted—with considerably more effort than usual. Korden reached out and touched the band running across the dead man's forehead, ready to yank it back at the slightest sign of trouble. The metal was cool, but the flesh around it room temperature.

Korden closed his eyes and let a few lines of poetry come together in his thoughts, enough creativity to get a trickle of artcraft flowing. Then he sent a single, tenuous thread of his consciousness into the other man's mind, but found nothing inside for him to commune with. All the areas of the brain normally lit up with emotion and musing were quiet and dark. The experience was like descending into a black cave and trying to find his way around by feeling along the walls.

This was futile. He could do nothing with a lifeless mind. As desperation set in, Korden gathered his will in the center of the dead man's head and sent out the one command he could think of, drenched in all the artcraft he could muster.

WAKE UP.

# OVERRIDE

## 1

"The images you're seeing are from outside Wonju, in the Gangwon Province. These people have all been forced to flee their homes in the middle of the night when the black cloud—what some are calling 'the Shroud'—spread to their city. They now join the larger mass of displaced citizens taking their children northwest through South Korea."

"Dan, at this point, is there even anywhere for them to go?"

"Well Stephanie, we're being told that Kim Jong-hui is standing firm on his stance to keep the border closed and has ordered North Korean military to fire on anyone who attempts to cross. But thousands of commercial and private boats have descended on South Korean shores to ferry refugees across the Yellow Sea. The Chinese government is also working on a way to perform aerial evacuations, but the logistics for such an undertaking are just so daunting, and, of course, time is a factor."

"What about the South Korean military? Are they planning any sort of counterstrike in Wonju? Are any forces being sent from the International Coalition to help combat the spread of these 'Incarnates?'"

"At this point, the government would much rather use military resources to assist with evacuation. If you believe the reports we've received from around the world, long-range, tactical weapons are useless against these creatures, and the effectiveness of individual firearms varies from person to person. I think the prevailing military opinion is that fighting the Dark Filament has become a waste of human life. Of course, that begs the question, if we can't fight them, then what do we do?"

Hesitation crept into the voice of the female anchor. "I...I understand we also have a live feed of the Shroud?"

"That's correct, and we want to remind viewers that, even aside from the death and devastation, what they're about to see can be...unsettling."

The holographic screen changed from the line of downtrodden, disheveled Asians to a high point of view, likely from a news aerocopter. Spread out below and maybe a mile or so in the distance was an urban city full of skyscraping apartment blocks, squat commercial districts, and boxy industrial factories.

Or rather, what was left of it. Fires raged across the landscape. The roadways were choked with abandoned vehicles. Even from this distance, the bodies lying on the ground and dangling from windows and lampposts like deli meat were visible, most of them so small they could only belong to children.

And, above the scene, a horrible, smoky mass swirled in the sky, darker than any storm cloud, darker than night, darker than the coldest depths of space. It cast a shadow across the foreign city so deep, it looked more like ink raining from the sky.

Staring into that pitch-black malignancy stoked an ugly fire inside Harris Stebens. One that made him recall things he'd tried to bury deep under a layer of apathy and self-denial. Like the time he'd snuck away from his mother's hospital bedside when she lay dying of cancer to attend a retro film festival across town. Sure, she'd been sleeping off some heavy meds and never knew he was gone, but, for god's sake, the featured selections had been those ridiculous, hundred-year-old movies where the undercover cop and the criminal with a heart of gold become best friends after racing cars through buildings and out of airplanes. Marinating in that goofy, twenty-first-century kitsch was comforting, but not worth the guilt that plagued him for years.

Now, because of 'the Shroud,' that old shame glowed front and center in his thoughts, making his stomach churn.

And he wasn't the only one retreating into past transgressions, judging from the sniffles and uncomfortable grunts coming from the rest of the breakroom. Everyone knew what looking at the Shroud did to you—it was one of the reasons so many people believed this was Armageddon leaping right off the pages of the Bible—but no one wanted to talk about it.

Because that would mean admitting all those terrible secrets you kept locked away in an interior vault; or, at the very least, admitting that vault *existed in the first place*, which was just as bad for most people.

As the holovid monitor changed to an image of President

Ghorbani encouraging United States citizens not to panic, Kristen Piven spoke up in a quavering voice from over by the espresso machine. "Turn it off. Please, *please*, turn it off."

"What're you so scared of?" Mateo demanded from his seat at one of the tables. Despite his brash tone, Harris thought the engineer's dark skin had taken on shades of green. "That don't have anything to do with us. It's on the other side of the goddamn world."

"Maybe she feels some sympathy for other people, jack-ass," Breanna muttered.

"I do too, but I ain't gonna get all worked up about someone else's war!"

"'Someone else's war?'" The words slipped out before Harris knew he intended to say them. Nervous acid burned his stomach, but it was too late to back out now; a hush fell over the crowded breakroom as all eyes went to him. He cleared his throat and stared at the tabletop in front of him while he asked, "You heard what that reporter said. They're not even trying to fight them anymore, just giving up and retreating. So once those things get finished chewing through Asia and Europe and Africa, where do you think they'll go next? Or do you believe all the televangelists who keep saying 'the chosen people of America will be spared the cleansing?'"

"Well…maybe we will." Mateo shrugged. "Maybe that's why the Filament only spreads west instead of coming the other way to hit us."

"Just because you're last in line on the smorgasbord, doesn't mean you won't get eaten."

"Yeah, Harris? What episode of *Star Trek* did you learn that nugget of wisdom from?"

"Maybe the same one where a scared little boy thinks burying his head in the sand will keep the big, bad monsters away."

Mateo stood up abruptly, sending his chair screeching back from the table on the tile floor. "Why don't you come over here and I'll show you who's scared, you tubby bitch!"

Harris hadn't been in a fight since the tenth grade (he lost), and he certainly didn't intend to have one on a Tuesday morning in the breakroom of the company he'd worked at for the last six years, since getting his masters in neurorobotics. Luckily, a passerby in the hallway saved him from coming up with a response by poking their head into the room and hissing, "Boss incoming!"

People scurried about their business, the room emptying out as everyone rushed back to workstations. Mateo shot Harris the finger as he stormed out. Harris took his time finishing his orange juice while he watched the news broadcast, which moved on to a different segment discussing yet another new mammalian species that had been discovered, this one in the middle of downtown Des Moines. When he was sure Mateo wasn't waiting for him outside, he got up from the table, tossed his bottle in the closest garbage can, and headed for the breakroom exit.

In time for Denise Moambati, CSO of Moambati Industries, to hurry into the room.

2

She was dressed as casually as always—flowery blouse, white capri pants, and sandals—but compared to Harris's jeans and grubby t-shirt, she might as well be ready for the prom. Her rich, ebony skin absorbed the light from the overhead fluorescents, as if she were a living shadow. The braids running down her scalp were aligned in such tight, perfect rows, they could've been stitched on by a machine. The woman was two years his senior but looked ten younger. As her deep brown eyes fixed on Harris, his legs went rubbery. He couldn't help it; outrageously beautiful women always had that effect on him. Denise made a beeline toward him, each movement coated with a grace usually reserved for felines.

"Harris, there you are." Her lovely, Haitian-accented voice turned his name into something exotic. "I have been searching for you."

"And here I am," he said, trying to sound nonchalant while making a furtive attempt to suck in his stomach.

"Charlotta asked me to find you. She wants you to run another test as soon as possible."

"Already?" He shook his head. "I don't think there's any point. We haven't upgraded the code substantially so the outcome won't be—"

"We need to get a handle on this project," she interrupted, frowning gently. "Surely you recognize how important this work could be. What it could mean for the world?"

Harris glanced at the holovid screen. "Yes, of course I do." Besides being reminded on a daily basis by the two women he reported to, it was all he'd been able to think about since he agreed to oversee the research.

"Then I have confidence in you. I am sure there will be an advance." The frown became a winning smile as she reached out and gave his doughy bicep an encouraging squeeze. "Charlotta will expect the data on her desk before the end of the day."

Her touch melted him, as she surely intended. She had most of the people in the office wrapped around her finger with her warm, friendly, overly-caring personality, and Harris was no exception. "Um, okay. Sure. Not a problem."

Denise turned to leave. Only when she was gone did Harris relax and allow himself to fume about the task at hand. *Another* test? When they hadn't made any significant breakthroughs? Wasn't the definition of insanity doing the same thing over and over and expecting a different result?

Then again, if he himself believed everything he'd just said to Mateo, then time was very much of the essence. A new data set could reveal something he'd missed before.

He left the breakroom and headed downstairs through the glass-and-steel headquarters of Moambati Industries, located in the heart of New Orleans, Louisiana. Harris came from Missouri, and he hated living here. He hated the humidity. He hated the twenty-four-seven party atmosphere. He detested Mardi Gras. But this company already stood on the cutting edge of cerebral research when he graduated, and everyone in his class applied for a position.

Of course, that was before the Dark Filament. Back when the world made sense. When news coverage wasn't a constant barrage of that cloud eating up a few hundred more miles of the planet every day as human beings scrambled to get out of its way, and the stars themselves hadn't shifted out of alignment, as NASA claimed. Hard to feel lucky about landing a dream job when the possible end of all civilization was staring you in the face.

"Not if I have anything to say about it," he murmured. Because Denise wasn't just blowing smoke up his ass. His work really *was* important. He believed, to the core of his being, that it could play a part in stopping the Filament.

And, because of that, the end completely and totally justified the means.

That's what he told himself so he could sleep at night, anyway.

As he passed the accounting offices on the first floor, lost in thought, he heard a low, *"Psst! Harris!"*

James Chung, Senior Acquisitions Accountant (and Beldroc the Orc in Harris's monthly *Dungeons and Daggers* game) leaned through the door of his office. Harris went toward him, a sudden sinking sensation in his flabby gut. The other man grabbed hold of his arm when he got close, pulled him inside the office, and shut the door.

"I found it," Chung declared.

"Where?" Harris asked, not sure he wanted the answer.

Chung picked up a folder from his desk and fanned the papers inside for Harris's inspection. "Colorado. Initial delivery to Crested Butte, but it looks like the actual plot of land is somewhere up in the Elk Range of the Rockies."

"Colorado?" Harris had hoped things would become clearer once Chung completed the covert research project he'd put the man up to, but this piece of the only puzzle deepened the mystery.

Chung pulled out some photocopied forms from the folder. "Charlotta's signature is on all these invoices. So why is the CEO funneling millions of dollars under the table to have major automated construction equipment delivered to a plot of private land in another state? And, out of the same account, she purchased controlling interest in a company called Further. I looked them up; they're a cryobiology lab. Does that make any sense to you at all?"

"Not a bit." Harris sank into a chair as his mind worked. He'd only stumbled onto the trail himself last week, from a stray equipment requisition that never should've crossed his desk.

"You sure about that?" The suspicion in his friend's tone grabbed Harris's attention.

"What do you mean?"

"I mean, does this have anything to do with the super top-secret project they've had you working on for the last two years?"

"Not that I know of," he answered. Which was one-hundred percent true.

"Then it must be tied to one of the others."

"Others? What others?"

"Are you kidding me?" Chung snorted. "This place has so many locked-down labs running right now, it makes Nazi Germany look like a high school chemistry class. David Hearn let it slip that they've got him doing some kind of DNA hereditary mapping."

"What for?"

"He wouldn't say." Chung sighed and raised a hand to squeeze his temples. "We have to blow the whistle on this."

"What? No!" Harris leapt up from the chair. "We don't need to do that, we don't know that she's even doing anything wrong!"

"Harris, at the very least, this is misappropriation of funds. Maybe even embezzlement. If I sit on this now that you've dragged me into the middle, it's *my* ass."

Harris swallowed and laid a hand on the folder of evidence. "We have to tread carefully here."

"This *is* me treading carefully!"

"Just...think about their mother."

Chung sneered. "You don't believe all those 'voodoo priestess' stories, do you?"

"No." Harris managed to sound incredulous even though he'd read all about Terese Moambati's legal troubles before he came to work for the deceased woman's daughters. That court case was *Twilight-Zone*-levels of weird. "But the woman went to prison for *murdering employees who defied her*. What if the apple didn't fall far from the tree?"

"Sorry, I'm not scared of the Moambati sisters."

"Sist*er*. Denise might not have anything to do with it."

"That's why we go to the authorities and let them sort it out."

Harris ran a hand through his shaggy black hair. "All I'm saying is, let me look into it a little more, see what I can find out. Maybe there's an explanation."

Chung answered with his jaw clenched. "Three days. Friday afternoon, I'm taking this up the ladder unless you give me a valid reason not to."

Harris thanked the man and left, continuing down to the sub-level elevator at the end of the hall while trying not to vomit all over the floor. This was bad. Oh, this was *really* bad. Why did he open his big fat mouth in the first place? He'd wanted to find out what Charlotta was up to, sure, but the last thing he needed was the FBI sniffing around this place.

He rode the elevator down to sublevel three, the lowest in the building. The doors wouldn't open unless he scanned his badge and pressed his thumb to the plate. Only three people in the company could access this floor. The rest of the research for his project had been chopped up and distributed to employees who had not the slightest clue what it was for.

In the antechamber, he stepped into a hazmat suit, zipped himself up, passed through the decontamination hoses, scanned his badge *again*, and at last gained admittance to the inner project rooms. Furious snarls met him as soon as the door cracked open. The next room was a tiled square with white walls and one other door leading deeper into the lab. They kept lighting dim in here—only an ambient luminosity from inside the walls that made them appear smoky—but the red glow coming from the eyes of the figure strapped to the exam table in the middle of the space was more than sufficient to see by.

"Hello, my friend," Harris said to Incarnate 7-B.

3

The subject on the table used to be an Asian woman, but now it was something else, an entity that, as far as anyone could tell, wore her skin like a suit. Harris hadn't believed such reports about the Incarnates (as in, *evil incarnate*, he assumed, and what drama queen came up with *that* moniker?) until he'd seen one for himself. Being a man of science, he didn't want to call them 'demons' like the religious nuts on the M-Net, but there was undeniably a mechanism at play that they didn't understand, be it viral, chemical, or other. This one—and the several others locked up down here—had been imported through legally dubious channels that the Moambati sisters did not disclose to him.

The Incarnate tried to respond to his greeting, but the words were unintelligible around its mouth restraint. He could guess at the content though. Yada yada release me, blah blah we come to extinguish the light, et cetera et cetera slaughter those who hinder our quest. Repeat ad nauseam. These things had a one-track mind that would rival a thirteen-year-old boy who'd just seen his first *Playboy*. Harris suspected that Charlotta had interrogated some of the other Incarnates in private sessions, but he doubted any useful information could've been gleaned. They didn't get scared or anticipate pain, even though they definitely felt it.

Which was part of the problem he was having with them as test subjects.

Harris approached the table without hesitation. He'd feared these creatures once, but that faded with time. They were stronger than regular humans, but they couldn't break steel restraints. The real danger was in one of them dying during these tests and attempting to 'jump bodies.' Videos all over the M-Net showed black smoke squirting from the eyes of one of these Incarnates as they expired and entering another person, who then picked up the rampage without missing a beat. Harris didn't know for sure if hazmat suits would prevent such an infection, but he'd insisted on them when he agreed to take on the project.

The Incarnate's red eyes followed him. Harris ignored its attention, focusing on the metal band clamped around its forehead. He felt sure that many experiments involving these creatures were going on all over the world right at this very second—brilliant minds trying to discover what they were, where they came from, and, most importantly, how to destroy them—but the only contribution Harris himself could make to the cause was *controlling* them, and this thin metal tiara was the key.

It was referred to in project documentation and internal memos as an 'override,' but, back when Moambati Industries filed the patent based on his original design, it'd been called the Muscle Memory™. The neural interface allowed transplant of donor or vat grown limbs, which could then be flawlessly controlled by the recipient. Hell, with one of these things, you could attach a human head to a new body in the morning and have them running a marathon by the afternoon. Such a bridge was the next evolutionary step from the telepathically controlled robotic prosthetics currently on the market.

And, since he'd reworked it to allow an outside user to control the wearer down to the smallest twitch, it was also a blatant violation of the Cerebral Research and Standards Act.

*This* was the reason he couldn't have the company getting caught up in an investigation. The authorities might start out digging at the corporate finances, but it wouldn't take much for them to discover what went on down here— with both Incarnate *and* human test subjects—and then Harris would be escorted to a cell of his own.

No matter how much he claimed that he was trying to save the world.

He logged in to the control computer on the counter nearby. Might as well get the test over with and mull the rest of his problems later. Maybe if they could get this thing working, Charlotta and Denise could hand it over to the military or whatever they intended to do with the technology, and then it would be out of his hands. Harris input a command string and sent it to the band on the Incarnate's head.

*C'mon honey, make a fist for Daddy*, he thought.

At the end of the steel restraint, 7-B's hands continued to struggle and claw at the table.

As the data uploaded automatically, Harris accessed the stimulator of the override and gave the subject a little goose to the parietal lobe.

7-B roared as electricity surged through its brain, but it did not obey the command.

"This is going to be a long session," Harris muttered.

## 4

It took two hours to run the sequence, with no discernible change in the Incarnate's behavior. Big surprise. Harris let the data collate with past results while he considered Chung's claims.

Other secret labs here in the building. Probably on the locked subfloors right above this one. His nose had been so buried in his work these last eighteen months, he hadn't noticed the odd changes happening in this company. Harris suddenly wondered if his project was but another piece of something larger that *he* was being kept in the dark about, some vast machination that only Charlotta Moambati—and possibly her sister—knew all of.

On a sudden impulse, he spun to the computer and worked the keyboard, not an easy task with the gloves of his containment suit. Harris's speciality might be neurorobotics, but he knew his way around a mainframe. He'd done his fair share of M-Net hacking in college, and this place sure didn't have Pentagon-level cyber security. Within minutes, he'd accessed a trove of documents and project updates on locked drives throughout the system.

Harris picked one labeled 'CISTERN.' One of the files in it was a schematic for something that resembled a miniature cement mixer made from aluminum alloy stitched with electrical conductivity wiring. He skimmed the accompanying documentation, but the science sounded like fiction to him.

"'Serocraftide harvesting?'" he read. "What the hell *is* this thing?"

"The results are still inadequate, I see."

Harris jumped, scrambling to hide his snooping as he looked up. Charlotta Moambati stood at the window of the lab's observation deck overhead. She was every bit as gorgeous as her sister, but packaged herself in far more formal pantsuits, like the dark plaid ensemble she wore now. The short lanks of her bobbed hair hung around her face as she stared down at him with hands clasped behind her trim waist. Harris's mind raced, trying to come up with excuses, until he realized she meant the override.

"That, um, that was, you know, expected," he stammered, speaking loud enough for the microphones in the ceiling to catch his voice. "I told Denise there hadn't been any significant progress."

"Why, though? Why does it not work on *them* like it does the uninfected?" The question's delivery sounded rhetorical, but the CEO's glare drilled into him from her high perch. The staccato syllables of her Haitian accent came across like machine gun fire. "The Incarnates possess a human brain, do they not?"

"Well…yes and no. Biologically, they're indistinguishable, but whatever drives these bodies when the…the *other* takes over, the alpha waves are totally incomparable. It's like…like this other consciousness is being *broadcast* into their heads."

Charlotta nodded thoughtfully. "From another plane of existence," she murmured.

"I don't know about that. But I do think, if we can tune the override to the right frequency, we should be able to gain control."

She made a clucking noise and shook her head. "I'm afraid that is no longer an option."

A cold tingle grew at the base of Harris's spine. "What do you mean?"

"Denise and I feel this project has reached a failed conclusion. Although it *has* yielded some findings we will make use of."

"Uh…that's good, I guess. Then what about me? Am I fired or what?"

In the room above, Charlotta gave a humorless laugh.

"Fired? Oh no. Since you are so keen on digging into things which do not concern you, we can never let you go. Fortunately, there will be a place for you in the new world we are building."

The cold tingle spread up his spine so fast it could've given him whiplash. Before he could feign ignorance about the accusation, Harris heard the door to the rest of the lab open behind him.

Six people entered the room, dressed in matching black Spandex bodysuits and moving in spooky unison, like trained military cadets on parade. Their coordination wasn't surprising though, considering they were all crowned with overrides. He even recognized their faces: the human test subjects he'd worked with before moving on to Incarnates. Their results had met with one hundred percent success, despite the extreme discomfort they reported from being under remote control. As far as Harris knew, all of them were sent home after signing NDA's, but he saw now how stupid he'd been to believe such tales.

Something about them looked different. As the synchronized squad drew closer in the dim light, he glimpsed their bloodless skin and cloudy eyes, and his dread grew into outright horror.

"You see Harris, your invention continues to work even with expired hosts," Charlotta explained, "creating servants that need no sleep, no food. It is quite efficient. They will serve us well in the struggles to come. As will *you*."

Harris turned to run. His clumsy feet got tangled and tossed him into the counter. Strong hands seized him from behind before he could get his balance. He squawked as they lifted him off his feet.

The undead test subjects carried him to the vacant exam table next to 7-B while he kicked and screamed. All six of them tore at his hazmat suit, ripping the plastic away. Harris got a flash of those old flicks they'd loved so much in the decades around the start of the millennium, the ones where the dead clawed their way out of the grave to feast upon the living. Beside him, the Incarnate twisted to watch while making a muffled gagging noise that could only be laughter.

"Do not worry," Charlotta's voice purred over the speakers. "The override must be put in place while you are conscious, but then an energy current directed through the frontal lobe will end all your suffering. I cannot guarantee it will be painless, but it will be quick."

Harris's arms and legs were held down. One of the test subjects produced a shiny new override. Harris gibbered as the metal band was shoved down on top of his head, the circumference so tight it tore through his skin as it locked into place on his skull. He screamed. A moment later, ion voltage ripped through his body. Pain filled him up, blotted out his vision with white light.

Then it ended, and everything went dark until a godlike, irrefutable voice swam out of the void and commanded him to WAKE UP and—

"*You crazy bitch!*" Harris screamed, continuing to struggle even as he came to the realization that the person crouching in front of him wasn't Charlotta Moambati, but a young white kid dressed like a peasant from a LARP event.

## 5

The dead man's mind flared to life, color and light filling up the dark recesses of its consciousness. Korden threw himself backward as the corpse bellowed and began to flail, trying to get out of range of those stun nodules on its palms, but quickly saw there was no need. The dead man wasn't aiming for him, but swinging blindly at the air, as though fighting an invisible enemy. His hysteria gradually subsided, and he sat squinting around the room in confusion.

"Where am I?" he croaked, rubbing at his dulled eyes. "Where…where's the lab?"

"Easy," Korden told him, approaching slowly on his knees as he tried to think of how to respond. Was it a trick, or had he somehow broken this man free of the band's control? "Stay calm. Do you have a name?"

"'Do I have a *name*?'" the dead man repeated incredulously, his tone implying the question was a dimwitted one. "Uh, yeah, it's Harris. Harris Stebens. Who're you? Why does this place look like a colonial village recreation? How did I get here?"

"His emotional cloud is manifesting," Zeega pointed out from across the room.

The dead man—Harris—noticed her for the first time. "What the hell is *that*?" he exclaimed, trying to scoot away. His movements had none of the grace or coordination he'd exhibited before.

"It's all right, she won't hurt you!" The riftling's observation was correct though; this man had an aura now, one rife with confusion and anger. "My name is Korden, sir. Um...what's the last thing you remember?"

"Oh, I remember *everything*, and I'll be more than happy to tell it to the FBI or grand jury or anyone else who wants to know!" Harris hunched toward him eagerly. "I remember Charlotta defrauding the company to fund her off-the-books project! I remember her and her sister co-opting my designs in order to force me to make illegal modifications! I remember them allowing human test subjects to die and then sending them after me to...to..."

His hands flew to his forehead and encountered the metal band. Korden saw his eyes widen in alarm even as disgust darkened his aura. He tugged at the device gently, then felt around the edges where the skin had grown over, fusing it to his skull. Then his gray-pallored hands caught his attention at the ends of the black garment's sleeves, and he looked down at his own body.

"Oh my god," Harris whispered. He grabbed at his chest with one hand and his neck with the other. "I feel weird. What's wrong with me? Wait, I don't have a heartbeat. *I don't have a heartbeat!* Am I...*dead*?"

Korden stared at the man, an odd mixture of glee and horror bubbling inside him. "You're from the old world. *Really* from the old world. And I woke you up somehow."

Harris glared at him. "I'm not sure what an 'old world' is, but you and your little talking octopus better start explaining, or I'll make sure you're part of the lawsuit I file."

6

Korden stood in the window at the front of the house, which looked out on the short stretch of porch and the road running by. Harris sat on the wooden ledge out there, hunched over a rain barrel, staring between his watery reflection and the black nodes imbedded in his hands. Korden had babbled at him for ten straight minutes about anything he thought might help the poor man make sense of the situation, fully aware in the back of his mind that any explanation would be grossly inadequate. Harris listened with a slack expression, his milky eyes unreadable, but his *mohol* revealed his growing anguish. After Korden finally stopped talking, he'd gotten up and walked out of the house without a word.

"Korden and Zeega should go," the riftling reiterated from the mantel. "They have lingered here far too long."

"What about him?"

The space that passed for a brow above several of the riftling's eyes arched quizzically.

"We can't just leave him here."

"Zeega sees no reason why not."

"He doesn't know where he is or what's happening!"

"That is neither Korden's nor Zeega's concern."

"But it is. I woke him up or brought him back or whatever this is, so that makes me responsible for him." Seeing that the argument wasn't persuading her, he added, "Besides, the whole reason I went into his mind was to learn something about the Moambati sisters. Well, he actually *knew* them."

The riftling bristled. "And what if the band on his head allows control to be retaken from him? Or perhaps to track his whereabouts?"

Korden studied the man outside. The idea hadn't occurred to him. "That's a chance we'll have to take. Stay here. Let me try talking to him again."

He pushed open the door and stepped outside.

## 7

Harris had decided none of this was real.

Not this deserted town, which looked like a movie set created by a production designer that couldn't decide if the film took place in medieval England, or the old west. Not those mountains rising sharply in the distance, which didn't resemble any part of Louisiana he'd ever seen. Not his reflection, which seemed to confirm his previous hypothesis that he'd somehow become a walking, talking corpse.

And *definitely* not the insane story the kid told him upstairs.

It was a dream. Or a hallucination. It *had* to be.

Because to believe otherwise implied a fundamental shift in his worldview so massive, so life-altering, he could find no way to fully process it.

The door of this rustic little house squalled open as the boy stepped on to the porch with him. Before the kid—what was his name? Korman? Korben?—could say anything, Harris shook his head adamantly and held up one of his pale hands. "Nah uh. Stay away from me. Every time you open your mouth, a little more of my life gets destroyed."

"I wanted to see if you were all right."

"Let me put it this way." He paused to swallow, the action taking incredible effort. God, his throat was so *dry*. But so were his eyes and his skin and everything else. "This morning I woke up like I always do…ate some Lucky Charms…watched an episode of *Commander JuJuby*…went to work…and now you're telling me that the Incarnates took over the world and reset civilization to the Dark Ages."

"They haven't taken over the *whole* world," Korden told him sheepishly. "Not yet."

"Christ!" Harris barked laughter. "How am I supposed to respond to that, huh? That everyone I know and love has been dead for three hundred years?" Although, now that he thought about it, there was more emphasis on the *know* than the *love* in that question. He had no family, no girlfriend, not even a pet. Other than his *D&D* group—which he suspected Chung had invited him to out of pity—his free time was spent streaming holovid and surfing the M.

Both activities which no longer existed, apparently.

"I'm sorry," the kid said.

"And, on top of all that," Harris continued, ignoring the apology to look down at the black skinsuit he'd been squeezed into, "you claim I've been some sort of undead slave of the Moambatis all this time, and that you woke me up with, what was it? Artwork?"

"Art*craft*. I told you, it's a form of magic that—"

"Yeah, no. I'm gonna have to stop you this time, kid. I'm a scientist. I don't believe in magic."

"But it's true!"

"Sure it is. I'd ask you to prove it, but then you'd tell me something like, 'It only works during the full moon of an eclipse during a leap year,' so—"

A gout of blue flame exploded from the kid's hand at the same time as a wooden rocking chair beside him flipped a somersault and slid off the porch.

Harris shrugged. "Oh, c'mon. I've seen better tricks on a Vegas stage." At the crestfallen expression on the kid's face, he waved a dismissive hand. "You know what, fine. It's a little more Jean Grey than Gandalf, but for the sake of argument, you're a wizard, Harry."

"Who's 'Harry?' Isn't that you?"

"Ugh, it's like high school all over again." Harris chuckled and slumped on the porch steps. He could sense himself giving in to anxiety and outright despair. It was too much, too big for his mind to take in. He needed to narrow his scope, deal with the parts of the situation he could get a handle on first, so he let his thoughts unspool as his mouth ran commentary. "Yes, for all intents and purposes, I appear to be clinically dead, as batshit crazy as that sounds. I don't have a heartbeat. I don't even seem to have a need to breathe except when I want to speak. Charlotta figured out that the overrides will work on dead tissue, which isn't that surprising, considering the human body is just a puppet whose strings are pulled by the brain. And that's obviously what the bitch did to me, but it doesn't explain how I'm *me*, awake and operating without the control impulses the override provides."

"What's an override?"

"This thing," Harris tapped the band right at the dent

beside his temple, annoyed to be interrupted, and continued talking to himself. "So, when the kid damaged it, *something* happened. Maybe…an ion surge from the stimulator caused feedback through the temporal lobe, sort of like a defibrillator? Enough to generate a spark of consciousness preserved by the neural network?"

The boy frowned as he listened to Harris rant. "You know a lot of about those bands."

"Yeah, I should. I invented the damn things."

Harris only understood he might have said the wrong thing when an invisible hand grabbed his neck and shoved his head back into the porch railing.

## 8

Fury consumed Korden. Artcraft burst out of him before he could control it, seizing Harris by the throat. He could feel that cool, stiff flesh in his mind, as disgusting to touch mentally as to do so physically. Thank the Upper his well was mostly drained, otherwise he might've torn the man's head off before he could get himself under control.

"*You?*" he demanded. "*You* created those…those obscenities?"

"*I never…they weren't…*" Harris wheezed, unable to get the words through his constricted throat. He pawed at the air around his neck, as though trying to find whatever held him.

"A horrible man used one of those bands on me. Took away my free will. It was one of the worst things that ever happened to me." Korden's jaw clenched so tight, his teeth ached. "Give me one reason why I shouldn't grant you a second death this instant."

He eased the pressure so the man could speak. "*T-they were meant to* h-help *people!*" Harris sputtered. "*I invented them so amputees and paralysis victims could control new limbs! Charlotta and Denise took the designs and made me create these overrides! Then they turned around and used one on* me!"

"*GRRRAAAAA!*" Korden bellowed in frustration as he released Harris. He stomped off the porch and stood in the road with fists clenched and chest heaving while he stared into the dark sky.

"I'm sorry," Harris said softly. His *mohol* dripped with guilt. "I never meant for any of this to happen. They told me if the Incarnates could be controlled, we could stop the Filament…"

Korden raised his arms and waved at the houses around them. "You see this town? It used to be full of people. But the Moambatis took them all. Put your overrides on them to make themselves more slaves. And they're going to keep doing it. The Dark Filament is horrible, yes, but the Moambati sisters are every bit as bad."

Harris watched Korden warily. "I don't know what you want from me, kid. *I* didn't do it."

"Maybe not." Korden rounded on him. "But you helped cause this, so you're going to help me stop it."

"Okay." Korden recognized the word from books, knew it was an archaic term of agreement, but the only other person he'd ever heard say it aloud was Heater Kay. "Tell me how."

"You worked for them. You must know something."

"Kid." Harris held up his pale hands as though to preemptively ward off Korden's anger, those black nodes jutting from the base of his palms. "I don't understand any of this. You said Denise and Charlotta did all those things. But it's been three hundred years, right? How could they possibly be alive?"

"You're from their time, and *you're* still alive. Sort of."

"Yeah, well, I can't see the two of them voluntarily going through what I did."

Korden sighed. "I believe they're Crafters, like me. The magic would've given them very long life." Of course, he'd also suspected this about the Prophet, and that had turned out to be very wrong.

Harris snorted at this theory. "Hey, I'm willing to accept that you're a sorcerer, but please listen when I tell you the Moambati sisters are *not*. I worked for them for six years, and the most magic I ever saw them do was increase stock price fifteen percent overnight." He frowned. "Now, if we were talking about their mother…"

Korden thought he had his emotions reined in sufficiently to risk approaching the man. "She was a…a 'voodoo' lady."

Harris's eyes widened. "How do you know that?"

He ignored the question as Stone's history lesson came back to him. "They said that she could raise the dead. And now her daughters…they're doing the same thing."

"In a way, I suppose, but they sure didn't do it with magic." Harris shook his head. "That all rumors, anyway. She was a brilliant but messed-up woman who murdered a man—and possibly a little boy—under mysterious circumstances, went to prison, and died there.

Her daughters just inherited her tech company, that's all."

"Then maybe they hid their crafting, or it developed later. But they've spoken to me and a lot of other people through our dreams, and they keep urging me to come to them in the Skyreach."

"You lost me again. 'Skyreach?'"

Korden pointed at the jagged peaks on the horizon. "I think you would call them 'the Rocky Mountains.'"

A look came over Harris's pale, mold-crusted face as his aura faded into light blue tones of epiphany. "Are we…in Colorado, by any chance?"

Korden thought about the last location Stone gave him. "I think that's what it was called."

Harris clapped his hands in excitement. "Finally, *something* that makes sense! Earlier today—or, I guess, the day Charlotta killed me—I found out she had some secret construction project going on in the mountains of Colorado, near a town called Crested Butte."

The shock of hearing that name stole the breath right out of Korden's frail lungs. "What was this project?"

"I have no idea, but she stole millions of dollars from her own company to build it. That could be where they're telling you to go."

Korden deliberated for a long moment. "The band on your head—this *override*—could they use it to trace your movements?"

"Sure, insert a geotracker chip. Simplest thing in the world. But it'd be a little redundant with the ocular feed."

"Ocular…*feed*?"

"When the override is tapped into a subject's brain, all

of the senses can be monitored through a computer or even wired directly into the cerebral cortex of the controller to be experienced firsthand. You can literally see what their eyes see, hear what they hear, et cetera. With that level of observation, you wouldn't need to track where they are with a chip, especially if you sent them there in the first place."

The explanation was technical, but Korden pulled out the most important fact. "Then...they could be watching and listening to us right now."

"I suppose." Harris touched the dented part of the crown at his temple. "Unless you damaged it when you did this, of course. And because the sensory feed runs through the same neural strand as the control input, that's a distinct possibility."

Korden nodded, considering the danger. As he'd told Zeega, it was a worthwhile risk. This man was too valuable to not have by his side. "Get up."

"What? Why?"

"Because you're coming with me. And we're going to put a framming stop to the Moambatis for good."

"Sure. Yes. Sounds good." Harris nodded. "One question: what the fuck is a 'fram?'"

## 9

Tarmon Doaks kept his commandeered horses at an all-out gallop on the open plains southwest of Wilton, constantly checking over his shoulder to ensure that none of the creatures pursued him. The town was lost to the night, and there were no signs of other people; he might very well be the only one who'd escaped whatever fate awaited the rest of those droolingly cheerful breedmonkeys. And not even *he* would've made it if he'd listened to Mr. My-Curse-Don't-Stink Holcomb back there.

The nerve of that witless rubo, asking him to distract those monsters. What did he look like, a damned *hero*? An older, fatter version of the boy? Doaks hadn't gotten this far in life by sticking his neck out for other people, and he sure wasn't going to start with a man that spat on him every chance he got. Hells, Rand held higher regard for his worthless, jinkoid brother.

Though he appeared to've broken free, Doaks didn't dare slow down. The more distance he put between himself and those things under cover of darkness, the better. On his right, off to the west, the plains unrolled for spans, back toward the river savannah where they'd crash-landed two days ago.

He kept a tight hold on the reins of the other two horses he'd taken, forcing them to match his mount's furious pace. If he could get to a trading post, he could swap them for ample provisions to venture back into the Valley to reclaim Gwenita. And, after he got his precious girl back, all this business with that infernal kid would become a sad, distant…

Doaks gaped at the land ahead, allowing the horses to slow. The waning baker's moon revealed a familiar shape just a hundred pargs away. He urged the horses to drift closer, certain he must be hallucinating.

Gwenita stood on her spider-like legs in a thicket of low brush, as if waiting for him. He honestly would've believed it a completely different vehicle, if not for the weathered remains of 'DOC APOCALYPSE' visible across the torn bonnet, and the dented-in front corner where the boulder had smashed into them outside Ida.

How was it possible? Had she…had she come to *find* him? Perhaps been summoned by his fervent wish?

*The boy.* His mind latched on to this explanation. *He changed his mind about coming with you. Used his magic to bring her here.*

Despite its ridiculousness, this idea sent an ecstatic thrill up Doaks's hunched spine, and not just because of the scratch they could make together. He realized, with some surprise, that he *missed* the boy.

Filled with excitement, Doaks dismounted the horse and limped up the steps to the control deck. He noticed that Gwenita's tank was bone dry, not so much as a single ion rattling around inside. But that was all right, they could mount some wheels under her, and use the horses to pull her to the closest fueling station.

Oh yes, this could work. He'd be back on his feet in no time, selling ear wax and ground-up toadstool as toothpaste. You couldn't keep the Armageddon Sawbones down, no sah.

"Korden?" he called out, as he muscled open the power-less door into the bonnet. "Korden, where are yah, rubo?"

Something moved in the darkness of the wagon, and it was not the boy. Fear squeezed Doaks's guts. A shape slithered out of the shadows, a twisted, blackened figure dragging useless legs behind it and trailing blood like snail mucus. Doaks backpedaled, trying to run, but the thing reared up and clawed at the air, making a wet, angry, gargling sound.

He felt the invasion of his mind and the pressure at his temples for the barest of seconds before his thick head caved inward in a massive rush, squirting one eyeball out and splattering the control deck with liquified brain matter.

## 10

"Mmm *mmm*!" Heater crowed, his form flawless again as he stepped over Tarmon Doaks's corpse. "You were a conniving little fram, weren't you? But hey, being devious requires imagination, too. Nobody knows that better than us."

The trip out of the desert had just about killed them. The wagon lost its juice in hours, leaving Heater to keep it running on a trickle of pure fantasy. By the time they emerged from the sands—straying far enough south that they didn't run into the Incarnate convoy—Loathe was insane with hunger and devouring Heater in chunks.

They couldn't let themselves become so desperate anymore. What they'd just siphoned from the man named Doaks needed to be preserved for the task at hand. So, rather than waste it by continuing to power the wagon, Heater jumped down and climbed on one of the horses.

"We'll head to Farrowbend, see if we can pick up his trail," he said, retrieving the information from Doaks's newly acquired memories. The statement was met with a chorus of encouragement from the endless voices inside him. "With a little luck, kiddo...we'll get to you before the Incarnates."

# Atop the Skyreach

# ZOMBERS

## 1

"Rand, wake up, man! C'mon drude, you gotta snap out of it!"

His eyes were smoldering coals when he opened them. Meech hovered over him, but the light was so dim, Rand could see only hints of the other man's face. His brother sighed in relief and helped him sit up from the cold surface beneath them with his one good arm.

"Lillam," he gasped, recalling the brutal shock of the electricity in his last moments of consciousness. "Is she all right? Where is she?"

"Don't know. She wasn't in here when we woke up."

"In *where*?" Rand turned his aching head. He could make out a forest of legs standing on the hard floor around him. Sobs and soft murmurs reached him, too numerous to separate out.

"They're some sorta transport boxes," Meech told him softly. "They hover, like Gwenita, but they're made of metal. Those monster people musta loaded us all up after they knocked us out."

Rand got to his feet. Bolts of pain shot through his body with every movement. Now that Meech had explained, Rand could detect the same sort of too-smooth gliding sensation beneath him that the wagon always produced. They seemed to be at one end of a rectangular space which reminded him of the barracks at the Prophet's home, illuminated by stark shafts of daylight that pierced through small holes in the ceiling and ribbed walls. A few dozen Wiltonites were packed into the narrow enclosure—holding one another, comforting their children, huddling on the ground wherever they could find room—but most gathered around the circular punctures in the metal to peer out. Rand comprehended that these holes were to prevent them from suffocating, but the air in the cargo hold remained stifling and uncomfortably warm from all the bodies, smelling of fear and body odor.

"Did anyone see what happened to Lillam?" he called out in desperation. "The woman who came to town with me?" A few people shook their heads, but most ignored him in their misery.

He was about to ask again when he heard his name called out from the far end of the transport loud enough to ring off the metal ceiling. The tight crowd jostled and parted for Mellory to slip through.

"Good to see you up, Mr. Mayor," the tavernmaster told him. He had a black eye and a long, clotted gash across his forehead.

"I'm not the mayor of anything." Rand objected.

"You're sure the closest thing we got. And if you have some ideas 'bout our situation, I'd love to hear 'em."

"What do we know?" Rand asked eagerly. Working the problem would be the only way to keep himself from going insane with worry over Lillam.

"Not much." Mellory gestured to the narrow wall next to Rand with the leather-capped stump of his wrist. "There's three'r four o' these floatin crates strung out behind us, and one in front. More'n enough to carry ev'ry man, woman and child in Wilton. I hope my son's not in one of 'em, but I don't reckon that's the case."

"Any idea where they're taking us?"

Mellory shrugged wearily. "We're somewhere up in the Skyreach, I think. A pass with mountains all around. We drove through an old-world town 'bout ten minutes ago, but nobody caught the name." His gaze drifted away as he frowned. "I don't understand why Incarnates'd do all this."

"They wouldn't." Rand waited for the other man to focus on him before adding, "Your precious Sisters are responsible for this."

The people closest to them gasped. Mellory shook his head. "No. I refuse to believe that."

Rand grabbed the tavernmaster's broad shoulders. "Those things that attacked us? *Those* are what took the people of Farrowbend. I'd be willing to bet they're also what's kept the Filament away from the Skyreach all this time. And now they've turned on us for some reason."

Mellory said nothing, but Rand caught the hesitant flicker in his eyes.

"What? What is it?"

"Back in town, I didn't see much. Got beat up in the stampede and zapped from behind while I was runnin. But a few other folk...they're claimin those things *were* the people o' Farrowbend. Bobsy Puckett over there, he swears it was his own cousin that got 'im." Mellory lowered his voice. "But I don't know how much stock to put in that, considerin he also says the man was dead but *still movin*."

"He's right," Rand confirmed, releasing him. "I fought one of them. It looked like a corpse come to life. Smelled like it, too."

"Puckett called them 'zombers.' From some old story that got passed down through his family about dead people that eat brains, or some such horsecurse."

"There's more," Meech added. He shifted his weight uncomfortably and readjusted the sling around his broken arm before continuing. "A buncha these people said that they wore metal bands around their heads, man. Ya know, like the kind that Doaks used on Korden."

Rand thought of the glint he'd seen on the creature's forehead while it straddled him. "Then...they aren't living dead people at all," he surmised. "They're just dead people *whose bodies are being controlled*."

A shout of, "*I see something!*" came from the opposite end of the transport. Mellory and Rand rushed toward it, clambering and shoving through the crowd. When they reached the wall, each found a vacant airhole and peered through.

Rand expected to see some kind of control deck at the front of the transport, just as on the wagon, but there was no driver area at all, giving him an unimpeded view of the twisty road ahead, lined on both sides with rocky foothills that quickly grew into steep slopes. He could see the back of another transport fifty or so pargs ahead—a floating, rectangular box built of scuffed red metal—and, beyond it, the canyon path deadended at a sheer mountain face with a long steel door built into the rock.

The entrance was dark blue in color, and adequately wide to admit six of these hovering vehicles side-by-side. As their transport coasted to a gentle stop next to the first, Mellory murmured, "What is this place?"

With a rumble so deep it penetrated their bones, the door retracted upward, revealing a black entrance into the bowels of the mountain.

2

Harris's vision was impaired.

He'd always counted himself lucky in this area, since most people who stare at a screen ten hours a day need some form of optical correction, so the sudden deficiency threw him for a loop. It hadn't been that noticeable at night, but once the sun rose, the light glinted off the cataract-like crust on his eyeballs and dropped a layer of white gauze across his sight. He rubbed and rubbed, splashed river water in them repeatedly, but it made little difference. If the Moambatis *did* receive a visual signal from their drones, it must be extremely low-def.

And that wasn't the only problem he found himself dealing with since his 'awakening'. The fetid smell that hung around him was gag-inducingly terrible, but he only became aware of it when he inhaled, which wasn't all that often. Far worse was the fact that, any time he stopped moving, his joints stiffened up, to the point that they almost locked him in place and popped like fire crackers when he tried to work them again. Even after getting limbered up, he struggled not to fall behind as the kid set a swift pace through a series of wooded foothills beyond the empty town, nimbly avoiding brush and rough terrain that Harris blundered through. He hadn't felt this awkward and ungainly since...well, to be honest, that part hadn't changed much in his horrible new existence.

Most annoying, however, was the override itself. Just knowing it sat atop his head, futzing with his cranial circuitry, was driving him crazy. He longed to tear it off but didn't dare; for all he knew, it might be the one thing keeping him 'alive'. Until he could get to some proper equipment and run some tests, he couldn't afford to do anything that might upset this bizarre fluke.

*Would that be so bad?* a small, plaintive voice inquired. *Do you really want to go on like this?*

*It might not be as bad as it seems. There could be a cure.*

*A cure? For* death?

Harris sighed inwardly. Trying to reconcile all of this was maddening. *Just get through this business with the kid, then you can figure out what happens from there.*

Speaking of which, Korden had drawn so far ahead, he was about to disappear around a sharp bend in the road they were following. The kid had seemed to have no destination in mind other than east until they'd come across this broken trail of asphalt just past sunrise. Upon finding a road sign and consulting a laminated map from his messenger bag, the teenager excitedly declared that it should lead them right to their destination. He'd sent his talking pet to scout ahead, the little blob racing off on its gaggle of tentacles.

Before the boy could leave him entirely, Harris yelled, "Would you mind slowing down?"

Korden slowed and turned, his mouth tightened in annoyance, before something by the side of the road caught his attention. He walked over and hoisted the rusted remains of another sign. Harris had to squint and block the sun from his diminished eyes to read it: CRESTED BUTTE, 2 MILES. "How far is this?" Korden asked.

"Another hour of walking. Forty-five minutes, at your pace. What's your rush, anyway? Town's not going anywhere. I assume."

"I don't think the Moambatis can locate me when I'm awake, but since we don't know about you, it's best to keep moving. Plus...there was kind of an army of Incarnates trailing me last I checked."

"An *army*? How many is an army?"

"Seven hundred or so."

"Oh, is that all?"

"That's why it's best if we keep moving." The kid dropped the sign with a *clang!* and started back toward him. "Do you need to rest?"

Harris considered the question. He wasn't actually tired, just frustrated at the prison his own body had become. And annoyed by this damn leotard with the Moambati Industries logo on the breast. "Maybe for a minute. The way you described these dead drone people, they sounded quick and agile. But I feel like the Tin Man before he got the oil can."

Korden gave a confused frown, but Harris couldn't tell if it was caused by the assertion or the reference. "You were fast before…"

"Yeah, I don't doubt it. Data from the overrides showed muscle coordination and reflex improvement by over thirty percent in the hosts. Basically, they could turn a regular person into an Olympic gymnast with the strength of a gorilla. Of course, that was in *live* test subjects. I would imagine there are a lot of extraneous factors to compensate for with a corpse." To demonstrate this, he stretched out an arm and winced at the deep snap that sounded in his elbow joint. It was becoming harder and harder for Harris not to think the dreaded words '*rigor mortis*'. "But unless they also somehow slow tissue degeneration, it sure doesn't explain why I haven't rotted away to dust in three hundred years."

Korden hunkered in the middle of the road, sitting on a crumbling chunk of asphalt. "How does your invention work?"

"Hoo boy." Harris swiveled his right shoulder to work out another kink while he tried to think of a way to answer the question. "That involves a lot of technobabble that you probably wouldn't understand even if you weren't living the Mad Max life. No offense."

"Hard to take offense when I don't even know what that means."

"Touché." Harris snickered. Despite everything, he kind of liked this kid. "Look, to put it in layman's terms, you feed a list of instructions into the override, and it sends electronic impulses to the parts of the brain that control various systems in the body to get it to carry out those instructions."

The kid's eyes flicked up to the band on Harris's forehead. "Yeah, I got to experience that firsthand."

"And you'll definitely have to tell me *that* story sometime. But anyway, that's why the ocular feed is so important if you don't have any other eyes on the subject. It's the only way to have adaptive responses in real time. Otherwise, it's just pre-recorded actions that allow for a set of simple if/then statements. The subjects can come off a little… stilted." He frowned. "And that's another thing bothering me about your theory. The computing power necessary to operate hundreds of these drones—not to mention the control staff—would be *staggering*. If Denise and Charlotta had said that was what they wanted to do with them, I would've told them it was completely impractical. I figured they would be used as spies, something to infiltrate the Filament to give us tactical information, weaknesses, things like that."

"Then maybe I'm wrong…but I don't think I am." The kid took a deep breath. "If we *do* run into more of them, is there any way to stop these overrides?"

"Yeah, separate them from the host or break them."

"I mean some way to…to switch them off, all at once."

"Not unless you have an EMP blast handy. The only way to shut them down together would be to find wherever they're being controlled from." Harris frowned. "Can't you use magic to wake them up, like you did me? Not that I would wish this lifestyle on anyone, but…"

"I only got close enough to enter your mind after I damaged the band and incapacitated you."

"Uh huh. Here come those stipulations."

The kid said nothing, just gazed into the rough hillside running along the road. There was an almost unbearable intensity about him, a competence that made Harris feel a little less ridiculous taking orders from a teenager. When Harris was sixteen, he couldn't find his way to the corner convenience store without a direction app in hand.

"Since you know about technology…" Korden reached into the top of his shirt and lifted out a small, round pendant hanging around his neck by a leather strap. "Can you fix this?"

Harris squinted until he could make out the object. "Kid, I don't get you. You dress like an extra from a Costner epic, but you're wearing sneakers I would've had to save six months for. And you've never seen a movie, but you're carrying around a S.T.O.N.E.?"

"Can you fix it?" he repeated.

"Who cares? I know that thing is probably a barrel of laughs to you, but, trust me, in my time, it was retro trash. My father got one for Christmas when he was a kid, and he smashed it with a hammer a week later."

Korden blanched. "He was my friend."

"Then congratulations, Synthetics International just called, and they wanna make you their new poster child for A.I. relations sensitivity." Harris started to laugh, but slammed his mouth shut when tears shimmered in the boy's eyes. "I'm sorry. My shrink says I use sarcasm to…never mind, not important. Do you know what's wrong with it?"

"It keeps repeating that it needs service."

"Well, this is not exactly my area of expertise but…if we had the right equipment…maybe just a good interface…I could give the code a quick review, I suppose."

Korden nodded, satisfied with the answer. "Then after we're finished with the Moambatis, that's what we'll do."

Harris considered telling the kid he had no intention of following around someone with seven hundred Incarnates on their tail, but decided that conversation could be left for another time.

They resumed walking, but it couldn't have been fifteen minutes later when the octopus came scurrying up the road to them and stated, "The settlement ahead is empty. Zeega found no sign of the dead humans or anything else."

The three of them diverted from the road, climbing a nearby flat-topped hill that gave an incredible, sweeping view of soaring, snowdusted mountains which dominated the eastern horizon, and the town nestled at the base of them.

Harris gaped. The kid had told him the Filament was winning the war against humanity, but it was different to see it for himself. Crested Butte was nothing like the strange, western-infused, medieval hamlet they'd just left; here was a city he could *recognize*, that he could've been instantly at home in. A place that had undoubtedly been full of people like him, with cell phones and holovids and helperbots and M-Net coverage, now repainted with a heavy coat of apocalypse.

Encroaching forest overran the buildings that weren't charred or collapsed. Cars—both the ground and hover-tread variety—rusted in the streets. He thought of that news broadcast, those people shuffling away from their homes in the middle of the night while the city lay in ruins behind them. The sole difference between that image and this one was the lack of the Shroud hanging over it all.

But, according to the kid, that black spot burning in the sky beyond the mountains *was* the Shroud.

It had happened. The fabled End of the World, subject of so much speculation for centuries. Not from comets or diseases or water shortage, but simple population dwindlage due to body-snatching invaders murdering all the children.

The end came, and Harris had Rip-van-Winkled right through it.

He faced Korden, wanting to express the sorrow and desolation welling up in him, and saw the boy had gone pale himself. Except he wasn't looking at the town.

"What is wrong?" the octopus asked before Harris could.

"That mountain." Korden pointed at the most prominent peak in the range, one whose shadow lay across the remains of Crested Butte like the hand of a sundial. It was a skewed slope, growing more off-center toward the top. It reminded Harris of that ancient Christmas classic *The Grinch*, and the lopsided summit the green main character called home.

"Yeah? What about it?" Harris prompted.

"That's the place they've been telling me to go."

# DRAFTED INTO
# SERVICE

## 1

Once the door into the mountain fully opened, the
transports moved through into a bank of frigid air. Rand
blinked as the sunlight disappeared, momentarily blinded,
but plenty of artificial light existed beyond the entrance to
see their surroundings once his eyes adjusted. A short crete
ramp led downward, then they entered a cavernous hollow
so spectacular it caused many of the shivering Wiltonites to
gasp in surprise, their breath pluming in the cold.

The walls were rough stone that climbed thirty pargs
overhead to a ceiling peppered with dangling rock columns
that tapered at the end like icicles. Blazing yellow lamps
were installed among the hanging pillars in neat lines, their
combined glare so bright they made Ida's flickering electric
torches look wan in comparison. While the rest of this
cavity appeared natural and unrefined, the floor, however,
was comprised of some slick, black material, glossed until it
reflected the lights as perfectly as a mirror and interrupted
only by thick towers of the same substance that stretched
up to the roof of the cave, presumably for support. From

aboard the smoothly hovering transports, they could've been gliding across a sheet of midnight ice.

A good portion of this interior space was taken up by rows upon rows of huge, squat, electronic monoliths thirty pargs tall and ten wide, full of blinking lights and emitting a collective hum that grew deafening as they moved closer. More of the walking corpses—'zombers,' for lack of a better name—crawled all over them and clung to the nearest rock columns, using various tools to make adjustments to the buzzing equipment. Their supernatural agility and matching black garments made them seem far more animal than human, like a pack of monteelas. Or spiders in a nest. In this brighter light, Rand could confirm Meech's claim that the pale creatures all wore metal crowns like the one strapped to Korden's head when they'd met, silvery bands that pressed cruelly into the flesh of their brows. He felt certain he'd been right before, that these things were merely puppeteered carcasses going about directed tasks.

But, if so, where was the hand that controlled them?

An unsettled wave went through the townsfolk in Rand's transport at the sight of the monsters who'd dragged them from their homes in the middle of the night, scared whimpers and bleats of terror. But none of the zombers gave the transports the slightest attention as they floated through the cavern. Several narrow, tunnel-like openings in the walls appeared to lead beyond this chamber, deeper into the mountain, but their destination was the corner, where floor-to-ceiling cage walls created a huge holding cell.

The boxy transports maneuvered up to one of these barriers in neat rows. Their narrow ends connected perfectly to hinged windows set into the bars. Rand and Mellory jumped away as both the window and the door of the transport swung open together, giving them an entrance into the cage.

"*Please exit immediately*," a cold, uninflected voice boomed from above.

Meech appeared at Rand's side. "I d-don't wanna go in th-there," he whispered through chattering teeth.

"I don't think we have much choice," Mellory said.

People reluctantly hopped from the transports. Rand stepped down onto that slick, black surface, then helped Meech by steadying his broken arm. At the same time, he studied the row of transports and disembarking passengers until he noticed a group of pregnant women stepping carefully into the holding cell, their bellies all varying degrees of swollen, and among them was—

"*Lillam!*" He shouted her name as he ran to her, pushing through the growing crowd. She met him with open arms as he swept her up. "Did they hurt you? The baby—!"

"We're all right," she told him. "Those things didn't shock me. They didn't do it to any of the pregnant women, apparently, but I don't think I was far enough along for them to see. After they broke down the door, I told them I was with child, begged them not to hurt me. They forced me to go with them and loaded us all up onto these floating barges." Her body quivered against him, either from fear or the freezing temperature of the cavern. This chamber was even colder than the one the sandman had created for them beneath the desert, but it smelled much danker, almost rotten, with an underlying acrid stench that must be emitted by the humming technology towers. "What is happening, why'd they bring us here?"

"I don't know."

"Rand, back in town...when that first creature attacked me...how did you—?"

He rushed to cut her off as the empty transports closed and backed away from the cell. The barred windows shut also, sealing the populace of Wilton into a space that three houses from the settlement couldn't have fit in. The next few minutes were filled with cries of joy as families and friends who'd come in separate transports found one another in the holding cell. Rand saw Gaulbriel walk through, holding Onjel on his shoulders. Lillam waved to Grayhm and Nancer while Mellory swept Harek up in a crushing embrace.

"This is bad," Meech told Rand from the side of his mouth as they watched the reunion.

"That's an understatement."

"I wish Korden was here. Everything has a way of workin out when that li'l drude's around."

"We should've listened to him," Lillam agreed forlornly, cradling the tiny bump in her stomach. "We were fools to believe this place could keep us safe."

Rand nodded forlornly and murmured, "Whatever we want in life, we'll have to fight for."

"*Your attention, please!*"

A hush fell over the crowd at the shout, followed by a brief round of screams when the speaker was found. A squad of sixteen zombers gathered around a ground-level door to the holding cell. The creatures stared in at them with blank, white eyes. Knowing that they were just manipulated corpses made them a bit less terrifying for Rand, but still awful to behold. Besides their deathly pallor, touches of rot, and foul reek, many of them appeared roughly-used and battle-injured. The one in the front—a woman with a bloodless gash across her side that cut through her bodysuit and deep into the meat beneath—began to speak in a distractingly normal voice. "You have all enjoyed the grace and protection of the Moambati Sisters, but now you have been drafted into service against the Dark Filament."

Rand shot a glance at Mellory and whispered, "Still think this has nothing to with them?"

The female zomber continued. "This is for the good of humanity, to set us free from the Filament's occupation of our world. Take comfort in the fact that your sacrifice will be remembered for generations to come."

There was something comically formal about the pronouncement, but no one laughed. A few seconds of uneasy silence passed, then a voice from the crowd called out, "What does that mean?" Grayhm followed this by bellowing, "You 'napped us all and put us in a cage! Don't matter if you represent the Sisters or not, we ain't doin jackcurse for you!"

The dead woman didn't acknowledge these shouts before making her next announcement. "Please have all children below the age of eighteen step forward to the door."

This time, protest *erupted* in the holding cell. Everyone talked and shouted at once, their voices echoing in the artificial cave. Parents shoved their pre-agers behind them, shielding them with their bodies. Rand stepped in front

Lillam and was quickly joined by Meech.

"Your children will not be harmed," the zomber assured them. "They will be cared for, allowed to come of age, and drafted into service only if they are needed. Those of you who are pregnant will be evaluated on a case-by-case basis when time permits, to determine if the same offer can be extended."

"*You're not takin our kids!*" a hysterical female voice cried out. To Rand's surprise, the vow was met with strident agreement by all of Wilton.

The zomber did not ask a second time. She and the rest of her group moved forward as one. The door opened on its own in front of them, as if sensing them by some hidden mechanism. They entered the cage two-by-two and spread out in a line. By unspoken agreement, the children and babies were ushered to the middle of the holding cell, and most of the adults—both those with *and* without offspring of their own—formed a protective barrier in front of them, a defiant line of balled fists and bared teeth. Rand thought of the crowd back in Ida, how they'd been willing to hand Korden over to the Incarnates, and realized he was witnessing a unity that few settlements would be able to muster. That sense of wholeness he'd felt back in Wilton was evident even though the security that generated it had been stripped away.

Lillam moved to stand with them, but Rand grabbed her wrist.

"Let me go!" she cried, struggling to free herself from his grip.

"You can't risk hurting the baby!" he insisted, dragging

her to the side of the cage where the other pregnant women gathered. Meech followed, doing all he could to help wrangle Lillam with his one good arm.

As the zombers closed in, the line of citizens broke. A large chunk of men and a few women charged their captors, outnumbering them four times over. Rand saw Grayhm and Gaulbriel among them, roaring with fury. The zombers waded into them without hesitation, spinning and dodging with unnatural speed, so nimble that none of the Wiltonites could even lay a hand on them. Their palms spit electricity, stunning anyone who got within range and filling the air of the cavern with that horrible crackling sound and an acerbic tang that Rand couldn't tell if he was tasting or smelling.

Those still standing quickly saw the futility, and the rebellion wound down to an embarrassing end. Dozens of unconscious bodies littered the floor at the booted feet of the zombers.

The creatures marched forward. There was no more resistance, no more fighting, but several women fell to their knees and pleaded before being shoved aside. Newborn babies were ripped from their mother's arms. Children sobbed and clung to their parents before being separated and herded back toward the door of the cage. Onjel pounded his small fists on the chest of one of the zombers and received a stinging blow across the cheek.

"Rand, *do* something!" Meech begged, his tone of voice conveying exactly what he expected his brother to do.

Rand took a deep breath and closed his eyes, concentrating, seeking the place in his head where all that power flowed beneath the surface, aching to be set free. But he found no conduit, no artcraft, no perception of Korden's blasted Upper.

*How the hells am I supposed to use it?*

The zombers ushered—and, in some cases, dragged—the screaming, crying children out of the cage, toward one of the tunnels leading deeper into the mountain. Mothers and fathers ran to the bars and stuck their hands through, reaching for their precious offspring.

The female zomber paused as the door closed and turned back to face the wailing parents of Wilton.

"The conversions will commence momentarily," she said, before striding away with the others.

2

Korden hiked down into the old-world city called Crested Butte with Zeega at his heel and Harris Stebens trailing far behind, partly because of his stiff, wobbling gait and partly because he stopped to goggle at everything. The man's jabbering was as constant as Stone's, and most of what he said made about as much sense. It might've been completely surreal to speak so casually with someone that had lived in the wonders of the old world, but Korden had grown up with the Olders' stories, so he was used to such grieving nostalgia. After they'd crossed several abandoned streets, he asked the dead man to be silent until they got a sense of the danger they were facing.

The settlement had obviously been the site of a battle in the distant past, most likely during the Purges. There were signs of fire throughout the buildings, blast marks on the crete, and skeletal remains in green uniforms strewn everywhere, but it seemed to be free of pathomes. Korden made his way through the destruction, keeping a wary eye on that familiar, canted summit looming over the far side of the city. It was so high up, a lone, rocky crag, but with less snow on it than in the Sierras, probably because of the higher temperatures here at the end of Burning Season. As he stared, something up there caught the morning sun at just the right angle to reflect a chip of light.

"What will you do?" Zeega inquired, as they crossed an intersection full of scorched autos. They were approaching the northeast fringe of the city now, and a break in the buildings let them see the green slopes leading up into the mountain range.

"I don't know," Korden answered honestly. "But they're up there. These *sisters*, or whatever they are. They've haunted me since I started this journey, and now I'm at their doorstep."

"If stopping the Filament is truly your goal, then they are but a diversion." Zeega used a claw to point at the street leading east out of the intersection. "Korden and Zeega should continue to keep your mind hidden while you sleep and slip past them, as you threatened."

Korden stopped, closed his eyes, and shook his head. "They're enslaving people. Killing them to use their bodies. They could attack Wilton next. I can't let that happen." He frowned as a new thought occurred to him. "Of course, if I do stop them, then Wilton and every other town under their protection will be vulnerable to the Incarnates."

"Hey, look at this!"

Down the street behind them, Harris stood next to the shattered window at the front of a building labeled 'Crested Butte Tourist Bureau'. On the other side of the glass was a wooden rack full of rectangular paper slips. He reached through the window to thumb through them. "If you need maps of the town, they've got plenty here. Some of them even show the hiking trails up the mountain. Oh, sweet, they have an arcade!" He grabbed a fistful of the maps and yanked them out to wave in the air.

"Um…Harris?" Korden pointed at the broken window.

The man raised a questioning eyebrow below the override, then turned to examine the shards of glass clinging to the frame, where a hunk of something white and fleshy dangled.

"What is…? Oh. That's…that's my finger." Harris let the maps flutter to the ground and held up his left hand, which now consisted of a thumb and three digits. The littlest one had been sheared away by the sharp glass, along with the side of his hand from knuckle to wrist. No blood welled from the wound; it was just a ragged, black-rimmed slash from which flashes of yellow bone peeked out.

"Does it hurt?" Korden asked, coming closer.

"Not really. There's sort of a…a distant throb…" Harris delicately lifted the finger off the glass with his other hand and looked at it on his palm. The lump of dead flesh made Korden's empty stomach twist. "What did they do to me? Those goddamned bitches, *what did they do to me?*"

"It's all right," Korden told him, glancing over his shoulder as the words rolled through the empty streets.

"That's easy for you to say!" The dead man's aura roiled

with anger and dark threads of hopelessness. "I'm falling the hell apart here!"

"We'll fix you, too."

"Kid, you see this? This is me putting my own finger in the pocket of this ridiculous leotard for safekeeping. How you gonna fix that?"

"There *must* be a way. Once my artcraft gets back to full strength, I'm sure I can do something. Help me with this, and then we'll figure it out. We'll figure *everything* out."

Harris's shoulders slumped. Korden wasn't sure if he was imagining it, but the spot of decay at the corner of his mouth seemed to be spreading across his upper lip. "Help you with *what*? I don't get what you expect me to do against..." He trailed, his cloudy eyes narrowing as he looked down the street over Korden's shoulder. "Do you see that?"

He stepped around Korden and waddled up the street as fast as he could. Korden kept pace with him, looking ahead, trying to understand what'd gotten him so excited. The weed-eaten streets came to an end in this direction, the buildings spaced farther apart as they reached the northeast edge of the town, where the steeper slopes took over. The very last structure—sitting on a crete-and-gravel lot—was a long, silvery building without a single window, just ribbed metal walls and a set of massive doors that took up the entire front. Its design appeared out-of-place in this otherwise rustic village, and much newer than any of the other buildings they'd seen.

"Do you recognize this place?" Zeega inquired, sounding suspicious.

"It's a hermetic warehouse. Air-tight, germ-free. Essentially a vacuum-sealed time capsule. Moambati Industries uses them to store medical equipment at distribution hubs around the world, to keep delicate parts from aging."

"Does this one belongs to them?" Korden asked eagerly.

They approached a smaller, person-sized door at the very corner of the building, and Harris pointed at an emblem painted in black upon its surface: the same outline of a wrinkly brain that adorned the breast of his bodysuit.

"I'd say chances are good. Charlotta was always big on branding." He frowned. "I don't see why they'd need one this big though, with hangar doors and all. You could fit a commercial stratoliner in there."

"Can we get inside?"

"I doubt it. Even if the power's working, we'd need an authorization strip keyed to the right frequency."

"If only the disembodied one were here," Zeega remarked.

"I'll pretend I know what that means." Harris reached for the handle with his injured hand, caught sight of the missing finger, and switched to the other. "We could try to break through, but it might—"

Something inside the door gave a sharp buzz. There was a click, and the barrier swung open a few cupits.

Korden looked at the dead man.

"It's gotta be the override." Harris touched the dented metal band around his forehead. "They must've wanted the drones to have access. That means there's power, too." He pulled the door the rest of the way open, revealing a small vestibule with gray polymer walls and crete floor.

An identical door waited on the far side. "That's a de-con airlock. We'll get a microburst of radiation to kill the germs while the warehouse fills with air."

"Will it hurt?"

"Naw, you won't feel a thing. C'mon." He went inside.

Korden paused, unwilling to enter another automated building with few exits, but his desire for information about his opponents won out. He stepped through, and Zeega joined them. The door sealed shut, leaving them in darkness for a few seconds before bright lights popped on in the ceiling. There were various beeps and whooshes around them, the brief scent of something chemical, and then the next door popped open.

The interior of the warehouse was all one big, open space, occupied by an array of colossal vehicles whose rubber wheels were twice Korden's height. They were all colored yellow and striped with black and adorned with a strange array of mechanical arms and scoops and corkscrewed metal cones that baffled Korden until Harris explained.

"It's an automated construction fleet. This must be what they used to build whatever they have up there. I saw the requisitions when they were delivered, along with a ton of lab equipment."

"Why would they put them in a place like this?"

"Maybe to preserve them, in case they needed them again. If the rest of the country looks like what we passed through out there, it can't be easy to find equipment like this anymore." His attention was caught by a line of smaller, roofless vehicles parked next to the wall beside them, with two bench seats. "Hey, passenger carts! And they're fully charged! If we could get one of these outta here, we could ride for a while!"

Korden walked through the warehouse, admiring the huge machines, a part of him that was still very young aching to drive one. After a few seconds, he came across a stack of dark metal crates painted with a large 'DANGER!' warning in red, and 'LX42 PRECISION BURN' in smaller text below. "What about this?"

Harris had to get his face within a few cupits to read the tiny print on the boxes. "Oh god, that's ion thermite. That stuff burns as hot as the sun. It can melt steel like butter, but it's so exact you could shave with it." He rubbed at his stubbled jowl with his uninjured hand. "I wonder if I still need to shave…"

"Could we use it to destroy whatever they built?" Korden asked.

Harris laughed. "You could destroy the *mountain* with this much IT. But if you don't know how to control the blast—which we don't—I would make sure I wasn't anywhere close when it went off."

Korden put a hand on one of the crates, considering, when Zeega called his name from the door they entered through.

"We must go outside," she insisted. "*Now.*"

Back on the street, the riftling faced that high, slanted peak and closed several of her eyes in concentration. "Zeega senses…humans. A large mass, deep within the base of the mountain."

"*Within?*" Korden asked.

"Yes. Somewhere far beyond the rock and earth." One

of her foreclaws reached out to grip Korden's pants leg. "The humans Rand, Lillam and Meech are among them."

"What? *How?*" Korden reached out with his mind, but whatever her delicate senses had caught was too distant for him. "What are they doing? Are they all right?"

"Their emotional spectra are filled with despair. Zeega can tell no more than this."

"Then...they've already got them." A wave of helplessness made Korden dizzy as the true meaning of that last dream came clear. "The Moambatis *already* took Wilton. They're the next 'sacrifice.'" He swung a fist into the metal side of the warehouse, producing a dull *clong!*

"What is it you wish to do?"

What he wanted to do was scream. To cry. To destroy something.

But none of those things would help.

"I'm going up there," he said. "To meet them."

"This is what they want."

"That's right. And I'll give it to them."

"Then Zeega will accompany you."

"No. I'm going alone."

The riftling bristled. "Zeega will not allow this!"

"Listen to me." Korden squatted in front of her. "I don't think the Moambatis know about you. They thought I was alone in the last dream, so maybe your lack of a *mohol* blinds them to you the same way your call does for me. I'll go up there, see what they want, and try to find a way to free the others. But if I fail...*you* must stop them. Destroy them with the crates inside the warehouse. Even if you have to kill me, too."

Her five-fold gaze lowered. "Zeega cannot."

"You've got to. They must be stopped, no matter what. I need you, Zeega. Promise me."

"*Hoshnitaths* do not have a concept of 'promises,'" she grumbled. "But Zeega agrees to your wishes."

"Thank you. You've done so much for me. I could never find a way to repay you." He slipped the strap of his carry pouch over his head and set it on the ground, along with the knife from his belt. He considered taking out one of the talkies to bring with him so they could stay in touch, but he would probably move out of range quickly and besides, he had no way to conceal it. "Watch my things for me until I get back."

Korden rose and faced Harris, who asked, "So what happens to me?"

"You're staying here to help her."

"I told you, I don't know anything about that thermite."

"Then figure it out. This is how you make up for inventing those terrible bands in the first place."

"Cripe man, I already *died*! Isn't that enough punishment?"

"If this had all ended with your death, yes. But other people are still being hurt because of what you did." Korden took a moment to phrase his next question carefully. "Do you believe in a god? *Any* god?"

Harris shook his head, the unruly straggles of what remained of his dark hair swinging against his thick neck. "Nope. Like I said, man of science here. Atheist all the way."

Korden thought of Bibb, talking of balance, and how immersion in one thing can shut a person off from many others. He was thankful that his mind was not so closed as this man's. "Well, I do. And I believe there must be a reason why, out of all their slaves, I found *you*, the one person who knew about the overrides. The one person who could help me. In my religion, we say that the Upper provides, and I believe that He provided you."

Harris gave a long, put-out sigh, but his aura soured with dark green guilt. "Okay. Fine. I'll stay with Squidward here. How long are we supposed to wait before we do anything?"

"If I'm not back by nightfall...assume I'm not coming back."

"All right. Then do me a favor. If it really *is* Denise and Charlotta up there, and you find a way to take them down...tell them Harris says hello."

"I can do that." Korden pointed back into the warehouse. "Now show me how to drive one of those passenger carts."

### 3

The holding cell filled with weeping after the children were taken, the lamentations ringing off the high-ceilinged cavern. Parents sat in traumatized heaps on the floor while Doc Timpett saw to those injured in the skirmish. Other Wiltonites stood at the bars of their cage, huddled against one another for warmth, and pleaded with the zombers as the creatures rushed about, performing unknown tasks around the chamber.

Lillam took Rand by the arm and pulled him over to a quiet corner of the cell. Her full lips had gone a shade of light blue in the frigid climate, but she did not shiver as she proclaimed, "I saw what you did. You pushed that creature away from me somehow. Like...like Korden would have."

Rand's heart thumped painfully behind his ribs. He couldn't speak, could barely meet her gaze.

"Tell me the truth, Rand. Are you a Crafter?"

He took a long, slow breath. This was worse than his admission to Hilton after they'd been caught breaking into the man's quarters, the hardest words he'd ever needed to speak. "I think I might be."

"So...you lied to me all this time we've been together?"

"Aged Lord, no!" he exclaimed, the words visible as a horrified fog in the cold air.

"Then when—?"

"It happened right before we left Ida." 'Happened' seemed a cowardly word choice, a way to shift responsibility away from himself. *Is it any surprise you can't use this power when you deny it every chance you get?* He rushed to clarify. "I don't know why. Korden thinks something must've awakened it inside me." Rand sank to his knees in front of her, clutched her waist, and buried his face in that bulge on her stomach, unable to bear the hurt look in her eyes. "I'm so sorry, Lillam. I couldn't think of a way to tell you. Please believe me, I...I didn't want this. And I'll honor your wishes if this is the last you want to see of me. But if you can forgive me, I swear, I'll never use it again!"

"You'll swear no such thing, you fool," she snapped. "What you'll do is use those powers to get us out of this terrible place!"

He raised his head to look up at her. "Sweetlove?"

Lillam caressed his cheek with a grin. "I told Korden I would be kinder to the next Crafter I met, and I meant it. I never expected it to be the man I love, but…"

"Do you still love me? *Can* you?"

"Rand, my silly boo-pup…I don't care what you are. I just want us to raise this child together. So get us out of this cage so we can do that."

"I can't," he told her miserably, a confession as terrible as the first. "This artcraft…it doesn't always work when I want it to."

"You're the only one who can help us, my darling. I know you'll find a way."

A spark flitted through Rand's mind as she said it. Nothing as big as that first pop back in Ida when this all started, but something like a door creaking open the tiniest bit in the deep recesses of his brain. But, before he could wedge mental fingers into that gap and attempt to pry it wider, commotion near the front of the cell drew their attention. Rand stood, and he and Lillam drifted closer, taking a position next to Meech as the female zomber and her crew returned.

"We require ten individuals to begin," she announced. "Volunteers should step forward."

"Volunteers for what?" someone asked.

"A Filament army is approaching this installation. If these walls are breached, they will slaughter your children. All of you will be converted into soldiers to counter them. Volunteers will be used for calibration and testing, to ensure the process goes smoothly for the rest."

A deep silence unfolded in the chilly cavern. Then, six

men emerged from the crowd and lined up at the door. The female zomber nodded and pointed at four more, one of which was Mellory's son, Harek. "All of you as well. Come now, or there will be consequences."

"No, I volunteer in his place." The tavernmaster rushed forward, shoving his son backward when Harek tried to stop him. As he came to stand in front of the door, the zomber's white eyes moved appraisingly down to his missing hand. "Don't worry yerself none about this," he said, holding up the stump. "I c'n do more with a stub than most men could with three hands." This must've satisfied the zomber, because the cell door opened, and the ten men filed out.

Mellory gave Rand a wink as he passed by. "Take care of 'em, Mr. Mayor."

They followed the zombers across the room and through one of the openings deeper into the mountain.

4

The passenger cart hovered, which was good, because the terrain quickly turned rough. Korden steered the tiny, two-seat craft along the grassy slopes of the Skyreach, following one of the trails on the maps that Harris found, which should take him near the summit of the tallest peak. As morning became noon, hunger cramped his stomach, but he did not slow down to eat. His every thought was for Rand, Lillam, Meech, and even Doaks, along with anger at himself for bringing them to this place and letting them stay when he knew it felt wrong.

There might not be much snow in the upper ranges of

these mountains, but the temperature dropped so far as to have him shivering. His lungs hitched at the thinning air until each breath took effort. As he drew closer to the vertex, it became evident that the slanted mountain held not just one summit, but *two*, a natural split in the rock forming a set of prongs that stabbed at the heavens. When he strained his vision, he could make out a few more details of the glittering structure up there. It looked like a horizontal glass tube stretched across the gap, built in such a way that the stone cradled it, but there didn't seem to be a point of access from the sheer cliff face below. Before he could get so close as to discern what might be inside, the trail wound around to the north face of the mountain, away from the structure and the town of Crested Butte.

He passed the remains of cabins from ancient campsites, and still climbed upward. When the ascent became too steep for the cart's puttering engine, Korden left the vehicle and walked, hugging himself for warmth and wishing he'd thought to bring his coat. By this point, he no longer needed the map or the trail; two *mohols* waited ahead, flickering atop the mountain like candle flames, and he headed straight for them.

Upon struggling up a narrow earthen gully, he reached an open plateau where the wind blew across in frosty gusts, so stiff they made him stumble. He was so high now that the spot of the Shroud to the northeast looked near enough to reach out and touch. The slanted crest of the mountain was visible a few hundred pargs above, but the path in front of him deadended at a vast wall of rock. There was no way around it; however, a small, polymer door was set *into* it, as out of place as a duck amid a herd of ramlars. When he came within twenty pargs of the white surface, it swung open, halting him in place. Korden stood straight and tall on the rocky shelf, refusing to let his exhaustion or breathlessness show, as the owners of those two auras emerged.

It was them. Exactly as they'd looked in his dreams aside from their dress, which was far more demure than the revealing smocks. He'd half-expected them to be elderly and wizened in real life, the female equivalent of the Olders, but their dark forms were every bit as sleek as portended. The moment felt so queer and dreamlike, he suddenly wondered if he might've fallen asleep while piloting the cart and slipped back into their realm without realizing.

"Are you real?" he demanded through chattering teeth, as a gust of wind sliced through his tunic. "Are you *actually* Denise and Charlotta Moambati? Daughters of Terese Moambati?"

"Oh yes, Korden, we are very real." Denise wore a cream-colored, short-sleeve dress that hung to her knees, the hem whipped by the wind, and a pair of white shoes that were little more than slippers. Her tightly woven braids created crisp lines down her scalp. She wiped at tears of joy as she added, "And you are here, you are finally here, I cannot believe it! We are…we are just *so* happy to see you!"

Her sister stood beside her with arms crossed, wearing furred white boots, a crisp pair of gray pants, and a black, long-sleeve blouse, the latter two fitted so tightly to her curvaceous form that they held not a single wrinkle. Charlotta's smile wasn't as grand and emotional as Denise's, but her *mohol* revealed equal amounts of joy tempered with smug triumph. "Come inside, Korden," she invited, her exotic pronunciation breaking his name into two distinct, unfamiliar syllables. "You will freeze to death out here."

"I didn't come because you asked me to!" he shouted, unleashing his anger and trying not to feel like a very skinny sixteen-year-old child. "You have my friends, and I want them back!"

Charlotta frowned. "Your friends?"

"Yes! You took them with the rest of Wilton!"

Denise's mouth fell open in what seemed like genuine shock, the emotion mirrored in her *mohol*. She glanced at her twin before answering, but Charlotta's eyes never moved from Korden. "I swear we did not know. When you closed your mind off to us, we could not follow you or see where you parted with your companions."

"Liar! You always wanted me to leave them, from the very beginning!"

"That is true, we did not want them to accompany you here, and we tried to frighten them away from you, but we meant them no harm beyond that. If they were swept up with in the raid, it was unintentional." She clasped her hands in front of her, as in the dream. "Please believe me, we would never harm you!"

"*Harm* me?" Korden scoffed. "You stole my artcraft and sent those things to capture me!"

"Because we thought it would be the quickest way to get you here, where you would be safe!"

"Obviously, we should have sent more," Charlotta added, raising an eyebrow. "Watching you defeat those three without magic at your disposal was quite impressive. May I ask what happened to the remains?"

"I destroyed them." The lie slipped out before he could reconsider it. He didn't know if these two read *mohols*, but, if so, how much of the truth would be revealed in his? Would it be silver, like Doaks? At least this seemed to confirm that they were unaware of Harris's awakening.

"That is good," Charlotta said. "Our tech can be dangerous in the wrong hands. As you know."

Denise bowed her head. "Yes, we have made mistakes, Korden. But you must see that our intent was to protect you. We warned you about Loathe when you encountered that horrible entity in the redwood forest. We filled you with power, so you could defend yourself to get here."

"It doesn't matter! You're hurting people, taking entire towns to—"

"*Enough of this!*" Charlotta stepped in front of her sister. The wind blew her short hair around her head in a halo. "Time is too short for this bickering. I refuse to beg you, Korden, so I will make you a deal: come inside, be civil, listen to what we have to say...and your friends will not be harmed."

Korden hesitated, checking for sincerity in *her* aura. "What about the rest of Wilton?"

"Them as well. Nothing more will be done until we have our discussion."

Denise made a balking noise to get her sister's attention. "But the numbers—"

"Are fine," Charlotta barked over her shoulder. "We have more than necessary to fend off the coming attack.

Converting the population of Wilton was always about the next step." She returned her stern gaze to Korden. "Speak with us. Hear what we have to say with your mind, rather than your heart. If, after we have finished, you wish to leave with your friends, with *all* of that town…we will allow it. But I do not think that will be the case."

Denise leaned to peer around her sister. "Please, listen to her, Korden. We have so much to tell you. So many answers to give. And so much that we can offer."

Korden stood for a long moment, watching the two blackenwomen, whose faces were so similar but everything else about them distinct. He could see no alternative to their offer besides walking away without the others—an unthinkable conclusion—or attacking them with artcraft outright, here and now, and they'd repeatedly proved themselves his better in that regard. Hells, any *real* power he'd obtained over the last few weeks had been given to him by them.

They held all the advantages in this situation.

*Not all*, he told himself, trying not to think of his instructions to Zeega and Harris.

"All right," he relented. "I'll give you one hour."

"I would ask for no more," Charlotta agreed, standing aside to invite him through the door.

## 5

For a short time, they'd heard screams echoing from the mouth of the tunnel where the ten volunteers were taken. All of Wilton waited nervously for what felt like hours. Many of them fell asleep; not surprising, considering that, aside from the time they'd been stunned, the town had been awake for more than twenty-four hours.

Rand sat against the bars of the cell beside a snoring Meech with Lillam reclining on his shoulder. He'd intended to try faithing, but the cold was too distracting, and every time he closed his eyes, sleep threatened to take him also. After surrendering to a fitful doze, more cries from inside the cage brought him flailing back to consciousness.

Mellory stood outside the door. His clothes were gone, replaced by one of the black zomber garments, and a metal band was clamped over his head so tightly that the scalp had split around it. Blood stained his face from the injury, reminding Rand of some of the rituals of those who followed the Saint of Christ. The people closest to Mellory scrambled to get away.

"Dad?" Harek strained against the bars, reaching for his father. "Dad, are you all right? Talk to me!"

The tavernmaster didn't give his son even a glance. He looked as dull-eyed and blank-faced as Korden had all those weeks ago in Ida, when he performed in Doaks's show. How ironic that, after freeing the kid from that fate, Rand and Meech would soon end up just like him.

Mellory stared into the cell and said, in a voice very different from his usual twang, "Please make yourselves comfortable. Conversions have been suspended until further notice."

# ARGUABLE THESIS

## 1

Korden walked into a pristine white hallway made of large tiles, every surface spotless and sparkling. The squares that formed the walls were lit from within somehow—creating a cool, diffuse illumination—and made of a polymer so glossy, he could see his own ghostly reflection in their shine. He goggled at the effect, shivering and wheezing deep in his chest, while the Moambati sisters entered behind him and closed the door, shutting out the howling wind.

"Welcome to our home." Charlotta's *mohol* revealed her pleasure at his amazement.

Denise surprised him by stepping closer and slipping her arm through his. "Oh, you are freezing!" she exclaimed. She gave a preoccupied, straining frown, a muscle in her forehead twitched, and then nebulous purple shimmers pulsed out from her chest. They swept down her arm and crossed over to him at the point of contact. Korden's shivers ceased and his breathing eased as a cocoon of pleasant warmth enveloped him.

Body heat, transferred from her to him on waves of artcraft.

"You're...you can..." Even though it was precisely what he'd believed all along, seeing their Crafting abilities with his own eyes left him flabbergasted.

"Show off," Charlotta muttered.

Denise stuck her tongue out at her twin and then smiled at Korden. "You must be famished. Come with me, my darling." She kept their arms looped and took his hand, intertwining her dark fingers with his light ones to create a pattern that reminded him of piano keys. He faltered at the show of affection but allowed himself to be tugged down the dazzling hallway and into a maze of similarly flawless passages before they entered a room that stupefied him all over again.

It appeared to be a rectangular living or dining space, but everything in here was white as well. An immaculate leather couch in front of a recessed hearth outlined in smaller white tiles; furry, deeply-padded chairs without a speck on them; and a long, polymer table which held the only variation of color in the room: a feast of various meats, cheeses, breads and desserts that made his stomach give an audible growl. But he couldn't take the time to concentrate on any of it because, while three of the walls were of the same material as the hallways, the fourth boundary across from the entrance was nothing but a sheet of glass that curved down from the top.

On the other side was the most breathtaking view he'd ever seen.

An endless field of pure azure waited directly on the other side of the glass; a boundless vista of sky. From what he could tell, a straight drop began at the floor's edge on the other side of the convex window. Far, far below, the mountain slopes of the Skyreach spread out across the land for spans upon spans. A tiny huddle of buildings in the umbra of the mountain marked the location of Crested Butte, but the view extended even beyond that, to the banks of the river he'd followed with Zeega and Harris. In fact, through a break in the foothills, even the tallest roofs of Farrowbend were visible.

Korden realized he now stood inside the glass tube he'd seen from below. At this height, the two women who'd built this gleaming, futuristic palace could look down upon the entire world.

And all the settlements they used as their personal stock of bodies.

"Please, sit down and eat!" Denise led him to the head of the table and released his hand to gently push him down into a chair. The plush seat felt heavenly beneath his sore legs. She slid platters of food filled with roasted pheasant and sugar-glazed pastries toward him. The smell alone made his mouth flood with saliva, but he dared not touch any of it.

Noting his hesitation, she knelt beside the chair to put their eyes on a level. He tried (and failed) not to notice how the hem of her cottony dress slid up her taut, ebony thighs. Holding his gaze, Denise said, with a solemnity that her aura matched, "You have my word, Korden. No harm will come to you while you are here. We have no desire to trick you or force you to do anything. Quite the opposite. So eat, my darling."

Her liquid brown eyes were mesmerizing. He wanted to hold on to his suspicion, but it was hard in the face of such gracious reception. His blood pumped loudly in his ears, and his mind raced with thoughts that made certain parts of him go firm and rigid.

Then embarrassment warmed him as he wondered how much of this yearning they could sense.

Or how much they welcomed.

Korden nodded, not trusting himself to speak, and turned to the banquet. He would already be distracted throughout this encounter; might as well get rid of these clawing hunger pains to give himself a better chance at focusing on whatever they had to tell him.

He picked up a leg of turkey and took a bite. The meat was juicy and spiced and unlike anything he'd ever tasted. His craving grew even sharper. Within seconds he'd picked the bone clean and began wolfing down everything else he could lay hands on.

Denise laughed, sliding into the chair at the corner of the table next to him. "Slow down! It would be silly to come all this way to choke now!"

"It's very good." He swallowed a mouthful of warm bread as a new thought occurred to him. "Did you... *craft* this?" The amount of knowledge it would've taken to conjure such extravagance was unthinkable, but he also couldn't imagine either of them in front of an oven.

His question elicited another musical, clear laugh. Everything about this woman was lovely and disarming. "No, I am afraid not. We could, very easily, but it would be a waste of resources when we have...well...servants to tend to that."

It took him a moment to catch her meaning. "Servants. Is that what you call them?"

"Servants. Soldiers. Subjects," Charlotta offered blithely. She'd sat down upon the leather couch facing him with her legs crossed and arms draped across the back, her dark form a steep contrast to the white material. "They are what we require them to be."

"They were people before you put those awful things on their heads." He could feel his indignation rising at her callousness. "Before you killed them and used their corpses as your slaves."

"We try to end their lives humanely," Denise's words—and her aura—were contrite. "They must be conscious for the overrides to interface, but as soon as they are converted, we do not want them to be aware of what is happening, or to suffer a lingering death."

"I'm sure that's a big comfort."

Charlotta seemed amused by his anger. "We learned much about you through your dreams, Korden. For instance, we know you were forced to wear one of those overrides, and for that, I am truly sorry. It must have been an early prototype, left behind in our rush to relocate here from our former labs during the last days of the Purges. If it is any consolation, one of the three servants we sent to retrieve you was the man who created them."

"Why would that be a consolation?"

"You destroyed him, did you not? While that was unexpected, we *did* know that you would not come without a fight. So we gave you an opportunity to take out your anger on the man responsible."

"Just because he created them doesn't mean he's responsible for the way people use them."

"An arguable thesis." She gave a languid shrug, as if none of this mattered to her in the slightest. "In any case, a man like this 'Doaks' should never have gotten his hands on our property. His behavior has understandably prejudiced you against our work."

"I don't see how he did anything different with his than you have with yours."

"We are not using ours to make money with parlor tricks."

"No, just to cook your meals," he argued, shocked to hear himself defending Tarmon Doaks.

The only physical sign of Charlotta Moambati's growing irritation was a small crease down the center of her perfect brow. "Your dreams also revealed that you believe the best way to beat the Dark Filament is for people to resist. To rise up. Well...we have found a way to make them do that."

"I want them to make children again, not be made to fight against their will!"

"And for the last fifteen years, our soldiers patrolled the lands around these mountains, from one end to the other. They have driven off the Incarnates. Made it safe for people to do that."

"Only so you can use them to make yourself even more dead slaves!"

"That is right," Charlotta snapped. Red flashes of anger pulsed in her *mohol*. "Up to this point, we could afford to employ only guerilla tactics, but sooner or later, open warfare will be required to repulse the Filament. And wars require armies. The people we took, we have given their insignificant lives purpose, used them for a cause more glorious than they could ever imagine."

"Oh yes, nothing more glorious than becoming a putrid corpse!"

Now her anger wasn't just in her aura; it poured out of her in indigo undulations that made the platters on the table vibrate. Even from this distance, he could see the veins that pulsed on her dark forehead like worms beneath her skin. "They are faster and stronger than any human could be. Far superior to those who fell before the Filament centuries ago. And you will be very thankful for them in short order, boy."

"All right, stop this, both of you." Denise glared at her sister reproachfully. "Fighting will not help to convince him."

"Convince me of *what*?"

The two sisters took part in a brief staring contest until Charlotta relented. She held up a hand and looked away, into the unlit fireplace. Those purple ripples in the air faded, but a gnarled stretch of vein still throbbed along her temple. With her face in profile, Korden could trace those jagged seams down, through the sheaf of her bobbed hair, where they led to a small, metallic circle embedded in the flesh behind her ear.

"Please, finish eating," Denise urged.

He pushed the food away. "I think I'm done."

She nodded sadly, watching him with those large eyes as her aura filled with an affection that made him uncomfortable. There was a rose-colored tint to it that reminded him of Debress. Who, he realized, was being held along with the rest of Wilton, ransomed in exchange for his attention. He needed to keep in mind, securing their freedom was his sole objective here. No matter what these two women said or how friendly they seemed (or how much he loved looking at them), they were every bit as ruthless as the Incarnates they claimed to be fighting.

As if to prove him wrong, an amiable smile graced Denise's full lips. "It is nice to be able to speak to you without rhyming. Neither of us are poets, as you probably guessed."

"Then why did you do it?"

"As we told you, such an artcraft connection between minds only remains steady if the creative part of the brain is piqued. Most people understand poetry, even if at a mere subconscious level, and, since your personal creativity lies with words, rhyming was the easiest solution."

"But *how* did you do such a thing? I lived with men who crafted their whole lives, and they couldn't do half the things that you can."

Denise hesitated and turned to her sister. Charlotta made them both wait before she rejoined the conversation. "All will be explained in the proper order."

"Then at least tell me how you're even here! You were the leaders of a technology company three hundred years ago! My teachers came from the same era and used artcraft to stay alive, but they grew incredibly old! Yet you're both as…" He stopped short of saying, 'beautiful.' "…as young as you were then."

Charlotta considered this with her head tilted back and chin jutted forward. "Very well. That answer is easy to give."

She waved a hand. A soft purr came from behind Korden. He spun in his seat, instantly on guard.

A panel on the shorter side of the room was sliding

aside, revealing a recessed space inside the wall. Two silver cylinders lay within, mounted at a slanted angle on domed, white bases and emitting an obnoxious lime green light. Korden stood and walked toward the strange objects, his curiosity too great to deny.

Each was big enough to hold a single adult. The tops were made of glass, and he could see padded beds inside, surrounded by gauges and wires and technologic machinery that seemed to be source of the sickly green radiance. Controls were set into the bases, displaying numbers that looked like times and dates.

"Cryonics," Charlotta explained from the couch, her accent blurring the R. "A way of suspending the body in time, arresting the aging process."

Korden put a hand on the glass, then jerked it immediately away. The surface was so cold it burned his palm. "You invented such a thing…?"

She gave a throaty, rough laugh. "That tech is far outside our expertise. We merely purchased a company that perfected the process, and, after building this place where we knew we would be protected, we put ourselves into hibernation in the year 2135."

"For us, the last three centuries passed as but a single night's sleep," Denise added.

"'Dead is a state we didn't ever know.'" He quoted from the dream where he'd met them as he moved back to the table. "But…why? Why would you do that?"

"Because we did not fool ourselves about the Filament, as so many others from our time did. We knew what was coming, what they would do." That crease returned to Charlotta's brow as she shifted on the couch, leaning forward to clench a fist in the air. "Unless someone found a way to *fight back*. And that is what we set out to do: send them back to whatever hell they crawled out of. To take back the future they stole from humanity."

"We developed a plan." Denise's eyes shone. "A last, desperate gambit. But unfortunately, it required time to prepare. So, when the final war against the Incarnates was lost, we put that plan into motion, and went to sleep until it came to fruition."

"But three hundred years! How could you be sure the Filament wouldn't conquer the world by then?"

A single thread of annoyance unspooled in Charlotta's aura. "It was not intended to be so long. Our calculations were…flawed. We were very lucky that something seems to have stopped the Shroud in its tracks."

Denise reached out and grasped one of his hands in both of hers. "In truth, we might still be asleep…if not for *you*, Korden. You are very special."

He frowned, hating the flutter in his stomach at her touch but unable to deny it. "What does that mean?"

Charlotta stood and moved her lithe form past the table, back toward the door. "Our hour grows shorter," she said. "And we have so much more to show you."


2

The ion thermite was potent; two of the flat, brown rectangles could fit comfortably on Harris's palm, but, according to the warning labels inside the crates, an undirected blast could incinerate everything within fifty square yards. When synced, they could be set off one at a time, or all at once. He took twenty of them, along with primers and a wand-like detonator, and packed them into a metal tin, a clumsy task with one of his hands now missing a finger. The mechanics behind the explosive looked simple, but he wished there were some way to search for a how-to video on MeTube.

"I still say playing around with this stuff is a bad idea," he muttered, an hour or so after the kid set out.

"Zeega does not care what you say, dead human," the kid's pet—had Korden called it a 'riftling?'—informed him. Though his primitive hindbrain was disgusted by the thing, Harris's scientific curiosity left him fascinated; it had the body of a giant amoeba, the legs of an octopus without the suckers, and sounded like someone gargling acid as it spoke. Even that it *could* speak was bewildering, both from a physical and psychological standpoint. "Zeega wants only to do as Korden commanded."

"Zeega should also want to learn some pronouns," Harris muttered.

She came to his side as he packed the thermite and demanded, "Is the dead human certain that is sufficient?"

"The 'dead human' thinks this much thermite could shave that mountain's mohawk into a buzzcut in about three seconds."

Four of her eyes cut over to him without blinking, their scrutiny as sharp and penetrating as a diamond-tipped drill. "Zeega does not comprehend this measurement."

"It'll be big," he assured her.

They put the explosives in the back of one of the passenger carts along with a few MREs from a box in the corner of the hermetic warehouse. Looking at the bricks of food made Harris realize that he hadn't experienced hunger since his awakening either. He could recall the sensation, but the memory was as distant as a scraped knee he'd gotten in the third grade. His body apparently no longer needed calories any more than it did air. He'd tried drinking some water to relieve the perpetual dryness in his mouth, but it still sloshed in his stomach an hour later. There was a lot he needed to figure out about his condition.

To kill time, he wandered the warehouse and found a computer with power in a separate bank of offices along the rear wall, which had been used to program the auto-construction fleet. The M-Net was out, of course, but the hard drive held plenty to peruse. And the security protocols were a joke; the Moambatis probably figured there would be no one left to access their secrets. Within minutes, he'd pulled up an interesting set of schematics for what he judged to be the facility atop the mountain. It appeared to be some kind of lavish lab-slash-condo, but, beyond that...

"Uh...Zeega?" he called out. When the riftling skittered into the room, he showed her the blueprints.

"What does this mean?"

"It means the base of the mountain is hollowed out with tunnels and chambers, and a long elevator shaft connects them to the structure at the top. It's complicated, and I haven't had time to read all of it, but there appears to be a huge door at ground level that leads inside. I bet your other friends were taken through there."

She considered this for a moment before declaring, "Zeega and the dead human must find it."

"What? No, no, the kid said to wait here until nightfall."

"Korden went to the mountaintop to confront the Moambatis in order to save the humans from the settlement of Wilton. He was unaware this could be accomplished by an alternative method."

"Fine. You want to go, be my guest."

"You will accompany Zeega."

He swiveled to face her in the office chair. "What if I say no?"

She moved forward, lightning fast, and snipped a chunk out of his bodysuit at the ankle with her lobster-like fore-limbs. "Then the dead human will be missing more than a finger."

Harris sighed and rolled his eyes. "Great. Now I'm taking orders from something that looks like it should be on my sushi platter."

Ten minutes later, they'd left Crested Butte behind on the packed hovercart. They headed the same direction the kid had gone, but instead of taking the trails that wound up the mountain, they followed a paved road through a narrow valley pass much better maintained than any of the streets in town. Eventually, the riftling ordered him to pull off the road and into a deep stand of trees on the upslope. She jumped from the cart and stared east, deeper into the mountain range.

"The others are close. Somewhere ahead. Perhaps—" She wheeled around and cocked her squishy black head like an alert sheepdog. "Someone approaches."

Harris heard it a moment later also: multiple, quick footsteps on the road. He'd gone to several marathons in his life—spectating, never participating—so he knew what dozens of people running on tarmac sounded like. The two of them crouched low inside the tree line, peering down at the road in the direction they'd come from.

Around the last bend came a gaggle of the undead drones in matching black bodysuits, their overrides glinting in the afternoon sun. They sprinted with a blank, single-mindedness in tight formation, moving far faster than any normal human was capable of on foot, perhaps twenty or twenty-five miles per hour. As the group flew by their hiding spot, Harris squinted his clouded eyes to study them. The technology didn't seem to have advanced much from the ones who grabbed him in the lab, and—

"Oh my god, that's Tammy from HR," he whispered. The skinny, unpleasant woman who'd once reprimanded him for streaming anime on his work computer was missing most of her left arm, which ended in a jagged shard of bone. "What did Charlotta do, enslave the whole damn company? Use them as a starter set for her army of the dead?"

"They must be followed," the riftling said. "Zeega will keep pace to see where they go. You follow and bring the explosives." Then she was gone, so fast that she all but left a flash of dust in the air like a cartoon character.

Harris grumbled but complied, taking the thermite tin and tottering along the slope on his stiff legs to stay out of view of the road. He didn't make it far before Zeega returned, urging, "Over the next rise, hurry!"

It was a good thing they'd stopped driving when they did, because the road ended ahead, at a long, rectangular opening into the mountainside. From here, they could see little past the entrance, but even more drones milled around outside, too many to count, all of them working together to prepare rudimentary fortifications like spiked blockades.

Harris strained to get a better glimpse. "It's completely illogical. They *must* be running a preprogrammed subroutine of commands. That's the only way they could control a group this size for such complicated tasks without just as many operators. I mean, the coding it must've taken…"

"Zeega and the dead human will go inside," the riftling declared.

"You mean…inside *there*? That place looks like the lair of a Bond villain!" Harris shook his head. "No way in hell. Snip off whatever you want, I'm not doing it."

"If Zeega and the dead human infiltrate, they can seek the others and ready the explosives at the same time."

"Yeah, and if they catch me, they could…!" He didn't finish, *couldn't* finish, but, somehow, she knew his fear anyway, as though plucking it right out of his mind.

"You are scared they will take away your consciousness and return you to your slave status."

"Well…yeah."

"Zeega sympathizes with this. She, too, was a slave, but Korden freed her. She will make sure the same does not happen to you."

"Oh, gee, thanks," he said. The words dripped with sarcasm, but only to hide that he might've burst into tears if his eyes were capable of producing moisture. *I think you're getting awful close to a mental breaking point here, Harris ol' buddy. The sanity tower is slouching, so you better get this shit over with before the bricks start popping free.* "Look, how would we even get in there anyway? Those things are everywhere!"

"Yes. And you resemble one of them."

It took a full ten seconds for him to catch her drift. "Are you telling me," Harris began, "that you want me to just stroll through the front door?"

She merely blinked at him; an arduous task with five eyes.

"This is ridiculous! I'm supposed to walk past them holding the thermite like a doof while you sit out here? I'm not going to—!"

"The dead human will do it *now*!" she hissed. One of her tentacles swiped the metal tin out of his hand and jammed it into her mouth, which widened disproportionately to admit the container. Then she scrambled up his leg and squeezed herself into the crevice beneath his gut like a wad of Play-doh, her dark color blending in with his jumpsuit. Normally, this would have tickled and/or disgusted Harris, but, of course, his dulled nervous system registered nothing. He thought he detected a note of panic as her voice drifted out from the new hiding spot below his belly. "Begin moving immediately!"

"All right, geez! Why are you so freaked out all of a sudden?"

"Because Zeega's former masters are approaching."

## 3

Something was happening with the zombers. They'd launched into a flurry of sudden activity over the last half hour, running back and forth across the black floor, carrying strange equipment and crates, and covering themselves in bronze-colored polymer plates that fit as snugly over their bodysuits. To Rand, they resembled the determined movements of soldiers preparing to go into battle, which concurred with what the female had told them before. They also opened the large hatch into the mountain, spilling stark daylight throughout the cavernous room while they buzzed in and out, setting up a progressive line of barricades along the road outside.

Rand did his best to ignore them as he sat beside the entrance to the holding cell, faithing just as Korden had showed him, and trying to make something, *anything* happen.

*Where the fram are you?* he demanded of the conduit, jaw clenched. *I didn't believe in the Upper before when I did those things, so OPEN, damn you, and let me use some artcraft!*

"Drude." His brother's voice sliced through Rand's concentration, sounding urgent. He and Lillam sat to either side of Rand while the rest of Wilton slumbered, huddled in pathetic balls on the chilly floor.

Rand opened his eyes to find one of the male zombers walking directly toward them, a heftier specimen than most of his fellows. He also moved much more stiffly than the others, and his white eyes roamed with a nervous awareness that the others did not possess, as though taking in the surroundings.

As he neared the cage, he stepped into a small area concealed from the rest of the room by one of the black columns and a high stack of polymer crates. There was squirming movement at his waist, then a familiar bundle of gelatinous black jelly plopped onto the floor in front of them.

"Zeega!" Lillam whispered excitedly.

The riftling's dark coloration camouflaged her on the floor as she scuttled up next to the bars. Rand unfolded from his faithing pose and scooted toward her with Meech and Lillam, all three staying low to avoid attention from both inside and outside the cell. "What are you doing here, where's Korden?"

"He has gone to confront the Moambati sisters atop this peak in an attempt to win your freedom."

"Oh, that dumb kid," Meech groaned.

Rand went weak with relief. "That's good then. We can just...just wait and let him take care of it, right?"

"Perhaps, but there is a more pressing factor: the Incarnate army we met in the desert is indeed coming, as Korden foretold."

"And we probably shouldn't stick around to greet them," the zomber behind her added.

Lillam gasped. Rand had been so thrilled to see the riftling, he'd forgotten all about the dead man she was riding.

"Drude...is that thing talkin for itself?" Meech asked.

"*Thing?*" The zomber repeated. "You're real judgmental for apocalypse survivors, you know that?"

"The dead human is named Harris. He is an ally." Zeega dismissed the man with an irritated claw wave. "The Incarnates will be here within the hour. Zeega believes the enslaved corpses are preparing to battle them."

"Then you have to get us out of here." Rand told her. "*All* of us, the whole town. The last thing these people need is to be caught in the middle of a war."

Zeega gave one of her curt nods. "Is there a mechanism to release the door?"

"The zombers just walk up and it opens."

The riftling turned her yellow gaze on the one she'd called 'Harris.'

"Yeah, yeah, Masters in Neurorobotics, but that's all I'm good for, opening doors," he muttered, coming forward. When he reached the cell entrance, it swung smoothly open.

Rand grabbed the bars and pulled them most of the way shut before anyone noticed.

"All right, we can get outta the cage. Don't see what good that does with all *them* around." Meech nodded at the rest of the zombers.

"Once the fighting begins, you may have an opportunity to escape in the confusion," the riftling advised.

"We can't go out that door," Rand argued. "We'd be walking right into the Incarnates."

"I did see another exit on the blueprint," Harris said. "I think. It looked like some kind of long tunnel through the north side of the mountain. I have no idea where it would be from here though."

"Zeega can search for it as she carries out her mission."

Rand frowned. "What do you mean? What mission?"

"Zeega and Harris must venture farther into this compound to set explosives. Korden ordered this place destroyed if the Moambatis do not cooperate. And perhaps even if they do."

"The children." Lillam reached through the bars and took Zeega's claw. "They took all of the children from Wilton somewhere else. You have to find them."

The riftling gave a curt nod. "Zeega will return with more information." With that, she scurried up the zomber's leg and hid beneath his protruding belly.

Harris looked at the three of them with obvious embarrassment, shrugged, and said, "It's a living." Rand quickly lost sight of the odd man amid the commotion as he walked away, then turned to Meech and Lillam.

"Spread the word among the others. As soon as the fighting gets underway, we make a run for it."

# SEROCRAFTIDE

## 1

They left the feast behind and escorted Korden through the luminous white halls. The tubular structure was even larger inside than it appeared from below, the passages opening onto rooms full of computers and humming machines and technologic apparatus. He yearned for Stone's presence to give him information on their purpose. In every space that faced westward, the outer wall was comprised of that same glass bubble, looking down upon Crested Butte and the lowlands beyond.

Soon they came to a small widening of the corridor, with double steel doors on one wall next to a control with a single button on which glowed a downward-pointing arrow. Korden recognized it as an 'elevator' from his trip through the power station outside Ida. And from here, at the tip-top of the Skyreach, such an elevator could only go one place.

Zeega had said she sensed the others deep in the *base* of the mountain. If Korden needed to find the residents of Wilton himself, this is where he would start searching.

The sisters stopped beside a circular pedestal in the center of the lobby. Resting atop it, facing the elevator doors, was a bust of a human head made from chalky white alabaster, its features smooth and plain, no more than anonymous suggestion. It reminded Korden of a foto Skewtz had shown him, a nude sculpture of a man named David, except the flesh and skull was removed above the ears to display a wrinkled expanse of brain.

"This sat outside our mother's office for years." Charlotta ran a slender finger along the grooves in the colorless cerebrum. "Terese Moambati devoted her life to studying the human brain, at the expense of all else. And do you know why?"

Korden shook his head.

"Because she was a Crafter. Like you."

"Yes. I knew she must be."

"Oh? And how did you figure that?"

"I have—*had*—a S.T.O.N.E. He gave me information on her. It wasn't hard to puzzle out."

Her eyes cut down to the cradle around his neck. "Then let me enlighten you on what you could not have gleaned from the M-Net." Charlotta circled the statue as she spoke, her nimble steps like a prowling panther. "Her abilities awoke at a young age, although she did not recognize them for many years. She loved to dance, and that creative expression allowed her powers—her *artcraft*—to develop. In her homeland, she became a medicine woman. She studied anatomy on her own, day and night, so she could use her abilities to heal others in the poor village where she born. And for that...she was demonized. Ridiculed. Labeled a 'voodoo priestess.'" The corners of her mouth pulled down into a disgusted frown. "Because mankind always fears that which they do not understand. Eventually, she left Haiti in disgrace and came to America to continue her studies."

"She wanted answers, you see," Denise explained. "About why she could do these things. And, more importantly, she wanted to find *others* like her."

"Her artcraft gave her keen insight of the human mind. Soon, she was considered one of the top experts in the field of cerebral research. By combining her abilities with scientific knowledge, she founded a company that created the most revolutionary medical advancements the world had ever seen. She considered them a perfect marriage of technology and magic."

Korden thought of Stone's explanation, the way Terese Moambati's inventions resembled wizardry. "Tash—my *den-so*—he always told me that such things stood separate. That technology is what killed artcraft."

"I am sure he spoke of many things he did not understand." Charlotta's voice grew haughty, a regal shade of violet seeping through her aura that he surmised was superiority. She stared at Korden as though waiting for him to argue.

Denise rushed to pick up the thread of her sister's story. "But our mother did not find the answers she sought, or a single other Crafter. So she became pregnant, hoping her abilities would prove hereditary." In contrast to her sister, Denise's *mohol* darkened with shame. "Within a few years, however, it became apparent that her twin daughters... shared none of her gifts."

"But how can that be?" The challenge exploded out of Korden. "You've been sending me artcraft all this time! I just saw you craft with my own eyes!"

"Yes, you have," Denise confirmed, choosing her words carefully. "But it was not always so."

"She would force us to paint," Charlotta said. "To write. To sing. Anything that might spark the same power in us. And when we proved to be another dead end, she shoved us aside." The story made Korden think of Rand, and their fruitless lessons in the desert. "We returned to Haiti with our father and did not see the woman for almost two decades. Not until her trial." Charlotta blinked, lost in memory. "The case made for prominent news. Our mother's face loomed everywhere. Reporters hounded us without mercy."

"What did she do though? I mean, what did she *really* do?"

He waited for more ire, but the woman merely raised one sculpted eyebrow. "There is not much to tell. In a way, Terese Moambati could manipulate minds and control bodies also; I suppose you could say such interests run in the family. She killed to protect everything she built. I would have done the same, in her place. And when she was caught for her crime, she trusted her company to us rather than see it destroyed." Charlotta snorted. "Our mother died in prison without truly fathoming the nature of the power inside her."

"But...how *could* she fathom it?" Both women stared at Korden, waiting for him to elaborate. "You can't use science to...to qualify artcraft. It can't be converted into facts and figures. Artcraft flows from the wellspring of the Upper through the conduit, and His nature—His will—can never be understood, not even by those who worship him." He stopped and frowned. "She *did* worship the Upper...right?"

The Moambati sisters glanced at one another again. They communicated so much between themselves without needing words. Then Charlotta looked back at him with poorly concealed mirth lurking in her eyes, the kind that Korden always saw on Fortholm's face when the old man tried not to laugh at something he'd said.

Except hers held an air of condescension that put him instantly on edge.

"What?" he demanded. "What is it?"

Denise reached out and ran a soft hand down his face to cup his cheek. Pleasant jitters ran through his stomach... but her next words sobered him quickly. "Korden, my darling...this next part will not be easy for you to hear. But it is important that you have the truth."

Before he could ask what she meant, Charlotta was off, speaking rapidly. "The reason our mother never found more Crafters is because she sought them *too soon*. For all we know, she was one of the first. But when we took over the company and continued her work, we combed the world for stories of people with amazing abilities. And we began to find them, with increasing frequency. When the Dark Filament appeared, that ratio escalated even faster."

"Because we rediscovered the Upper," he insisted. "The power was given back to us so we could defend ourselves."

Charlotta glossed over the comment. "Denise and I met as many of these people as we could. Tested their abilities, studied their genealogies, performed every medical examination in existence. And with such a large data set... patterns emerged."

"What kind of patterns?"

She countered his question with one of her own. "What do you know about the brain?"

"Well...not much, I guess. It's what we use to think."

Charlotta's laugh was more boisterous than her sister's, ringing off the sterile walls of their complex. "That is true. There are many different parts that do the thinking, but they are divided into two hemispheres. Our mother used to say that the human mind is a country at war." She stood on the opposite side of the statue, facing him, and brought her hands down on it one at a time as she elaborated. "The right hemisphere is responsible for creativity, while the left deals with the analytical...but it also contains a lobe of the orbitofrontal cortex that processes one of our most important emotions: hope."

Korden remained silent. Something inside him suddenly screamed for him not to listen, to cover his ears and run from this house of cold technology and uncompromising science. The blank eyes of the statue regarded him with indifference as its innards were used for illustration.

"Hope is vital to the health of the human brain. It is a driving motivator, protecting against anxiety. In fact, depression and sadness are no more than the *absence* of hope; too much of them can shut down the mind." Her fingernails scraped along the left side of the statue's exposed cranium. "Hope, however, is formless. Unique to the individual. Anything can inspire it, so achieving the effect it has on the brain can often be inconstant. That is why the success of medicines meant to recreate its effects varied from person to person. But there is one concentrated form of hope that humanity clings to in its hour of need. Do you know what it is?"

He did. The answer swam into the forefront of his thoughts, but when he spoke it, his voice seemed to come from someone else's lips. "Faith."

"That's right!" Charlotta came to stand in front of him. She and her sister measured a mere six cupits taller than Korden, but, in that moment, she loomed over him. "What if I told you that your 'artcraft' is nothing more than a potent mixture of neurochemicals produced in certain right-brained individuals during highly creative periods?"

## 2

The zombers (god, even *Harris* was using the term now, and George Romero must be rolling over in his grave) paid no attention to their overweight brother as he walked among them, as Zeega predicted. They were far too busy strapping on leather-and-polymer infused armor and equipping themselves with an array of swords that appeared to be crafted from carbon steel. It all looked completely archaic, like something out a Greek epic, and even more baffling for one fact: if ion weaponry, tanks, even *napalm* had little to no effect on the Incarnates when the entire world was fighting them, why did the Moambatis think a bunch of drones with claymores and scimitars would make a difference? Did this have something to do with all those rumors going around on the M-Net, about only those with faith being able to kill them? If so, these brain dead, remote-controlled soldiers didn't look like they'd be attending church any time soon.

Harris tried to act like he belonged as he made his way out of the server farm in the main chamber (which was impressive, but still not enough computing power to run this many overrides) and entered a corridor carved through rough stone, where the black floor ended and the only light came from bright LEDs that dazzled his cataract-ridden eyes. The passage led to a network of similar tunnels that made Harris wish he'd taken more time to study the schematics. He couldn't imagine the amount of money and effort it had taken to build this ant colony.

*Who cares about that when you have an army of the undead to do it all for you?* he thought.

*Yeah, an army* you *gave them.*

*Hey, that line is getting mighty old,* he shot back at this interior accuser. *Everyone wants to lay the blame for this at my feet, but I'm just as much a victim here. My responsibility for what the Moambatis did with my invention has to end somewhere.*

*Oh really? Let me know when you get there.*

He continued going deeper into the complex, away from the buzz of activity, with Zeega clinging to his waist like a fleshy belt. Eventually they entered a wide room where three long box cars sat atop a gleaming metal rail.

"Dear god," he whispered, after making sure they were alone. "They brought a *maglev* down here?"

Zeega let go of her perch beneath his stomach and dropped to the ground at his feet. "Explain."

"It's a...a conveyance," he told her, inspecting the

smooth train cars. He'd never ridden one, but he'd watched a documentary about the super-fast transports of the twentieth-first century. Their exorbitant cost meant that they'd never caught on, and once the AIN came online, abundant, cheap energy rendered them obsolete. Each car measured fifty feet long and ten wide, powder blue in color, with a line of oval apertures for windows. Only the first car had seats inside, while the last two contained open space for cargo. The single track beneath them led into a much larger tunnel and out of sight.

"And where would this conveyance go?"

"Wherever the rail leads. I'm pretty sure that's the passage I saw on the schematic that went north. It's probably how they shipped in all the equipment."

"Could it transport all of the people in the cage?"

Harris performed some mental calculations. "It'd be a tight squeeze, but...yeah, I think so."

"Then Harris and Zeega should complete their task." The riftling abruptly hunched over, gave a deep retch like a sick dog, then spat out the thermite tin, covered in some dark, clotted fluid. "Where should they be planted?"

Harris tried not to gag as he picked up the sticky container. "In confines this close, I don't think it matters. But for maximum damage, we should spread them out as much as possible."

They set the first one together, Harris clumsily demonstrating how to seal the thermite, attach and arm the primer, and tune it to the detonator. Then they divided the remainder and pledged to meet back after distributing them.

"Be extremely careful," he cautioned. "If these things go off, they'll bring the whole damned mountain down on top of us."

Harris plodded on, taking turns at random, planting the explosives in places least likely to be discovered. The corridors remained deserted; the zombers were concentrated around the main entrance as they prepared to fight the Incarnates. The thought of seeing more of those creatures instilled a frantic urgency in Harris. He had a sudden, irrational (or maybe all *too* rational) fear that they would know what he'd done, how he'd experimented on their brethren.

He had one thermite packet left when he walked into a space with another cell wall stretching across the mouth.

A large group of bedraggled children of all ages stared out at him from the other side of the bars, some of the oldest clutching infants. Their accommodations were much nicer (and more long-term) than those given to the adults—padded walls, cots, drinking fountains, toilet stalls and even some toys—but it was obviously a prison. They whimpered when they saw him, the ones closest to the bars retreating in terror.

"Oh, hey, it's okay, I'm not like them," he said. The assurance did little to stop their cowering as they watched him. *Now I know what Frankenstein's monster felt like.* "I'm...I'm here to get you out," he tried again.

A girl with curly brown hair stepped forward, eyes full of hope. "C-can you take us back to our parents? *Please?*"

Harris frowned. No one had ever asked him a question filled with so much stark need. Since his mother died, the only person he'd taken care of was himself.

He wasn't the sort of person people depended on.

"Yes," he told the girl. "Yes, I will get you back to your parents." When he approached the door, it swung open as easily as the other one. He grinned, beckoning to the girl. She returned the smile hesitantly, before her gaze swept past him and a scream tore from her throat.

Harris spun in time to see the blade of a long broadsword pierce his gut.

He felt no pain, but the force of the blow sent him crashing back into the metal bars of the cage. Behind him, the children gave quavering cries of fear. The length of polished steel was buried deep in Harris's belly, halfway to the hilt. He looked up from the point of entry to the figure wielding the weapon...

And squawked in surprise.

James Chung gripped the handle, his dead, crusted eyes sparkling in the light like mineral-heavy rock. The accountant always loved playing *D&D*, but now—dressed in armor and carrying a blade as thick as his arm—he could pass for one of the characters in real life. A king, perhaps, with that silver crown upon his brow.

"James," Harris said softly. "It's me. Harris. Are you... in there somewhere?"

The other man responded by ripping the sword free, slicing Harris's stomach open on an upward diagonal in the process. Just like with his amputated finger, his body was far too desiccated to bleed, but a coil of something dark and squishy flopped out of the wound and dangled to his knees.

Chung reared back with the sword, preparing a blow that would lift Harris's head from his shoulders.

Harris flailed in an ungainly attempt to push the other man away. At the same time, twin arcs of sizzling electricity jumped from his palms.

Chung jerked and seized as the bolts zapped him. His white eyes rolled up into his head. He stumbled back across the room with smoke pouring from his override and crashed to the floor as Zeega scrambled through the door. The riftling took in the scene before asking as gently as her harsh voice allowed, "Is Harris all right?"

"No. He's goddamn well not." Harris numbly bent over, gathered the swinging loops of his own rotted intestine, and shoved them back through the gaping hole in his chest. He couldn't tear his gaze away from Chung's pale, moldy face. The man was the closest thing he'd had to a friend, and Harris had just killed him.

*Technically...you killed him* twice.

Behind Harris, the kids he'd promised to help sniffled and sobbed, some of staring at his exposed innards in horror.

"I...I can't do this anymore." He pulled the thermite detonator from his pocket. Offered it to Zeega. The riftling started to object, but Harris barked, "I did everything I told the kid I was gonna do! This is over for me now, I'm finished! Good luck with getting the rest of these poor bastards out, but I'm gonna stroll right through the front door before those Incarnates get here!"

He shoved the detonator into the riftling's foreclaw, then ran from the room as fast as his stiff legs would carry him.

## 3

"We named it 'serocraftide,'" Charlotta continued, her accent slicing off each syllable. "When utilized, it stimulates parts of the hope center of the brain that we believe have been dormant in humankind for thousands of years, allowing individuals like you to quite literally bend reality to your will. *This* is where your power come from."

Korden was shaking his head before she'd finished. "That can't be true. My S.T.O.N.E. analyzed me every time I used artcraft. He never sensed anything like that."

She sneered. "You expect a toy to be capable of perceiving the greatest scientific discovery in history?"

"But your own mother spent years of her life studying the brain and never came up with any answers, you said so yourself!"

"And with good reason. She was missing a vital piece of the puzzle. As was your mind-reading bauble."

"What piece?" he demanded.

Charlotta's nostrils flared. Her aura filled with that triumphant, superior shade; he suspected that she was *enjoying* this. "You are aware of the other planes, Korden. Dimensions that exist alongside ours which the Filament is capable of moving through. The American government became aware of them when the Incarnates arrived. We acquired from them the knowledge to detect—and even, to a certain degree, access—them. These planes are, theoretically, infinite and infinitely variable...and every Crafter possesses one of their own."

"I...I don't understand..." he stammered.

"Your 'wellspring' is nothing but your own personal, miniscule plane; your 'conduit' no more than an inter-dimensional link between it and your mind. As serocraftide is produced, it is stored in this plane until you summon it to work your *magic*...through the hope center on the opposite side of your brain."

"No. *No. No!*" Korden felt like he could go on saying it forever, until the force of his negations rattled the glossy white walls. "None of that is right! The Olders knew the truth, *Tash* knew the truth, he told me the Upper—"

"*The Upper is a fairy tale!*" Charlotta snarled. "Do you not see? Hope is the gateway to using serocraftide; what better way to produce it than with faith! And, as with the Incarnates, it does not matter *what* you have faith in, only that you *believe* in something! The Upper was made up by the first Crafters so they could stabilize their links, a pathetic security blanket they could cling to rather than face the truth!"

"I-I don't believe you!" In his head, he heard Mellory, talking about *religions of necessity*. "You don't know anything about magic!"

This time her laughter was harsh. "There is no magic, boy. Only mysteries that science has yet to solve."

A cold echo of Stone's words. Tears welled in Korden's eyes. His stomach churned, forcing rancid bile up his throat. A terrible humiliation began to steal over him at her scorn.

*They're lying.* He clung to this idea like a drowing man with a scrap of wood in a flood. *They want to break your faith.*

But the truth of their claims was irrelevant now. He could feel the seeds of his own doubt growing, seizing on to this explanation as proof of all the secret uncertainties and skepticisms he'd worked so hard to keep at bay. He thought of everything he'd told Rand in their teaching sessions, all the arguments he'd waged with Stone over his defense of the Upper, and his disgrace worsened.

*Never,* ever *let go of yehr beliefs,* Tash whispered, one of the last pieces of advice his *den-so* had ever given him.

Denise moved forward and took him into her arms, pulling him tight against her breast. "Must you be so cruel?" she asked her twin.

"There is no time for kindness, sister. We—"

Overhead, a soft alarm chimed.

Charlotta turned and sprinted away from them.

Denise broke the embrace. She gently lifted Korden's face. "I know you are in pain, but come with us. With *me.* Just a little further. All will be clear soon." She took hold of his hand, pulling him along as she ran after her sister. The hallways became a white blur through the sheen of Korden's tears.

This time, they ended up in another wide room whose far wall looked out over the Skyreach through the domed window. From the positioning, it seemed to be located directly in the center of the structure. Banks of monitors and control panels sat in rows like the barrack where he'd met the Prophet, except these were in pristine working order. They displayed endless graphs and lines of indecipherable text.

Charlotta stood at one of the stations with her back to them, quickly tapping keys. The view through the glass wall suddenly changed. In a heartbeat, they appeared to be rocketing toward the ground. Korden screamed and grabbed for the closest table, sure that the glass tube of their complex was plummeting from its lofty perch, but Denise gave his hand a reassuring squeeze. "It is an optical illusion. A zoom overlaid across the screen."

"Like...farviewers?"

"Exactly."

The glass wall now gave them an up-close view of the ground spans away. Korden recognized the streets of Crested Butte even from above. Incarnates marched among the buildings, a parade of blackened flesh heading straight toward them. The detail was so good that he could make out the rusted spikes on their armor. Of Heater, there was no sign, but the man must be out there somewhere.

Korden's heart seized at the thought of them finding Zeega and Harris. He never should've left them, but he didn't know these demons would arrive so soon.

"Could you see me, when I came through there?" he asked.

Denise shook her head. "We searched, but we could not find you. With your mind closed off, we only became aware when you arrived on our doorstep. But we have sensed *them* coming for some time." She smiled. "This is the first we have seen them, however. You were so brave to escape."

"They will be here in minutes. Do not worry though, our soldiers are prepared for them." Charlotta hit another button, and the window changed to an overhead view of a steep mountainside with a door at its foundation, where more of their drones marched out in neat ranks. She looked to Denise. "I have poured the vinegar as always, sister. Give him the honey, before the first battle of this war begins."

Denise walked past Korden to the corner of the room, where a huge, silver, lidded cauldron sat. The squat cylinder was ten pargs around, and a few cupits taller than Korden. A dense network of wires connected it to equipment built into the gleaming walls around it.

"Korden, my darling...this is the Cistern," Denise told him. "It is *our* wellspring."

# Freely Given

## 1

The armored zombers filed out of the mountainside door in orderly rows, hundreds of them marching into the afternoon sunlight in mechanical unison, carrying hooked, sickle-like weapons and five-parg-long broadswords of dark steel. The sound of their boots on the black floor reverberated like thunder. Rand had to admit, it was awe-inspiring in its own way; before Korden came to Ida, he'd never in his life seen anyone so much as raise a hand to an Incarnate, much less a coordinated effort like this. From the cage in the corner, he couldn't tell if the fighting had begun yet, but the cavern would be empty of the walking corpses in minutes.

All of Wilton gathered eagerly around the unlocked door of the holding cell, which Rand still held mostly closed. He'd feared one of the zombers would come to check on the prisoners and discover their deceit, but they evidently had bigger concerns.

"*Let's go!*" someone in the crowd hissed.

"Not yet," Rand insisted. He didn't add that he had

no clue where they should go once free of the cell. Zeega had yet to emerge from the tunnel she'd disappeared into, although Rand thought he'd seen her undead companion lining up with the other zombers to troop out the door. "Give them a little more time…"

"Fram that!" a bearded man near the front growled. "I'm goin to find my kids!" He shoved past Rand, barreling into the door and sending it crashing around into the cage bars as he hurtled through. The *clang!* echoed through the cavern.

Across the room, the back two rows of zombers turned to take in the situation, then broke ranks to start toward them. The man who'd caught their attention changed his mind, scurrying back into the cell as the rest of the prisoners froze.

Their last chance had been squandered. The rest of the zomber garrison left the mountain, but twenty of the creatures stayed behind to deal with the Wiltonites, more than enough to stun every last person in this cage. Then, if the Incarnates didn't storm the place and slaughter them, the town would be 'converted' into more of these soulless, blank-eyed slaves. Rand found that this idea didn't make him sad so much for himself, but the thought of Lillam and his unborn daughter being sacrificed was unbearable.

There it was. That same *spark* in his head as when Lillam said she believed in him, like the tiny flare of a flint striking steel. This time, Rand shut everything else out and rewound his thought process, trying to figure out what had caused it. He let his mind settle into that focused channel Korden taught him to strive for, then seized upon those words coming out of Lillam's mouth: *I know you'll find a way.*

With a roar that went straight down to the core of his bones, the spark found purchase.

A raging bonfire ignited inside Rand Holcomb's brain.

Energy slammed through him, a thousand times more intense than when Korden went into his mind to show him the way to the conduit. The surge came so swift and sudden that he threw out a hand to the bars of the cage to keep from being bowled over. The world leapt at him, every angle in sharp contrast, as though sharing a secret code meant solely for him. He heard Meech asking if he was all right, but Rand was far too busy piecing together what had changed to answer.

Lillam. He'd focused on *her* while communing, and the conduit blossomed as naturally as a rose. He could feel that connection, stable and secure, a bridge to a vast reservoir of unrefined power.

The truth that'd been staring him in the face all this time crashed down with undeniable clarity. There'd been a pop in his head that started all this, like a cork from a bottle… and it happened when she told him about the baby. The jolt that awakened his artcraft had been his need to protect her and the life inside her. And every time his subconscious used this power since then—on Doaks's fleeing wagon, amid the maelstrom, when fighting the scorpigator—he'd been far more worried about what would become of them if he died. They were, after all, the reason he'd left Ida to seek a better life, the only two things in the world that he would lay down his life for.

Faith. That was the requirement for opening the conduit. Korden drilled this into him over and over. But faith couldn't be forced, as the boy had tried to do with the nebulous concept of his Upper. It must be cultivated. Grown. Freely given.

Rand couldn't say for sure if the Upper was real, but he *did* believe in Lillam.

As she believed in him.

He gathered his wits and looked up. The zombers had sheathed their swords and were closing in with vapid intensity, electricity crackling in their palms. He moved through the door of the cell to meet them, shrugging off the hands that tried to pull him back.

That *energy*. It crackled all around him, inside him. He no longer knew if it was part of him or he was part of it.

But he thought he finally knew how to shape it.

Keeping Lillam in his thoughts and trying to remember his training, Rand directed his newfound artcraft at the zombers.

A green shimmer pulsed from his head and arrowed outward. The misty wave struck five of the creatures, sending them flying across the room like dry leaves in a windstorm. They collided with the black pillars and technology towers scattered around the cavern, their bodies falling into twitching heaps.

Gasps came from his fellow prisoners but Rand ignored them, intent on his mission. The other zombers swarmed toward him, moving with ghostly speed. Rand pushed outward with his mind again, imagining a giant hammer falling upon the creatures. He gritted his teeth and willed it to happen with all his might, then let out a startled squawk when eight more of the monsters were smashed flat to the floor, most of their bones broken.

That left seven, one of which, he noticed now, was Mellory. The tavernmaster's death was so recent that his skin retained a more natural shade than the pale flesh of the other zombers. Rand reached out with the artcraft, but this time, in place of blunt force, he envisioned his hands reaching for those silvery bands at their brows. A moment later, he could sense them in his head as surely as if they were pressed against his fingertips.

"Sorry, my friend," he whispered to the tavernmaster, then used those mental hands to tear the crowns away, taking a few rotted scalps with them.

Mellory and the rest of the zombers collapsed like marionettes with cut strings and lay unmoving on the floor.

Rand faced the people in the cage. He was both surprised and not surprised to find that the citizens of Wilton were surrounded by blazes of color, individualized at their centers but covered in a mantle of drab yellow that his instincts told him was a shared fear of their situation. Most of them stared at him with mouths hanging open in shock or disgust. His younger brother, however, shot him a lopsided grin, and Lillam nodded proudly with tears in her eyes.

"So...who's ready to get out of here?" Rand asked.

## 2

Korden didn't think he could take any more. The sisters' claims and explanations had blurred together to create an uncomfortable pressure in the center of his mind, like a head cold but sharper. He felt confused, disoriented, and a little nauseated every time he tried to resolve them, so much that he could scarcely concentrate to keep the conduit's eye open. Yet Denise began babbling again, oblivious to his discomfort.

"We are not Crafters," she clarified. "We do not have the innate ability you do. But we *are* scientists, and we learned to use serocraftide in much the same way. Except our supply comes from here..." She gestured to the giant vat she'd called 'the Cistern.' "...gets chemically translated through our computers, and we control it with these, wired directly to our orbitofrontal cortices." She turned her head to the side and lifted her braids to reveal a metallic circle behind her ear identical to her sister's.

Korden stared at the vat and the multitude of wires sprouting from it. "Then this thing creates...artcraft?" He couldn't bring himself to say this word of theirs, the impersonal collection of complicated syllables that stripped away the majesty and wonder of his gift.

"Not exactly." Denise pursed her lips uncomfortably. "We have had no success with artificial serocraftide."

"Then how...?"

"As we said before, Crafters appeared with increasing frequency as the Filament advanced. As if nature pushed the human race to evolve. With a continual stream of data, we pinpointed the Crafting genes, extrapolated factors that encouraged their inheritance through offspring...and even accessed the storage planes of these individuals to draw upon the natural serocraftide within."

"Draw upon...?" Korden blanched as the meaning of her words hit him. He thought back to what they'd done to him in that last dream, before Harris and the other drones attacked. "You...you stole their power."

"No, we did *not* steal," Denise said emphatically, but a hint of guilt crept into her aura. "We siphoned a small portion. Spacial distance is irrelevant between planes, so once we developed an algorithm to identify these Crafters, we were able to tap into their personal supplies all over the world, without them being aware in the slightest. It was for the good of humankind, Korden."

She reached for him, but this time he stepped away from her touch. "How is that for the good of humankind?"

Denise looked hurt by his rejection but answered the question. "The rate at which most Crafters produce serocraftide is so low, there is little they can hope to accomplish with it. You must understand, separated out, this power is insignificant, but if it can be brought together... used for a singular purpose..."

"You mean *your* purpose."

"We mean the purpose of fighting the Dark Filament." Charlotta interjected. "Which, I believe, is your purpose as well." On the wall screen behind her, the Incarnates broke into a final charge, sprinting to meet the assembled drones in the narrow valley leading to the mountain. He noticed that her monitor showed a point of view at ground level, a perspective that bounced toward the oncoming demons. It jumped to several different angles before Korden realized he was seeing through the eyes of the undead soldiers on the front line; their 'ocular feeds.' "The invention of the overrides gave us the prospect of soldiers, but the necessary time and energy required to direct them was another matter. The human body is a complex organism; not even the largest computer network ever assembled would be powerful

232 RUSSELL C. CONNOR

enough to command an army as large as we required, and we would need as many programmers to direct them."

"You control them with artcraft," Korden deduced, recalling Harris's claims.

"If that is what you insist on calling it. After the serocraftide is translated into electrical impulses, we can direct countless waves simultaneously and across great distances, as easily as if their bodies were our own. We can even use it to slow down the decomposition process in them, undoubtedly the same way it kept your 'Olders' alive."

"The one problem facing us was the time required for it to be produced so we could collect it," Denise jumped back into the conversation. "With the rate at which new Crafters were awakening, we created a timetable. Our projection was *ten years*. If humanity could hold out that long, we could farm sufficient serocraftide to come to its rescue. So, to avoid any other dangers that might arise during that time, we put ourselves and the soldiers we had amassed so far to sleep. That...was our miscalculation." She frowned. "The Cistern would have woken us when it reached capacity. That did not happen in ten years, or twenty, or fifty. It did not happen until a very special Crafter was born, one that produced serocraftide so fast that he finished the task we set three centuries before."

Korden continued backing away from them in horror, that pressure roaring in his ears. In his head, the conduit spasmed wildly, causing the flow of artcraft to flicker as unreliably as candle flame in a breeze. "How long has your creation been siphoning from me?"

"Since the day you were born," Charlotta said, with a hint of brazen pride. "The Cistern sought you out on its own and suckled at you like a pig on its mother's teat."

"But we gave you so much back!" Denise insisted, edging toward him with her hands out. "To ensure you could make it here! And we have used it to fight the Filament, just as you would have! As soon as we awoke and discovered the situation, we cast...an *enchantment*, for lack of a better word, over all the lands west of these mountains. A spell coded by our computers specifically to cut off the Incarnates' communication so that we could concentrate our efforts on this side of the country first. Dividing and conquering; that is how we will beat them!"

"I don't care!" he shouted. Crafting spells with a computer seemed like yet another perversion to him. "You are no better than Loathe, feeding on the energy of others like...like vampires! It wasn't yours to take, none of it!"

"We know that." She was still moving toward him, reaching for him, anguish on her beautiful face. "We never wanted it to be like this. We wanted to contact you years ago and encourage you to come to us, but until you left your village and its barrier, we could not reach you."

"But *why*? You obviously got what you wanted from me, so why drag me all this way here to tell me? Just to gloat?"

"Of course not! Korden...you are the key to the future." She jabbed a finger at the Cistern. "What we are doing here... this is not sustainable. We are burning through our supply at phenomenal rates. We need *more* Crafters as powerful as you, all of them producing serocraftide together. And now that we have found what factors encourage inheritance, we can manipulate offspring DNA to create them. Together, we can seed an entire generation of Crafters! To that end, we...well, we..."

"We want you to impregnate us." Charlotta perched on the edge of the console and favored him with a sly grin. "Artificially or otherwise. Whichever method you prefer."

"We can be yours." Denise reached him at last, took his hands, brought them to her sculpted lips, and gave the back of each a gentle kiss. The contact sent pleasant tingles slicing through the pressure in his head. "There is so much we can do for you, my darling. You will be our king, and we your queens. Our children will destroy the Dark Filament, and usher in a new world from the ashes of this one."

"We know you want us." Charlotta cocked her head to the side and ran a hand along her throat, then down to trace along the curve of her breast. "Most men do. But you could have us in ways they never dreamed."

Korden's breath grew shallow. The pit of his stomach pulsed with a hungry need no amount of food could satisfy. Denise continued holding his hands, and he received a vivid, overbearing image of using them to remove her dress.

Self-loathing washed over him. He despised what these women had done...but yes, he wanted them. It was a desire he had no control over.

As for the rest of their offer...if they could *truly* drive back the Filament...wasn't it his responsibility to help them? Perhaps this was why the Upper sent him on this journey in the first place.

*Except the Upper isn't real, if they're to be believed.*

"What about my friends?" he asked, surprised by the huskiness of his own voice. "What about the people of Wilton?"

"They can go free, as we promised," Charlotta told him. "We won't need to make any more soldiers...especially if we can encourage the other Crafters to breed as well."

"There truly are more?" His mind went to Rand, but he refused to expose the man's secret. "You can find them?"

Denise gave his hands a squeeze. "They are *so* many, spread across the land. Most of them are unaware of their power. But we can gather them together, offer sanctuary. We have a train far below that can bring us north, where many of them have congregated. All you have to do is...say yes."

He tried to swallow, but his mouth had gone dry. A new thought occurred to him, and he voiced it now. "My mother...she said that I had no father. That she became pregnant without ever... Do you know if that's possible?"

She frowned at him in what seemed to be genuine confusion, but the conduit had collapsed inside his mind beneath that pressure, and he could no longer see their *mohols* to be sure. "I do not. But there is much we do not understand, much that we can learn from you. The three of us can search for the answers together."

Korden nodded. "Yes. All right."

Denise squealed with joy. "I knew you would see things our way!" She surged forward and pressed her full lips to his. His breath seized as an electric jolt shot through his body. The action surprised him so much that his first kiss ended before he could respond to it, but the thrill left him gasping for air.

"There will be time for that later, when we celebrate." Veins throbbed across Charlotta's brow as she turned back to the console. Denise ran the ball of her thumb across Korden's mouth, leaving behind a fragrant, flowery taste in his mouth, then took up a position at the station next to her twin. "For now, stand back and watch as we turn the tide against the Filament once and for all."

### 3

Heater arrived in Farrowbend the morning after taking the horse. The abandoned city gave many of Loathe's personalities the creeps, but Heater saw its potential immediately. Here was a ready-made town for him to set up shop after this exhausting business ended and the next phase of his life began. There would be room to expand and housing for the people that came to work for him. He could make this place into a mecca, the capitol of the new world, and he would be the savior who used commerce to bring humanity back from the brink.

His pleasant daydream hit a brick wall when he realized that Bright wasn't there any longer. The trail had run cold, and Heater was stumped.

Luckily, that was about the time when his former buddies came trekking through. Torgas's men had apparently abandoned their caravan vehicles as soon as they left the Valley, either because they gave out or because the demons couldn't stomach the human tech any longer. They traveled on foot, most of them blackened with sunrot, which Heater couldn't help but feel the tiniest bit responsible for seeing as how he was the one that convinced them to chase the kid across the desert. But, considering they'd left him there to die, that made them just about even in his book.

He rode the horse parallel to their ranks as they pushed deeper into the foothills, following them from a discreet distance, content to let them do the tracking until he could sense the framming brat for himself.

The bigger ranges of the Skyreach stood ahead now, and he could see the glittering structure perched atop the tallest peak on the horizon. Bright was up there, Heater could practically taste him...but so was something *else*: a huge motherlode of concentrated creativity that made Loathe's many mouths water. Whatever it was, it was cold and raw and unformed, an amalgamation of as many minds as Loathe itself, but it reduced even the kiddo's expansive imagination to mere appetizer.

They just needed to make sure they beat the Incarnates up there to it.

Which didn't look like it would be a problem, because the *Exatraedes* were heading through a valley toward the base of the mountain, where another army was marching out to meet them. Heater could detect no brain activity at all from these soldiers, not even a blip of ingenuity. In fact, if he didn't know better, he would've said they were *dead*... and one of the personalities in his head—an electrical engineer in his former life—believed they were being remote-controlled via metallic bands on their heads.

This must be the mysterious Moambati that had been holding the Filament at bay. A legion of corpses piloted like robots with collars from Radio Shack. He might've found such a thing odd once, but it'd become par for the course since his path crossed Korden Bright's.

*never mind just go get up there only the source matters* Loathe's impatience had reached new heights since they'd caught a whiff of that stockpile above. But, as always, the entity depended on Heater to render their fantasies into reality.

Heater regarded the glass tube straddling the mountain, gauging the distance. The creativity he'd taken from Tarmon Doaks was dwindling, but it should be good for one last push to get him up there, if he used it wisely.

He looked at the horse beneath him and imagined gnarled wings of bone and bloody muscle springing from its back. The animal whinnied and squealed in agony as its body reformed. But it rose into the air when the disgusting appendages flapped, and Heater clung to his nightmare Pegasus as it bore him toward the summit.

<h1 style="text-align:center">4</h1>

On the screen, the endless lines of drones continued their measured advance to meet the charging Incarnates, who displayed no such discipline in their berserk charge. From this high vantage, both sides appeared small and inconsequential, but Korden recalled their standoff with the demons in the desert, and he had no desire to repeat the experience.

Charlotta was right: he *was* thankful for their army in that moment, no matter how they acquired it.

*Sure turned around on that fast, didn't ya, boy?* These

disgusted words belonged unmistakably to Winstid. *Ya came up here determined to blow this place to smithereens, and, with just an hour of butterin up from these two, you're ready to hop into bed with 'em. Figuratively AND literally. By this time tomorrow, you'll be puttin those infernal things on folk's heads yerself.*

Korden tired of voices barging into his mind. Of living up to the expectations of other people and computers and creatures. Maybe Rand had been right in the first place; morals and close-mindedness had gotten him nowhere. So he didn't respond to Winstid's chide, but only watched the screen and took solace in the synchronicity of the Moambati army.

"Are you sure your…your servants…can beat them?" he asked, recalling Denise's words outside about their numbers.

"They have seven hundred; we have close to a *thousand*, with another five hundred that could be here within the hour if summoned. Soon you will see exactly what all of this has been for." Charlotta glanced over her shoulder to smirk at him. "Unless, of course, you still have objections to our methods. Perhaps we should send them back to their trivial lives."

Korden ignored the gibe. "But how will they kill the Incarnates without faith?"

"They have faith. *Our* faith. Faith in science, technology …and ourselves."

"The armies of our time tried to fight them with guns and bombs, but that was their mistake," Denise added. "The farther away you are from the fight, the stronger your faith must be to break their hold on the bodies they inhabit.

But, by fighting hand-to-hand, our soldiers carry our faith directly to the Incarnates."

Charlotta nodded. "And they do not risk being infected by every one they fell. It is all the benefits of melee combat with none of the drawbacks."

The frontlines of the battle collided like two opposing waves, both sides comprised of bodies borrowed to wage war. Korden strained to see what was happening, but the frenzy of activity was no more than a blur from this distance. Then the screen performed another of those dizzying zooms until they were in the center of the skirmish, and he saw their soldiers in action.

They moved with an agility that bordered on elegance, leaping and dodging, intent on defending themselves until they found the perfect opening to thrust or slash with their swords. The fighting style resembled dance more than combat, a graceful wonder to behold. By comparison, the Incarnates were lumbering maniacs, rushing forward to swing wildly, teeth bared in snarls, relying on brute tactics that served them well with humans that could be intimidated. Korden remembered fighting Searda and her cohorts, the relentless way they'd come at him.

And the demons fell with each slice of the drones' swords. It seemed to Korden that for every one of Moambatis' soldiers that fell, the others slaughtered at least ten Incarnates. Bodies piled up as the undead drones held the line. Wisps of black smoke drifted up from their enemies' covered eyes, but these miniature clouds only dissipated in the fury of battle.

Their soldiers would win. Easily. It was plain to see,

victory a matter of minutes away.

He was truly beholding an army that could save the world from the Dark Filament. An ecstatic cheer built inside him.

"What about Heater?" he asked eagerly. "How will you deal with him?" He would take no small amount of pleasure in seeing the butcher and his inter-dimensional sidekick given their comeuppance.

The sisters tore their attention away from the control panels to look at him.

"Who?" Charlotta asked.

Denise frowned quizzically. "The man that you killed? The 'triker?'"

"He...he isn't dead," Korden said, as a terrible heat bloomed in the pit of his stomach. "Loathe saved him. Heater released it from the stone arch in the forest. Last I saw, they were working with the Incarnates to catch me."

Charlotta's brown eyes sprang open wide. "Loathe? You knew that creature was coming here and *you did not tell us?*"

"I thought you already knew! You're the ones that warned me about it in the first place!"

Denise shook her head patiently, but the calm façade was belied by a slight quaver to her voice when she spoke. "We only detected Loathe when you entered its domain, my darling. We tried to delve into its consciousness, the same way we did yours, but...it was confusing. A myriad of fractured minds blended together into one identity. We learned enough to ensure it could not deceive you. If it is free and inside a human host...we know little about its capabilities."

"It is no matter!" Charlotta proclaimed. "Our soldiers have won the day! There are less than two hundred of the demons remaining! What can this Heater hope to accomplish against us?"

As if waiting for these words, the window screen in front of them blew inward, throwing shards of glass and polymer across the room like a hail of arrows. Korden fell backward onto the glossy white floor before the fragments cut him to ribbons and heard one of the Moambati sisters cry out. Alarms wailed overhead. Freezing wind whipped into the room, along with a large mass that looked like a bloody, winged horse. It smashed headfirst through several of the consoles, leaving a trail of wires and circuits and destruction in its wake as it skidded across the tile, then came to rest in the center of the room. Korden sat up before the animal erupted in a gory explosion that threw blood and entrails in all directions.

Heater Kay rose from the carcass, long beard flapping in the wind, not a speck of blood on his leather outfit.

"My ears are burning," he said, with that sadistic grin Korden would never forget. "Were you three talkin 'bout little ol' me?"

# WORSE THAN DEATH

## 1

Korden sat perfectly still on the floor, afraid to twitch so much as a muscle as he stared at Heater. He couldn't believe this was happening, it had all the panicked trappings of a nightmare, but the cold wind gusts and rising goosepimples on his arms assured him he was awake.

The Moambati sisters had no such problem. Both ladies were standing before the debris settled, rushing back to their consoles. The shattered wall screen had gone dark around the hole in its center, that magnified view of the battle below extinguished.

"*They are offline!*" Charlotta screamed over the wailing alarm. Blood dribbled down her face from a deep cut across her forehead, the flaw an obscenity on her otherwise perfect features. "*The control grid is down! We have to close the door!*"

"Let's not." Heater waved a hand. The computer console in front of Charlotta appeared to melt, transforming into runny goo that sagged and oozed into a white puddle. She jumped away with a squeal of surprise as the alarm cut off in mid-howl.

"There. That's better." Heater stepped out of the gruesome remains of the horse and dusted shards of glass from the sleeves of his *jhaken*. His eyes locked onto Korden as he strolled across the control room, his boots leaving bloody footprints on the pristine floor. "The least you could do is look happy to see us, kiddo. We've hounded you across half the godsdamn continent, after all." The man waggled a finger in mock scolding. "But, we gotta admit, you ran a good race. We were beginnin to feel a little like Darth Vader, always walkin into a room as the Millennium Falcon blasts off." He chuckled. "We know, we know, you don't get the reference. But you will soon. Once you're in here with us, you'll know *everything*."

*drain you dry mine now no escape warned you*, Loathe taunted in its hideous choir of voices.

Charlotta swept into the man's path and raised both hands, the fingers hooked into claws. "*Be gone from our home, creature!*" she commanded. The veins thumped at her temples as furious purple artcraft streamed from her palms.

Which had no effect on Heater, other than to make him smack his lips.

"Not bad," he declared. "A little bland for our taste, but hey, a meal's a meal."

Charlotta's mouth dropped open in shock, blood dripping down the side of her nose. Over her shoulder, Denise stood silently, face betraying no emotion.

Heater reached the spot where Korden cowered, bent to grab his wrist, and yanked upward, forcing him to scramble to stand up; it was either that, or have his limb pulled out of socket. The triker put a friendly arm around his tense shoulders and jerked him closer until their heads were side by side. Korden cringed at the sensation of the man's greasy beard against his ear as Heater hooked a thumb at the sisters. "We take it these two are the famous 'Moambati' everyone keeps blabbin about. Niiice work, kiddo. They got a real young-Grace-Jones-meets-Rihanna-thing goin on. If we weren't more about the outties than the innies, we'd totally throw 'em a fram too."

"You are a vile, disgusting monster," Charlotta fumed.

Heater's face went stony. "You got that motherframmin right, lady. And don't you forget it." He let go of Korden and stalked toward her, looking from one blackenwoman to the other. "Twins, eh? Small world. We had a twin once. We're wearin him now, actually." He stepped up to Charlotta, standing nose-to-nose with her. "If you wanna see how it feels to wear *your* sister's skin, keep jawin."

"Leave them alone!" Korden shouted, finding his voice at last.

Heater spun and frowned at him, brow wrinkling.

Pain exploded through Korden's head. Something was inside there, clawing at his brain, sucking his very thoughts out with such force that his skull creaked and bowed inward from the sudden vacuum. Even as he screamed, some distant part of him discerned that this wasn't Loathe swallowing up his artcraft as he released it, but rather drinking directly from the source, as with the animals in the redwood forest.

The mental torture abated as suddenly as it began, but Heater was on him before he could recover. The triker raised one hand and brought it down across his cheek with a brutal *crack!* that made the room spin.

"*Did you think we'd let you get away with it?*" Heater roared. He struck Korden again, a blow that split his lip and sent warm blood cascading down his chin. "*Burning us, breaking us, leaving us for dead? NO ONE does that to Heater Kay!*"

The third blow would've put him back on the floor if Heater hadn't grabbed the front of his tunic and lifted him off his feet. Korden writhed in the man's grip as that psychic presence invaded him, feasting on his mind, siphoning out his imagination, each second of the agony lasting an eternity. Above it all, Loathe laughed in a thousand crazed voices and, among them, Korden could swear he heard Doaks. When the torment stopped this time, Heater cried, "Oh GODS, but you taste good, kiddo! A banquet fit for a king! And you better believe we're gonna make it last, too! Savor each bite of your imagination while we take your body apart piece by piece! Then we'll go after your friends, your little pet squid, and anyone that's even dared to *smile* at you, includin these two cradle-robbin wombies!"

"Stop," Denise said, speaking for the first time since Heater's entrance. The single word was neither command nor plea, but something in between. Perhaps that was why it cut through Heater's tirade, caused him to look over his shoulder as he held Korden aloft. When she spoke again, her voice remained calm and even. "We want no quarrel with you. Surely there must be an accord to strike."

"An *accord*?" Heater scoffed. He shook Korden, who flopped like a wet rag, unable to hold up his head. Blood ran down his swelling face and dripped onto Heater's hand. "You don't seem to be gettin it, this little fram is *ours*.

There's no bargainin for that. Even if there was, you damn sure couldn't pay the cost."

Denise's gaze flicked to Korden for a moment before resettling on Heater. "Then take him and go."

"Yes!" Charlotta cried eagerly, her eyes wild. "Yes, take the boy, he is nothing to us!"

"W-what?" Korden rasped.

Heater lifted him up and tossed him away as nonchalantly as a chewed tynar root. Korden braced himself to hit the floor, but a great, invisible force swept him up in midair, propelling him backward until he slammed into the rear wall of the room beside the door. Before he could comprehend what was happening, he sank through the partition, the glistening white panel melting into molasses like the console. The polymer flowed over his limbs and torso before it hardened, locking him inside the wall with only his face sticking out. He tried to scream, but more of the white liquid slid over his bleeding lips and then *into* his mouth, gagging him, cementing into place around his teeth and tongue, so that he could do no more than whimper.

"Hush now, the adults are talking." Heater faced the sisters. "You say he's nothin to you, but the three of you were sure cozy up here. And you best think carefully before you speak; we catch even a whiff of a lie, and those big, pretty eyes'll be under my bootheel before you can blink."

Denise stiffened her back and squared her shoulders. She seemed to be going out of her way not to look at Korden now. "It is true, the boy is a key component of our plans...but not a crucial one. There will be—there *are*—others. As I said, you are not our enemy. If giving him to you brokers peace...so be it."

The words might as well be another punch, this time to Korden's gut.

Heater snorted laughter. "Translation: you're willin to throw the kid away to save yourselves. That's cold-blooded, lady. But we can appreciate that. Okay, fine. Your cooperation is noted. You and your sis might live through this yet."

The tension drained out of Denise's body. She allowed herself a relieved grin. "Excellent. Now, if you will allow us, we must close the door of this facility before the Incarnates overrun it."

"Sounds great," Heater agreed. "But first..." Without looking away from them, he raised a hand and pointed two fingers into the corner of the room.

At the gleaming bowl of the Cistern.

"Let's talk about whatcha got boilin in the kettle over there."

## 2

After his display of artcraft, a few of the Wiltonites gave Rand suspicious, wary glances as they streamed out of the holding cell. Most of them, however, turned to him for direction, waiting for him to lead the way. "Head deeper inside!" he urged the crowd, pulling Lillam and Meech away from the bottleneck at the cage door so they wouldn't be trampled. "We'll search for the children and find another way out!"

"You're just fulla surprises, *Mr. Mayor*," Grayhm told him with a wink as he escorted Nancer past. Several others shouted their agreement, and one woman gripped his hand briefly to bless him. Gaulbriel, however, showed no such restraint; the dark-skinned man threw his arms around Rand in a full embrace, gave him a smacking kiss on both cheeks, and muttered something in Mex that sounded like, "*Gracias, el Padre de Cielo*," before hurrying away to seek his son.

"Don't thank me yet," Rand mumbled, glancing at the cavern's main door. He'd expected the large steel shutter to lower after the army exited, but it remained wide open to the bright afternoon. Even from outside the cell, they could see only the backs of the zombers as they marched away through the narrow valley beyond the door, though they could hear distant snarls and the clang of weaponry. Rand had no experience with large-scale battles, but he figured this must be their music.

His scrutiny was interrupted as Harek split off from the main group of Wiltonites and ran to kneel beside his father's body. Rand followed and laid a hand on the young man's shoulder. "We have to go," he said gently.

"Why did he do it?" Harek sobbed. "It was supposed ta be *me*!"

"He did it because he wanted to make sure you survived. And if you get caught because you stayed to weep for him, it will've been for nothing."

It took the young man a moment to accept this, but he eventually nodded, stood up, and moved away with the others. The cell had almost emptied, the bulk of the townsfolk hurrying through the closest tunnel entrance.

"Uh, Rand?"

He turned at the note of concern in his brother's voice. Both Meech and Lillam were staring through the main door. Beginning fifty pargs from the threshold, the zombers toppled over in droves, as boneless as hot candlewax.

"What's happening to them?" Lillam whispered.

"Something bad," Rand answered.

Within seconds, the army was reduced to a massive field of unburied corpses. But now, with them on the ground, Rand could see farther up the road, where the last of the Incarnates they'd escaped in the desert were gathered. There must be a few hundred of the demons left and, after a moment of confusion about their enemies' sudden collapse, they regrouped and charged toward the gaping door into the mountain, gnashing their teeth as they waved rusted swords and splintery clubs in the air.

With nothing to stand in their way but a few unmanned barricades, the Incarnates would be inside the cavern in minutes.

"Go with the others and find a way out," Rand told Lillam and Meech. "I'll gain you as much time as possible."

Both balked before he could finish speaking, Lillam clutching at his arm.

"Drude, did gettin a little artcraft drive you crazy?" Meech demanded. "Even Korden said he couldn't fight that many!"

"I'm not going to fight them, I'm going to hold them back." Rand could still touch that power flowing into his mind; it made him feel like he could pull down the sky if he wanted it bad enough. "Now get going, you're wasting time."

"No!" The colorful cloud around Lillam—her *mohol?*—flooded with a shade of dark crimson. "You will not do this Rand, I...I *forbid* it!"

Rand reached out and caressed the bump of her stomach. "Only this matters. You need to get her out of this place, make sure she has a chance. That's why we went through all this. It's what parents are meant to do, no matter the cost." This time, the word 'parent' caused him no fear, only a swelling sense of pride. "You understand that...don't you?"

He watched the truth spread across her beautiful face, saw the ironclad will that rose to replace her fear and anger.

A potent reminder of why he loved her.

Lillam nodded. "Yes, I know. I'll go."

"Well, *I* ain't preggers with your dullard spawn, so I won't!" Meech bellowed. "I left you before, I'm not doin it again!"

"Damn it Meech, you can't do anything here!"

"I can too! You just have to trust me!"

Rand seized his brother by the back of the head and pulled him closer until their foreheads touched. "I *do* trust you." He swiveled Meech's head to make him look at Lillam. "I'm trusting you with *them*."

His brother said nothing, but his *mohol* filled with a turbid purple color Rand assumed must be anguish.

"Go." Rand released him and gave Meech a hard shove. "*GO!*"

With a hurt frown, Meech took Lillam's hand. She surged forward and gave Rand a brief kiss before allowing herself to be led away. Rand watched for them to reach the tunnel, then faced the door.

The Incarnates were almost here. Rand could hear their awful growls. He strode to meet them, ignoring the terror and the cold of this chamber as it worked its way into his bones.

*You were given the gift for a reason.* Korden's words to him, before they'd parted ways in Wilton.

"Time to find out if that's true," he murmured, and unleashed the power inside him one more time.

### 3

Korden's right eye had swollen shut, but, from his entombed position inside the wall, he could see Denise's calm, in-control demeanor falter as Heater crossed the room to their precious Cistern. Her neutral expression cracked like brittle ice.

"That...t-that is...you cannot..." she stammered, shooting another glance at her sister. Charlotta looked like a frightened child now, her dark eyes open so wide the irises were adrift in a white sea.

They watched helplessly as Heater brushed aside wires, opened his arms wide, and fell onto the huge cauldron as though embracing it. He laid his forehead on the smooth silver with all the gentleness of a lover and spoke while pressed against it.

"We can smell it in there." His voice sounded breathlessly excited in a way that unnerved Korden more than his false joviality. "Liquid creativity. Bottled innovation. Raw, unformed ideas. Countless lifetimes' worth. We don't know how you got it or what you're doin with it, but we want it."

"I...I am sorry." Denise composed herself but took measures to keep her tone respectful. "That is out of the question. The contents of that container are much more vital to us than the boy."

"That's too bad. For *you*, we mean." Heater pushed away from the Cistern and turned around. "Because, one way or another, we're takin it. Would've done it already, except this overgrown coffeepot ain't exactly a human head, so we can't quite figure how to get at it. We could probably crack it open like a crab claw, but, frankly, we're a little afraid of what that much pure, undistilled power might do if the release ain't controlled."

Charlotta set her jaw and tried again. "There must be a way we can compromise. Perhaps to share its contents."

Heater grunted and shook his head. "With that much imagination, we're gonna be able to reorder *the universe*. You don't share that kinda power. So you're gonna show us how to access it, or you're gonna die. Simple as that. Considerin how keen you were to save yourselves a minute ago, we'd've thought the choice would be easy."

"But taking that from us would be as good as killing us anyway!" Charlotta exclaimed desperately.

"Maybe. But you know what's worse than death?" Heater snapped his fingers. Both Moambati sisters shrieked and grabbed at their heads in unison. They thrashed as he fed upon them, sinking to their knees. The torture lasted but a few moments, but the trauma was so severe it left them both moaning.

"Pain," Heater told them. "Pain is faaaaar worse than death, ladies. We get the idea you two have spent so much of your lives in glass towers, you've forgotten that. But you're gonna get a long, drawn out reminder unless you give us what we want. *Right now.*"

Denise and Charlotta remained kneeling and caught their breath as they looked at one another. The latter gave her sister a meaningful nod. Korden tried to scream through the hardened polymer in his mouth, to beg them not to give this maniac any more power than he already had, but nothing beyond a whimper escaped him.

"All right," Denise relented. She used the console to pull herself wearily back to her feet and flapped a hand at a spot in front of the door. "You must stand there."

"Now we're talkin." Heater strolled toward the position they indicated. He paused in front of Korden long enough to say, "We want you to remember one thing while you watch us ascend to godhood, Bright: it coulda been *you*. Maybe next time you'll walk through the arch 'steada of bein such a spoilsport." He moved on, stopped in front of the door, tugged at his beard, and readjusted his leatherclad crotch. "Ready, ladies. I'm good and hungry, so hit me with your best shot."

"If you insist." Denise hit buttons on the console.

Above Heater, panels in the ceiling slid open, and two of the sleek, black energy weapons Korden was coming to recognize so well dropped down and pointed their barrels at the Triker. His mouth dropped open in surprise.

"Surely you did not think magic was all we used to defend ourselves," Denise said, before the blasters started firing.

# INTENTIONS

## 1

Many of the Wiltonites were injured from both the raid on the town and their short-lived revolt in the holding cell, so Lillam and Meech easily worked their way toward the front of the crowd as they fled through the much warmer tunnels carved into the bedrock of the mountain. They passed Doc Timpett before catching Grayhm and Nancer, the former now leaning heavily on his wife. Meech slipped his good arm around the man's waist to help support him while Lillam worked to protect her belly amid the tight confines.

"Stay together!" she encouraged. At every branch of the tunnel, people scattered from the main passage to explore the offshoots, desperate to find their children.

"Where are we going?" Nancer wheezed.

"I don't know." Every cupit of these overgrown rabbit burrows looked the same; Lillam had no clue where to even start hunting for the pre-agers. For all she knew, they had passed the youths by without being aware. And if there *were* no other exits...

Well, if there were no other exits, Rand would've sacrificed himself for nothing, and they would all soon be joining him.

Cries of joy from ahead interrupted her mournful thoughts. Lillam peered through the bodies and saw a gaggle of children running toward them. The tunnel became clogged as mothers and fathers surged forward to embrace their offspring, all of them weeping with relief. Lillam saw Gaulbriel sweep Onjel off his feet and crush the boy to his chest. She put a hand on her belly as tears blurred her own vision.

"Lillam."

She jumped to hear her name gurgled from above. Lillam looked up and found Zeega clinging to the rock ceiling by her tentacles.

"Thank the Aged!" she blurted. "Did you find another way out?"

"Down the tunnel branch to the right, there is a cargo transport. Zeega does not know where it leads, but it may provide an exit." The riftling's eyes swiveled in all directions to take in the crowd. "Where is the human Rand?"

"Back at the main door! The zombers, they just fell over, so he's trying to hold back the Incarnates to give us a chance to escape! Please, if you can do anything to help him...!"

Three of the riftling's eyes narrowed. "Zeega may have a way, but it will be dangerous to all. You must get the other humans on board the transport and be ready to depart."

"I will! Thank you!"

Zeega moved her jiggly head in a brief nod and crawled along the ceiling down the tunnel in the direction they'd come.

2

Heater had to admit, the clever bitches had caught him with his proverbial pants down. He thought they'd hit their breaking point and, even if a little fight still blazed in their skinny bodies, what could they possibly do to *him*? Now, that arrogance would cost him. Even as he registered the very real danger to his physical form, surprise stole the precious few milliseconds he could've used to mount a defense.

And then superheated streams of ion were scorching holes right through his chest.

*NOOOOOOOO*, Loathe roared, its many personalities aligned in their fury.

There was little blood and no pain—the light beams cauterized arteries and seared away nerve endings too fast for sensation to reach his brain—but Heater could very much feel the life draining out of him. In seconds, he would be dead, and, if he'd interpreted the rules of their coupling correctly, death was something Loathe couldn't undo. The entity needed a host to revise the world, and if that host bought the farm, resurrection would become a tad difficult, wouldn't it? So Heater threw himself backward, trying to get out of the firing line, but the cannons tracked him, spitting sizzling red bolts that continued tearing him to shreds.

*think of something heal yourself stop this do NOT die*

As he had when the Incarnate stabbed him in the Valley of Bones, Heater reached deep into his own imagination and rendered exotic patches of not-quite-human flesh to replace what was being taken from him, starting with the most life-threatening injuries. The fabrications weren't pretty, just misshapen lumps of freakish tissue that left him less and less human, but they would keep him alive, provided he could sustain them long enough to get out of this.

The cannons weren't letting up though; the damn things were disintegrating him as fast as he could repair the damage. Heater stopped healing long enough to send skewers of molten lava into the ion weapons, disabling them in dual explosions that rained sparks. But, in those few seconds of diverted focus, the lasers left him with a perforated lung, a bowl of charred soup where his organs used to be, and his left arm all but amputated at the shoulder.

Across the room, one of the twins released a shimmering purple river of artcraft at him. *Idiots*, Heater thought, as he continued his Lovecraftian stitch job. Did they never learn? He felt Loathe surge toward the magic, in desperate need of energy…and then get pulled back as Heater plugged one of the punctures in his lung.

Apparently, his incorporeal buddy had a problem eating and playing at the same time.

The wave of artcraft passed through him, leaving him physically untouched…but Heater experienced it in his *mind*, a mental taze that crushed his concentration and sent Loathe reeling like a punchdrunk fighter.

"*I can feel the creature inside him!*" the woman shouted. "*Help me separate them, sister!*"

Inside Heater's head, Loathe's anger fizzled, and an interesting bit of trivia slipped out into his wavering consciousness, a fact the entity had kept hidden even from him: this was how it'd been captured the first time. Weaken the host with grievous physical injury, and Loathe could be drawn out, where it was vulnerable.

Hands plunged into Heater's head, psychic fingers that gripped Loathe's conceptual form. A sudden wrenching sensation filled his brain as the Moambati bitches tried to rip the entity out of him, taking a handful of his psyche in the process. He bellowed in agony.

*NO STOP THEM HELP SAVE US* For the first time in their partnership, Loathe's many personalities sounded terrified.

Heater staggered to his feet—although 'feet' was more of a euphemism at the moment, considering his lower appendages were currently fused together in a serpentine tail that looked like it'd been nuked in a microwave way too long. He hurtled forward, ignoring his remaining injuries, using the pain as a motivator for this last Hail Mary. Now that the women had their mental claws in him, he could see where their power came from, trace it back to the source.

They were too busy playing tug-of-war with Loathe to even see him coming. Heater made it to the one in the skintight catsuit and, using his remaining arm to reach behind her ear, he tore the circular metal implant from her head.

3

Rand sealed the doorway into the cavern with a shimmering green curtain, as Korden had when the boy protected the wagon from shootfire during their escape from Ida. The artcraft streamed easily from him now, and he shaped it with his will, endowing the air itself with the solidness of steel.

On the other side of the magical obstruction, dozens of horrible, snarling faces leered in at him. The remaining Incarnates were packed five deep beyond the threshold, crushing the foremost in their eagerness to get at him. They pounded and slashed and beat on his barrier in a frenzy, their enraged howls far more animal than human.

Rand stood thirty pargs away, eyes closed in concentration, sweat coursing down the length of his body despite the frigid chill of the chamber. Every one of their strikes against his shield was an endless series of pinpricks applied directly to his brain. His hands shook as he lifted them to rub at his aching temples. As long as he kept Lillam in the center of his thoughts, the conduit remained open, the artcraft flowing through her mental image, but Rand could sense that wellspring on the other side deflating as it finally ran dry.

He became lost so deeply in communing that, when the gentle tug on his pantleg came, he screamed in surprise. The barrier flickered and then solidified as he glanced down at Zeega.

"Where are...the others?" he asked, pushing the words out through the pain. "Did they find...way out?"

"There is a transport down the tunnel, fourth branch to the right." She kept all five of her eyes rooted on him, as though purposely not making contact with her former masters at the door. "They await you there."

"Can't leave. Have to...hold them back..."

The riftling produced a black stick of rectangular polymer from the tangle of her tentacles and offered it up to him. There was a dial and several buttons on its face. "Zeega placed one of the explosives in the ceiling of this chamber. The blast should be sufficient to collapse the space. She also programmed the others to detonate in sequence exactly five minutes later. If you run, you should be able to arrive ahead of them. All you must do is press this button to start the cycle." Rand bent to reach for the device, but she pulled it out of reach. "Korden is atop this mountain. There is a mechanical lift, but it cannot be summoned from this level. However, Zeega has found an air shaft leading out to the sheer face of the mountain. It should not take her long to climb to the structure above, but you must give her as much time as possible to bring him back."

"Do...what I can..." he agreed.

She handed him the polymer stick and vanished in the next instant, racing back into the mountain at top speed.

Rand held the device in one hand and backed away from the door where the Incarnates gathered, one shuffling step at a time, while maintaining the shield. Seconds or seasons could've passed. By the time he reached the edge of the tunnel, pain wracked his mind, and the artcraft flowed in spits and jerks.

And then the shimmering green barrier across the door faded out. Incarnates spilled into the cavern, falling over one another like stage show buffoons.

"Right here, you frammers!" he shouted, waving his arms. The taunt was unnecessary; the seething horde wasted no time coming for him. He waited until they were all inside the large chamber, streaming past the electronic towers and black support columns.

"I gave you as much time as I could, Zeega." Rand pressed the button on the polymer stick and ran into the tunnel without looking back.

4

Korden watched Heater's transformation in horror. The man's body grew and stretched and melted and reformed in insane new combinations as the energy cannons mounted in the ceiling tore him asunder. Bones twisted, sinew shifted, and gnarled flesh unfurled to cover gaping wounds, the changes happening between the blinks of an eye and each one more terrible than the last. In seconds, the former leader of the trikers was unrecognizable as a human being, just a bloated, blistered patchwork of mismatched parts. A single reptilian eye peered out from a fold in the tumescent lump where his head should be.

*It really is like a nightmare*, Korden thought, struggling to draw breath inside the wall.

*Of course it is*, the voice of his father whispered. *Because that's what Loathe specializes in. You said as much yourself.*

Before he could consider that, twin explosions drew his attention. Both ion weapons went slack in their cradles. A moment later, Charlotta and Denise went at Heater with artcraft, shouting something about separating him. Korden wouldn't have thought such an attack could work against Loathe, but whatever they were doing, it caused the entity to babble in dread.

Then the Heater-thing lurched up and charged at the Moambati sisters.

With one distorted limb that resembled a giant eagle talon, it ripped the artcraft implant from the side of Charlotta's skull, taking most of her neck with it. A geyser of blood erupted from the savaged flesh, spraying across the control panel in rhythmic spurts. Korden saw her eyes roll back before she crumpled.

"*CHARLOTTA!*" Denise's anguished howl reverberated off the sterile walls. She rushed to her sister's side, splashed to her knees in the crimson pool growing around the woman, and pressed her hands to the gushing wound.

The Heater-thing held up the device it'd torn out of the woman. Several fine, twitching wires dangled from the gleaming metal disc, and a thin spike jutted from the back, covered in blood. After regarding the tiny piece of technology for a moment, the Heater-thing used it to stab the mound of mutated flesh right next to that single, slit-pupiled eye.

In the corner of the room, the Cistern issued a low, droning buzz audible even over the reedy whistle of the wind whipping in through the shattered screen.

"*YEEEESSSS!*" the Heater-thing roared, in a voice that sounded like he was speaking around a throat full of burning coal. It spun to face the metal cauldron and slithered forward. "*BY ALL THE GODS, THE POWER! IT'S DELICIOOOOOUUUSSS...*"

*Korden, you must get out of this place*, Redfen Bright told his son.

*The more we see through the illusion, the less power*

*they have*. That's what he'd said to Rand and Meech after their first encounter with Loathe. He thought of the way the Heater bugs flickered in and out of existence when he'd denied their reality. The way the entity recoiled when he asked it to take on his father's form, way back inside the cave where it was imprisoned.

Unlike his artcraft, which accepted and worked within the constraints of the natural world, none of Loathe's conjurings were real. They relied on the mind being fooled into accepting them. To rob them of their power, he just needed to *not* believe in them.

And, thanks to the Moambatis, he'd become an expert at doubt.

*I'm not inside this wall*, he thought. *I can't* be.

Breath rushed into his lungs as the hardened polymer inside his mouth faded away. A moment later he dropped to the floor, the wall behind him nothing but a solid white surface once more. His injuries, however, were apparently very real, because his legs threatened to fold when a wave of dizziness swept through his beaten head. He looked at the Heater-thing to see if it had noticed his escape, but the creature seemed absorbed in whatever it was doing, draping itself over the curved side of the Cistern as that electronic moan from within rose in pitch.

"Denise." He whispered her name so softly, he thought for sure it would be lost in the rest of the noise, but the woman looked up from her sister's corpse with dazed eyes. He motioned urgently for her to come with him.

She nodded, face slack, and moved to stand.

A rumbling tremor vibrated the soles of Korden's feet a

half second later. Its intensity grew rapidly until the room swayed back and forth in a violent, whipcrack seesaw. The floor squirted out from under him. Korden lunged to the edge of the door and clung there to watch as the Moambati's mountaintop home shook itself to pieces.

The bubbled window on the far side of the room dropped glass shards in a musical cascade, exposing the room completely to the elements. Something groaned within the structure, an exhausted concession. A horrible, yawning crack opened in the floor below the window. It raced across the control room, splitting the cylindrical complex in two. Korden could see nothing but open air through the fissure, an abyss over the sheer face of the mountain. Whole sections of those clean, white polymer tiles broke away as the quaking continued. They dropped into the chasm, widening the gap until both sides of the room sagged toward the middle.

Denise's face was drawn in terror as the structure crumbled around her. She'd latched onto one of the consoles to keep her footing, but now she let go and wobbled away from her sister's body before it slipped off the precipice. The vibrations abated but were still severe enough to make her roll an ankle. She twisted in midair, landing hard on her side. The ground beneath her hips gave way, and she screamed while sliding into the fissure.

Korden dove toward her. He got both hands around one of her wrists before it disappeared. Her weight nearly pulled him in with her, but he managed to snag the corner of a console with one foot. He ended up on his stomach, peering over the lip of the crack with his one good eye at the long fall to the ground below. Denise dangled from his hands, shrieking as her legs scissored.

"*Hold on!*" he told her. He hauled, but knew instantly he would never be able to lift her. Korden reached into his mind, seeking artcraft to aid him in the task. That uncomfortable pressure was still there though, a manifestation of the uncertainty the Moambati sisters had introduced into his faith. It blocked his access to the conduit in much the same way Zeega's hum did.

Denise seemed to recognize the futility also. The fear left her face. She gazed up at him with serene understanding.

"Our intentions were good," she said simply, before slipping from his grasp.

Korden watched Denise Moambati plummet away from him for a moment before scrambling back from the edge. The rumbling had stopped, but the floor felt unstable, and he thought he knew what had caused it.

The ion thermite. The explosives had detonated, although why Zeega and Harris set them off before the nightfall deadline, he couldn't even guess.

Across the room, the Heater-thing remained oblivious to all. It embraced the Cistern as if fused to it. While he watched, its appearance flickered, and he could see through the sham to the reality beneath: a gaunt, broken man whose jaw and throat were incinerated to the bone.

*I did that*, Korden thought, with sympathy and shame.

That hum coming from the Cistern rose to a piercing screech much like the sound Bibb's teapot used to make back home, growing shriller by the second. Something told Korden he didn't want to be here when it reached the crescendo.

He ran through the door, out of the room, and turned in the direction of the elevator.

# 5

*MORE MORE MORE MORE,* Loathe demanded, as they devoured the imagination streaming directly into their collective head. The entity had overridden Heater's tenuous control of the body they shared immediately after jamming the metal spike into their brainstem, giving them access to that limitless stockpile of creativity the Moambatis had been hoarding. Ignoring all else, they maneuvered their metamorphosed form toward the corner—where the transmission time would be shorter by nanoseconds—and wrapped themselves around the silver crucible like a leech attaching itself to warm flesh.

"Hey...slow down," Heater told them, in a voice he no longer recognized as his own. The influx of power felt like a constant stream of high-grade cocaine, and it showed no sign of slowing. He'd said there was enough imagination here for him to reorder the universe, but even that might be an understatement; he could remake *all* universes in his image, an infinity of planes with Heater Kay's face emblazoned in the stars.

But the rush was too much. Too fast. Heater loved it at first, but now he couldn't help thinking of a balloon filled far beyond capacity.

Loathe, of course, paid no attention to his objection. The entity had always been a glutton, and this proved a smorgasbord they could not abandon. Throughout the strange earthquake, and even as the framming kid slipped out of the room past them (which Heater witnessed from the corner of his eye) the feast continued. Heater tried to reassert control, but whatever those black bitches did inside his head had severed quite a few of his connections to Loathe. The entity felt...*unstable* inside him, a dislocated mental joint. Heater was afraid that, if he struggled too hard, the two of them would simply tear apart like fabric with a loose seam.

But he needed to do *something*. Not only was the godsdamn place falling apart around them, but that shrieking noise from the honeypot was spiraling higher and higher, a steam whistle from hell. Several of Loathe's personalities agreed that such a sound made by contents under pressure was never a good thing. Heater recalled what they'd told the Moambatis, about the damage that kind of power might do if its release wasn't controlled.

"We have to go," he garbled. "Somethin's wrong with this thing..."

*MOOOORE*, Loathe moaned, a million voices lost to ecstasy.

Heater took the initiative and tried to move, dragging their body away from the vessel. Bright, flaring pain sliced through the mutated remains of his skull. The tearing sensation he'd feared wasn't like fabric at all, but closer to a Band-Aid being peeled away from a raw, oozing wound. Loathe roared, but kept eating as fast as it could shovel the raw imagination in.

"*You...stupid...fram...*" Heater snarled.

Something deep inside the pot let go with a subdued, almost delicate *toomf!*

But there was nothing delicate about the undeniable

force that came blasting out of it.

A freight train smashed into Heater's mind, a nuclear explosion of psychic energy that momentarily blotted out every thought in his head, bathing his consciousness in a dazzling white light. The discharge kicked so hard, he was picked up and tossed across the room by the sheer weight of it. Frigid air rushed across his mottled skin; he deduced with a sort of clinical detachment that he'd been tossed right out of the sisters' little clubhouse.

And still the shockwave of mental power assaulted him. Loathe's personalities screamed in agony as they were ripped from Heater's head. He sensed the entity being shredded to tatters, infinite facets blown apart like a dandelion puff in a hurricane.

For a moment, with Loathe's presence gone, his mind collapsed in on itself, becoming a black hole of incalculable proportions. His consciousness fractured, reduced to mere sparks of intelligence. Distantly, he became aware that he was still falling, plunging through impossible leagues, but all was darkness, an infinite midnight that penetrated straight to Heater Kay's soul, and, as he waited to splatter on the unforgiving ground below, a light bloomed in that darkness, a strange, murky line like the horizon at twilight. He reached out for it, strained toward it with every fiber of his being, and then—

6

The concussion knocked Rand to the ground so hard, he felt ribs crack. Terrible pressure pounded at his eardrums until he thought they might burst. A fog of blistering heat rolled down the tunnel from the main chamber, stealing his breath. He looked back and saw the mouth of the shaft clogged with loose earth and boulders the size of oxen. It was utterly unthinkable that he could've caused such destruction with the push of a button. If the cavern had collapsed as Zeega claimed, the rest of the Incarnates must be pulverized.

*In five minutes, you're going to join them if you're still down here!*

Rand forced himself to get up and continue running, seeking the tunnel branch the riftling instructed him to take. His shattered chest throbbed with each breath. His brain was a strained muscle, the well of artcraft as dry as burnt bread. The floor gave a nervous mutter beneath his boot soles, an unsettling vibration that soured his empty stomach. The lights embedded in the low ceiling flickered, plunging him into brief moments of total darkness that he feared would never end.

He tried to keep track of the passing seconds in his head, but burgeoning panic made it impossible. Where was the transport? Had he taken the wrong turn? The polymer stick was gone, lost somewhere along the tunnel, or he might've sought a way to pause the sequence. He was on the verge of backtracking when he entered a long chamber that held three boxes on a rail, what he believed the people of the old world called a 'train'. The cars were like the transports that had brought them to this place, but much larger and more open, with windows and gaping entryways. The Wiltonites were crammed onto them, standing in tight herds with their children. A cheer went up when they caught sight of him.

Meech stood in the front car, beckoning frantically, with Lillam beside him. Rand flew up the short steps, into her arms.

"Where is Korden?" he asked when they parted.

Lillam frowned in confusion. "Korden? We haven't seen him!"

Rand put a hand to his forehead and moaned, "Oh Aged, what have I done?"

"What was that noise?" Meech demanded. "The whole frammin mountain moved!"

"The explosions have started. The last of those Incarnates are dead. Or whatever passes for death with them." Rand lowered his hand. The die was cast now, and they would all be doomed if they didn't push forward. "We need to get this transport moving before the rest go off."

"The controls are up here," Lillam told him.

She led him to a simple station at the very front of the train. There were gauges Rand couldn't read, but no levers, no dials. Only a single green button labeled **AUTO-RUN TO TERMINAL**.

"Where will it take us?" Lillam asked fearfully.

Rand peered into the tunnel ahead, where the train rail disappeared into utter darkness. "I don't know. But it has to be better than here."

He reached for the button. Meech grabbed his hand.

"Drude...what about Korden?"

"We can't wait for him. This place will be a tomb in minutes." Rand swallowed hard to get past the lump in his throat. "I...I held out as long as I could. He probably stands a much better chance of surviving on top of the mountain, especially with his artcraft."

Meech continued holding his hand. His hollow-eyed face was dipped in iron resolution. Rand nodded toward the rest of the train's occupants: Gaulbriel and Onjel, Grayhm and Nancer, Harek and so many others.

"We have to worry about them," he said softly. "It's what Korden would've wanted. You know that, Meech."

His brother considered this for a long time while precious seconds slipped away. Then he nodded reluctantly and let go. Rand pushed the button.

With a soft hiss, the train rose several cupits. A slow, melodic purr came from its undercarriage, and the cars began to glide smoothly along the metal rail into the black maw ahead.

At the same time, another of the explosives detonated somewhere inside the maze of tunnels.

## 7

The elevator doors opened the instant Korden touched the button. He stepped into a small, round space hemmed in by more luminous white walls and capped with a silver dome. A simple panel on the inside displayed an up and down arrow. He reached for the latter, but the thought occurred to him that the explosion might have damaged the lift or the passage it used. Even if it hadn't, the destruction below must be much worse than up here. He had no clue what he might be walking into.

But he knew that he was desperate to get away from Heater as fast as possible. And that he couldn't leave without confirming the others were safe.

Korden pushed the down arrow. The doors slid shut. His stomach fluttered at the curious sensation of the elevator dropping.

He waited, wondering how long it would take to reach the bottom, when a brilliant white light burst across his vision and slammed through his skull.

Korden cried out in surprise. He fell back into the elevator wall, sure that Loathe was feeding on him again or that another of the thermite bombs had detonated, but no pain accompanied this light, only a growing vitality and rejuvenation. When his vision returned, the world around him pulsed in time with his heartbeat, vibrant with color just as when he'd unleashed all his might aboard the crashing stratoliner, and he understood.

This was a thunderous surge of artcraft unlike anything he'd ever experienced, even more than the dreams Denise and Charlotta sent him. It flowed across his skin, rushed past him in an expanding wave, filled his depleted wellspring to overflowing, rampaged through his body until he seemed to be made of magic.

The Cistern. Something had happened to the Cistern, he felt sure.

Then the overwhelming sensation faded. The elevator slid to a smooth stop, the doors opening with a muted tone onto a place that wasn't nearly as nice as the upper complex. Korden stepped out into a dimly lit corridor with rough-hewn stone walls—

And was immediately pitched into one of them as another explosion rocked the mountain.

He stumbled away from the wall with his bruised head ringing. The floor beneath him shook so much he could scarcely keep his balance. A pall of fine dust rained down over him. An unearthly, grinding roar emanated from the very air itself, as though something hungry had awakened deep inside the earth.

Korden turned back to the elevator, willing to face Heater if it meant getting out of this hellish place, then fell back as something struck the top of the lift with a deep, bass gong. The domed roof caved in. Sparks spewed around the doors as they slammed partially shut and stuck there.

He stood in shock, trying to decide what to do, but a heavy slab of rock broke the trance when it cleaved away from the ceiling and crashed to the ground a few pargs to his left.

Korden ran. He didn't know where he was going, but mindless terror usurped all other instincts. His lungs hitched, refused to fill. That rumbling, all-consuming growl chased him as he fled, the tremors tossing him side to side in the corridor. Now fist-sized hunks of rock fell all around him, beating at his shoulders and back. He tried to open the conduit, desperate to use the artcraft that had overwhelmed him in the elevator, but that dull pressure blocked his attempt. He just couldn't concentrate to get around it. Instead he held his arms above his head as meager protection and kept moving.

The path took a sharp twist. Korden burst into a larger, cave-like chamber and spied movement on the far side. Some sort of boxy autos packed with people moved along a rail that led into a much larger tunnel. He recalled the train

Denise told him about at the same moment he recognized several faces from Wilton among the passengers.

Korden sprinted, blind to all other concerns except escape. The last of the cars pulled into the tunnel, and he leapt down onto the recessed floor where the rail lay and dashed after it. At the rear of the train, a wide doorway revealed the interior. Through it, he saw the townspeople shouting and pointing urgently at him, then the crowd parted to allow Rand and Meech to get to the entry, with Lillam behind them. Korden's heart leapt with joy when he saw them. Both men held out hands to him.

"*I can't figure how to slow it down!*" Rand shouted.

"*C'mon drude, jump!*" Meech urged.

Korden was a few steps behind the car, but having trouble keeping pace. He pumped his legs, pushing himself, ignoring the burn in his chest, concentrating solely on their hands. He reached forward, his fingertips brushed theirs…

With a sudden *whoosh*, the train put on a burst of speed that he would never be able to match. Korden came to a gasping halt and watched as it skated smoothly away on the rail. He could see his friends for another moment before the they faded into the gloom of the tunnel. His last image of them was Rand holding Lillam as she buried her face in his shoulder, and Meech falling to his knees, good arm held out, while he sobbed, "*I'm sorry, Korden! I'm so soooorrrryyyyy…*"

*Good luck*, he wished them silently.

Korden felt rather than heard another explosion go off. A massive ripple in the earth yanked away his legs. The ground rushed up to smack him in the back. Lights from the mouth of the tunnel winked out, leaving him in profound murk. As he lay there, blind and hyperventilating, something smashed into his hip, causing him to scream in pain. His hands found a chunk of rock the size of a garren fruit and rolled it away. No bones broken, but his right leg felt numb and useless. All around him, he could hear thuds as the tunnel collapse accelerated, burying him alive and alone.

No, not alone. His hand stole up to caress Stone's casing around his neck. The computer might not be conscious, but he was in there somewhere, and Korden tried to take some solace from the idea that they would be together for an eternity inside this mountain.

Another rock impacted near his head, sounding like it could've crushed his skull. He jerked away from it and realized he could see the shards scattered on the earthen floor. Now that his remaining eye had adjusted to the dark, he could make out a faint, lurid green glow coming from somewhere down the train tunnel. Korden got to his hands and knees and crawled toward it, dragging his dead leg. The light came through a narrow opening in the rock. When he reached it, he pulled himself through into another chamber and gaped at what was in front of him.

Then another thermite device detonated, even closer than the others, and the mountain dropped upon him.

# EPILOGUE I

Torgas strode through the empty halls of the Blackhold, marveling at his complete lack of options.

He was unsure what had transpired at the Skyreach, but he could no longer contact any of the Incarnates he'd dispatched there. The last updates from the Fearnaughts spoke of an installation built beneath a mountain, and a strange army of puppeteered corpses that Torgas ordered his soldiers to march upon. If his men had all been slaughtered—which looked more and more to be the case—that meant every single one of the *Exatraedes* under his command were gone, bodies extinguished or incapacitated, *animogas* sent back to the Outer Realm for new dispatchment.

And it was all his fault. Torgas had listened to that multi-voiced entity, gambled on its foolish plan, and now he was a general without an army. The sole Incarnate for thousands of spans. He might've considered ending his corporeal form himself so that he could join his men, go home at last, but he feared what kind of reception he would receive after such an unmitigated failure.

As he walked and contemplated, he experienced a sudden tugging sensation in his mind, a call he'd not heard in many years. His consciousness was drawn inexorably across countless spans to the comforting blackness of the Night Castle.

"Torgas." The voice that greeted him from the pitch was impossibly deep, a bass rumble that could never be produced by human vocal cords. "It has been long."

"Master." Torgas would've fallen to his knees if he'd physically existed there, but he settled for showing his deference by averting his mental gaze from the unseen form in front of him.

Sixteen years had passed since he'd last faced the Deadfather, Overlord of the *Exatraedes*, Emissary of the Stranger, and Leash Keeper of the Shadow Disciples. The fact that he did so now meant that the specter of this 'Moambati' must've ended at last, their spell of isolation broken.

Sudden terror gripped Torgas at the realization that he would be accounting for his decisions much sooner than expected. He hastened to prepare a contrite apology, but the Deadfather stunned him with his next words.

"You have done well," that voice from the murk rasped. "I lacked forces which could be devoted to this power that separated us. But you marshalled an army and ended the counterfeit *craeftus* magic, restoring our communications." There came the briefest of pauses before the Deadfather inquired, "That *was* your intent, I assume?"

"Of course," Torgas said. Better to take credit than admit confusion.

The Deadfather made a chuffing sound of doubt. "Then I would be most interested to hear why you didn't undertake the task sooner."

"I am sorry, my lord. I did the best I could with the resources available." Torgas rushed to change the subject. "What news of the Black Lands? Has the front line—?"

"The front line remains unchanged since last we spoke." The statement held a dangerous edge that made Torgas regret asking. "And the Stranger grows extremely dissatisfied with our progress on this plane. We face resistance across the allverse. And...Trofonag has been destroyed."

"What?" Torgas looked up in his shock before remembering to avert his gaze. "How is such a thing possible?"

"A rogue Facilitator. I have been ordered to bring the remaining Disciples here to help us finish our work. The Stranger wants everything in His power brought to bear on this insignificant plane."

"Of course." Torgas didn't dare express the thought that came to him: if this plane was so insignificant, then why was it putting up such a struggle? "If you would like to send reinforcements now that the way is open, I can continue my assignment here," he offered.

"That will be unnecessary. You will abandon the Blackhold and come to me through the bone portals. But first..." Torgas perceived movement in the eternal shadows as the Deadfather shifted atop his magnificent obsidian throne. "Tell me about the boy."

"The...the boy? H-how did you...?"

"*Have you stood in exile for so long that you forgot the Stranger sees all?*" the Deadfather leapt to his feet, his rage a palpable thing. That booming voice would've sliced at Torgas's flesh if this physical form had been there. "*His Emptiness is quite interested in this child which bested your soldiers again and again.*"

"He is nothing," Torgas insisted. "A simple *craeftus*. He defeated a few wastelings and outran my army, no more. I can no longer sense him, so he is likely dead already."

"Perhaps." The Deadfather settled himself once more. "But I want to know everything. Should he reappear, all *Exatraedes* will be ordered to bring him to me immediately."

Torgas hesitated. He hated to admit this next part since it defied their creed, but it seemed many things had changed in his absence. "In that case…I may have something to assist in this regard."

Minutes later, when the conversation ended and Torgas returned to his body, he continued through the Blackhold, but now his steps found more purpose, taking him to the crude prison his men had fashioned before departing. He regarded the pitiful form curled up on the dirt floor within.

"Rise, *craeftus*, and prepare yourself for a great honor," Torgas ordered the human named 'Tash'. "You're to become the first guest of the Night Castle."

# EPILOGUE II

The excavator claw bit into the rubble, its jaws closing around a half ton of earth before lifting it into the air. In the headlights, the mechanical arm resembled the head of some giant beast, tearing a mouthful of flesh from its downed prey. Then the upper portion of the excavator swiveled, and the claw deposited the debris onto a growing pile behind the automated construction vehicle.

"You see?" Harris Stebens asked, powering down the mighty machine with the yellow-striped controller he'd taken from the Moambatis' storehouse. The undead human had found a new set of garments in a Crested Butte shop to replace his black jumpsuit, but looked amusingly puffy beneath them with his midsection swaddled in a thick layer of gauze to hold his sliced belly together. "This thing is our best bet for clearing smaller wreckage, but each load is a drop in the bucket. Even if we program the rest of the fleet to break up the larger stuff and shore up the tunnels to keep them from collapsing right back on top of us...you're talking about a monumental undertaking here."

"The feat was accomplished once, therefore it can be accomplished again," Zeega told him stubbornly from where she crouched in the bough of a nearby pine tree. The riftling's yellow eyes never left the place where the door into the subterranean complex had been, now covered over by a massive landslide that filled in the valley for half a span.

She'd climbed the face of the mountain as quickly as possible after giving Rand the detonator, but the quake from the first blast had hit while she was a third of the way from the top. Several bodies fell past her—one dead, one alive, and one somewhere in between—but Korden was gone by the time she reached the glittering structure and crawled up through the crack in its middle. She'd narrowly survived after the subsequent explosions sent the glass tube tumbling down from its perch along with most of the summit, which lost a thousand pargs of elevation in minutes.

In short, she'd failed her only friend. She didn't mean to let it happen again.

Beside her, Harris gave an exasperated sigh. "Yes, I get that. We'd probably have an easier time digging down through the side of the mountain itself, but yes, it's possible. I'm just saying that, to quote the third best Beatle, it's gonna take a whole lotta precious time. Before we go through all that trouble, are you *sure* the kid's even alive?"

"His emotional cloud is...strange," Zeega admitted, directing her mind toward the presence she sensed through the spans of earth. "Weak and unchanging, as though caught in a dreamless sleep. But he is very much alive."

"Yeah, well, let's hope he stays that way until we can get to him." Harris regarded the controller in his pale hands, then peered back at her. His cloudy eyes glimmered in the moonlight. "You really think he'll be able to help me? Use his magic to keep me from...you know...rotting away?"

Zeega bowed her head, closed her eyes, and answered his question the only way she knew how.

"I believe that Korden Bright will find a way to do anything he puts his mind to."

# AFTERWORD

It's funny how the littlest things can completely change your life.

Almost twenty years ago, I was working on a short story about a school shooting. Back then, such occurrences were still relatively new and freshly horrible in our minds. To me, these acts seemed far more evil than anything a mere human being could undertake, and that's exactly how I wanted to depict them. I needed something to make it clear that my shooter was a creature hiding in a borrowed body, some kind of nonsense dogma for him to spout that would indicate he worked for forces beyond our reckoning, and I typed the words 'Dark Filament' for the first time. I had no idea that phrase—plucked from the mental aether where the Muses reside—would reshape the rest of my writing career.

That short story was "Goggles" (one of my first published pieces) and that merciless school shooter was the very first Incarnate. The short story quickly spun into a novel, *Race the Night*, and then, as the universe continued to expand in my head, into a short story called "The End of Things," which serves as a prologue to Korden's story.

And now, the volume you hold in your hands concludes what I like to think of as the 'Moambati Cycle' of the *Dark Filament Ephemeris*. As Korden said, the specter of these two women have hung over this journey just about from its beginning, and, though the story will be free to move in a different direction now, rest assured that their influence will be felt long after their deaths.

There were several goals that I had in mind when I began this series. Some of them can't be revealed just yet, but there are two that I would like to talk briefly about. First, I wanted these books to be standalone for the casual reader, but very much connected to my other work for those that wanted a deeper experience. For instance, if you'd like more background information about the allverse of the *Ephemeris*, I very much recommend reading the short story "Moambati" in my collection *Howling Days* (where you can also find "Goggles" and "The End of Things") Or, if you'd like to better understand the conversation between the Deadfather and Regent Torgas, check out the novella "Outside the Lines," available in ebook by itself or in my collection *Killing Time*. There are lots of Easter eggs scattered throughout my novels for those who pay attention.

Second, I wanted this series to be *weird*. Unclassifiable. A bizarre mixture of post-apocalyptic sci-fi, fantasy, and horror, where you never know if the next person the heroes meet will be an imagination-devouring multi-entity or a leftover sentient weather satellite. And from here on out, things are only going to get stranger.

But that's only if there actually *is* a here-on-out. I've poured my heart and soul and years of work into these books, but there's really no point in continuing to write them if there's no readership. While interest in the series has definitely increased in the last year or so, it still isn't selling nearly as well as my horror novels. That's where you come in.

What can you do if you'd like to read more of Korden's adventures? First and foremost: *review the books on Amazon*. With every review that comes in, it makes the next sale that much easier. A good ad campaign can only get a prospective reader to the product page, but they need to see positive reviews before they'll buy. You can also tell people about the books on social media; word of mouth is a powerful influencer. And be sure to follow me on Amazon, Twitter and Facebook to get updates.

Until we meet again, thanks for reading, and may all your choices be true.

Like this novel?

## YOUR REVIEWS HELP!

In the modern world, customer reviews are essential for any product. The artists who create the work you enjoy need your help growing their audience. Please visit Goodreads or the website of the company that sold you this novel to leave a review, or even just a star rating. Posting about the book on social media is also appreciated.

# About the Author

Russell C. Connor has been writing horror since the age of five, and is the author of two short story collections, five eNovellas, and fourteen novels. His books have won two Independent Publisher Awards and a Readers' Favorite Award. He has been a member of the DFW Writers' Workshop since 2006, and served as president for two years. He lives in Fort Worth, Texas with his rabid dog, demented film collection, mistress of the dark, and demonspawn daughter.

.

Made in the USA
Coppell, TX
29 January 2024

28349100R00171